TRILOGY
THE FREQUENCY

I0682388

Janja Srečkar

FLOODLIGHT

Are fame and wealth the things
you really crave?

(2nd book)

FLOODLIGHT, JANJA SREČKAR
Title of publication: Floodlight
Subtitle of publication: Are fame and wealth the things you really crave?
Original title of publication: V soju reflektorjev
Original subtitle of publication: Sta slava in denar tisto, kar si zares želite?
Author of publication: Janja Srečkar
Publisher: selfpublishing (Janja Srečkar), Ljubljana
Edition (printed): First edition
Year of printed edition: 2016
Printed by CreateSpace, An Amazon.com Company – Print on demand

Year of first publication (e-book): 2013
Year of copyright protection: 2010
Pictures and ornaments: Pia Rihtarič
Design and layout realisation: www.leparec.si
Translation and editing: Mojca Lorber and Alan Horvatič
This text is copyright protected in accordance with the provisions of 174. article of the copyrihgt law.

CIP - Kataložni zapis o publikaciji
Narodna in univerzitetna knjižnica, Ljubljana

821.163.6-312.9

SREČKAR, Janja
    Floodlight : are fame and wealth the things you really crave? / Janja Srečkar ; [pictures and orna-ments Pia Rihtarič ; translation Mojca Lorber and Alan Horvatič]. - 1st ed. - Ljubljana : selfpublishing, 2016

Prevod dela: V soju reflektorjev

ISBN 978-961-94018-1-1

284540928

TABLE OF CONTENTS

To all who have ever experienced the joy of cooperation with their brothers, sisters or friends. To my sisters Mojca and Špela for always shining a Light down the Life's path. To my friends Sara and Edis for paving that path with me. To Mojca and Alan, whose masterly work, invaluable support and effort cannot be measured. To Maruša and Dragica for inspiring me time again and again with their enthusiasm. To Pia, Katja and Grega, for adding important pieces to the mosaic of work and friendship. To Jonathan Jackson + Enation and David Bowie whose music illuminates heart's darkest corners. And to my brother Klemen who gave his life so I can know what eternity tastes like.

Part one

Jesse

I RAN UNTIL I LEFT THEM BEHIND ME. It seemed so real and at the same time so…impossible. I panted up the hill astonished at my own weakness. When I got to the edge I caught sight of her again and although I don't scare easily, I shrieked loudly.

»Get lost, you freak!« My threats didn't drive her away. She stood calmly on the edge of the cliff looking straight into my eyes. When I took a step forward she moved towards me. She was less than three feet away. I started to shake again. As her arm reached towards me I quickly got around her, ran ahead and found myself on the edge of the cliff. *My hallucinations have obviously come back*, I thought. *It doesn't matter now if this world is real or not.* I wanted to leap forward.

»You don't want to do that,« she continued.

»I said get lost,« I screamed and stared at the rocks. I would surely get smashed to smithereens if I jumped. I sensed her gaze at the back of my head and turned towards her. I cried in anger and fear.

»It doesn't have to be this way…Please understand…« she slowly drew nearer. Her pale face looked even more divine and more terrifying. I knew what she was capable of. She took another step and I instinctively drew back. Suddenly I realized that I had actually stepped into an empty space.

I panicked, because I wasn't ready yet. *I don't want to leave this world*, I screamed inside, *no matter how terrifying it is…*

It was too late. The blackness started to engulf me and I felt the pressure in my stomach – the kind one experiences on a roller coaster. Except that this time it wasn't a game…it was real.

I. THE SUPERMARKET

I stood in line considering my options. I gazed in my wallet and sweated. *I'm too honest, that's the problem*, I berated myself. If I had stolen at least one thing in my life, my conscience would've been better prepared for this world. And this way…I put a can of food on the conveyor belt and wondered what will happen…I took another look in my wallet. Three credit cards and not a cent of cash. If I could at least check my balance! An elderly lady was the only person in front of me – I presumed that she had been stocking up for the holidays. So was I, only my stock was…significantly smaller.

»Will there be anything else or just the stew?«

The saleslady's voice shook me out of my thoughts and I started sweating again.

»Hmm, just this.«

The elderly lady in front of me was still putting her things in her stupid paper bags; her hands were moving slowly and awkwardly. I had a good mind to step up to her, put her things in her paper bags and escort her to the door myself. Then I could talk to the saleslady about my stew.

»Two dollars and thirty cents, please,« she told me routinely.

»I don't have any cash at the moment, I'll pay with my credit card.« I made an excuse.

I smiled – this smile had helped me many times before – and quickly took out my credit card. She took it and slid it through the terminal. Although I was very nervous I tried to act as cool as possible. I had been secretly practicing that in front of the mirror a few times too. The machine beeped, but I didn't know whether that was good or bad. The look in the saleslady's eyes told me the card got rejected.

»Won't work,« she said. The elderly lady with paper bags raised her eyes. The shame started to burn inside me and I felt I wouldn't be able to hide it much longer.

»Yes, I see,« I smiled again nervously. I took out the next card and offered it to her. I wished that at least the old bat would stop staring at me.

As she slid my Mastercard through the terminal I remembered in desperation how my father had lent me 10 grand a year ago, after I described to him in great detail how I was going to make it. At the time I *knew* I was going to make it. I felt that I could truly become a famous musician. Rodney was radiant too when we almost signed a contract with a producer. Yes, *almost*. I hate that word. Because of it I haven't seen my home in a year, because of it I don't have the guts to look anybody in the eye, because of it I lie to everybody I meet. And because of it I don't have the money for the damn stew!

»Also denied,« saleslady looked at me. This time her voice was softer, while the old woman next to me, having successfully packed her things a while ago, occupied herself exclusively with me. She looked at me as if I was the most pathetic hobo in the street. I hate pity.

»Ah, no problem,« I pretended. The whole line that formed behind me, was staring at me. I took out my *last* credit card.

»Try this one,« I almost stuttered. I tried to steady the hand with which I was offering my American Express card as much as possible, so that it wouldn't show how much I was shaking. From the disgust of being poor. From the anger of suffering such a humiliation. And from my... completely crushed male pride.

The terminal beeped the same as twice before. A murmur went through the line behind me. A murmur of impatience, of pity, and I also heard subdued whispering. I was so mad I could easily punch someone. I decided to leave as quickly as possible.

»You know what? It's OK,« I said hastily and took back my last card. *They're all useless, damn it,* I thought. *I'll choose one to make a guitar pick from at home.*

»Keep the can. Thank you for your time,« I tried to be polite to mask my frustration.

»There's no need.«

The old lady, who still hadn't left, was holding a five-dollar bill in her hand. »Take it. And happy holidays to you.«

She smiled for the first time, so I could see her dental prosthetics. Her face was awash with enraptured faith in holidays, helping strangers in need and all that. *But I don't want her help!!!*

Now she was finally gone. The five-dollar bill was resting in the palm of my hand. The saleslady nodded at me.

»Anything else?«

»No, thank you,« I said quickly and thought to myself that enough people had seen my embarrassment.

I took the can that had caused me so much pain and swore to myself that Rodney would make the next ten trips to the supermarket. I pointed my eyes to the floor and quickly headed for the exit. I was shaking all over. I quickly opened the door and turned right, walking along the wall towards the rear of the building. Towards the delivery area. Where there is usually nobody around.

My wet eyes were searching for a place where I could finally unleash my anger. The rear of the supermarket was empty; the cars were parked in a fenced parking lot, so nobody saw me as I slipped past a small dumpster into an empty delivery alley. I dropped the bag with the can and started kicking the wall. The tears I had managed to hide for the longest time filled my eyes and the saliva started drooling from my mouth. If somebody were to see me now, they'd surely be scared. Just let them come. Their fear would have been justified!

I kicked the wall repeatedly, swearing. I was getting wilder by the second, because the images I saw so clearly in my head just a year ago were becoming blurry in front of my eyes, turning into the disgusting reality I was living. From a luxurious mansion – to the dump Rodney and me call a rented apartment. From the fact that one can make it with one single genius song – to the fact that one can try a thousand times and always end up on the bottom! From the situation when masses of people party around the stage and scream my name – to the hobo who can't afford a stew! Life can't possibly be so unbearable!

In a fit of rage, I forcefully punched the wall with my right hand. My knuckles hit the brick surface with a characteristic crack. I realized what I had done when it was already too late. Following the shock, pain came slowly in waves and it really hurt. I screamed from the top of my lungs.

The sand from the façade, which mixed with the blood on my hand, caused such strong and sharp pain that at least for a moment I managed to forget who I was and how pathetic my reality was. I fell to the ground and cried. Eventually I calmed down counting the drops of blood that dripped on the asphalt. The ringing of my cell phone brought me back to reality.

Since I was only able to use my left hand, I answered the phone before checking who it was. I was certain it was Rodney. I told him I would be back in five minutes and now I was gone for at least half an hour.

»Sorry man, complications at the cash register,« I quickly summed up. Attentive voice on the other side took me by surprise.

»Jesse, are you all right?« I heard a concerned woman's voice speaking in French. After a few seconds it dawned on me that my mom was calling and that it would be wise to quickly come up with something credible explaining why I answered the phone the way I did.

»Hey, hi mom,« I answered awkwardly. »I didn't know it was you. Everything's great,« I mumbled unconvincingly.

»Are you sure?«

»Yes, yes. Rodney and I went to the supermarket, there was a line, and

I thought you were him. He's waiting outside, you know, I have to go...« I tried to end the conversation as soon as possible. At the same time I was testing my voice and relaxing my vocal chords, so she wouldn't sense that I had been crying like a girl just a minute ago.

»Dad's asking if you're coming home for the holidays,« she wouldn't let me get rid of her. When I last saw him, I promised to come home for the holidays. Not by car though. By private plane.

»Yes, of course he's asking,« I quickly replied. I was considering my options. I had two options here: either let cockroaches eat me alive in that godforsaken hole or go on an involuntary hunger strike. Or both. In both cases I wouldn't live to see New Year's Day.

»Err, OK mom, I'll come,« I quickly summed up – unaware of the consequences, »But I can't talk now, I have to go. I'll call you. Say hi to everybody.«

As I ended the call I dropped the phone to the ground. I leaned my head against the wall. I slowly tried to move my right hand and concluded that I had probably broken a knuckle or two because it hurt like hell. The fact that I was going home hurt even more. If they knew that I was returning home to Quebec from the glamorous LA, the city of dreams, like a hobo, if they knew that I couldn't afford a can of food, much less a fare home, if I told people the truth...my life would've been – to put it mildly – even more unbearable than it already was.

I felt that I needed to stay in the game. I would find the way to get home. And to get some decent clothes. I used my left hand to feel the last two and a half dollars in my pocket and I felt a quiet satisfaction about the means I had left. Rodney would spend the holidays at Jessica's; he'd be all right. I had to prepare for the battle that could enable my thousand and first attempt at success...

II. PREPARATIONS FOR THE TRIP

I WAS LOOKING AT MYSELF IN THE MIRROR AND CAME TO A CONCLUSION that the man staring back at me as my reflection looked pretty good. The suit that almost fit gave the impression of someone who doesn't have a problem with dishing out some change for a new Armani suit. Middle-length blonde hair, slightly curled at the end, gave the impression ob boyish playfulness. Blue eyes, straight nose and symmetrical, full lips were well suited for gracing the front covers of music magazines.

I had stood many times in front of the mirror and rehearsed, especially before auditions and meetings with producers. This time the rehearsal was even more intense: I would have to convince my dad that I was perfectly fine, that everything was going according to plan and…I will have to find a pretext for another ten grand. Maybe finalizing the contract took a little longer than I thought it would. And I could pay him back double at the end of the year. Or maybe I need to invest in a new video. No, I'd need a single for that, already released and in stores, so my dad could see it and maybe even buy it. It should be played on the radio. But anyway, professional videos cost much, much more.

A knock on the door snapped me out of my thoughts.

»May we come in?« asked Jessica.

»Yes, sure,« I quickly replied and realized that it must've taken me a long time to get dressed.

Rodney, Jessica and her kid brother Jonathan entered the room.

»Hey, if I'd known that this suit looked that good, I wouldn't have lent it to you,« said Jonathan.

Jessica poked her 13-year-old brother.

»What did I tell you? This suit doesn't fit you anyway. You can stay here though, and I'll go and tell our parents who tested dad's electric razor on the neighbors' cat the other day…«

»No, no, it's OK Jesse, it looks great on you,« said Jonathan, »I don't like wearing stuff my aunt buys me anyway.«

I turned and faced them.

»Thank you both. Jonathan, you shouldn't have…When I get back I'll teach you some crazy Canadian hockey moves.«

»Cool, man,« he was pleased. At the same time I felt that he wanted to make an impression on me. I didn't think I was worth it. I should be looking up to him, stay at home, listen to my parents and maybe even take over the family souvenir store. That way I would never have to lie. But it was also true that I'd know the whole time that the world could be much more exciting than my little hometown and I'd eventually die of boredom.

»Are you ready?« asked Rodney. He nervously pushed away a lock of his black hair and pointed his oblong inquisitive face in my direction.

I looked at him and didn't quite know what to say.

»We'll make it, man, I just don't know how yet,« I patted him on the shoulder, »you just keep an eye on things, OK? I'll be back with the money.«

»Thank you too, Jess, I'm sorry you had to lie for us,« I turned towards her. »I'd never have raised enough money for the plane ticket and the trip if you hadn't come up with the idea of 600 dollars for a school project.«

»I did it for myself,« she smiled, »My boyfriend and his friend are going to be the most famous rockers in the world and I want to be there, when it happens!«

I admired her optimism. After a year without success she was the only one who still believed in us. Although I wasn't sure whether that was because of her love for Rodney or she actually liked our music.

I softly punched the kid who couldn't wait for his turn.

»We have a deal, don't we,« I said. I had a feeling like I had a kid brother again. Full of mixed feelings I turned away from him so he wouldn't notice my confusion.

I picked up the bag with my things and my plane ticket. As we walked down the stairs towards the front door I decided to say my goodbyes quickly and with a smile; I couldn't let them suspect that I was worried whether I would be able to come back.

»I'll call you, man,« I said quickly with a smile.

»Hang on, gang, we'll make it!« I shouted as I turned around in the street for the last time. My taxi arrived and I got in, waiting to be taken to the airport. Luckily Rodney found a cheap taxi service online and we were able to figure out precisely how much this ride was going to cost me. After I paid for the ride at the airport my only possessions left were my plane ticket, a few items of clothing and some food (Jessica had encouraged us to loot her parents' refrigerator) I took for the trip.

Finally in my seat on the airplane (a great last-minute offer), I thought back and remembered all the hard work over the last year. I couldn't imagine anybody else going through all the insults, dubious job offers and misunderstandings while searching for a producer. Nevertheless, deep down I felt I mustn't give up.

The plane started to move. As if a radio programmer could somehow read my mind, a song that was a hit a few years back came from the tiny speakers above my seat: »Bye-bye, Hollywood Hills, I'm gonna miss you...«. And I knew I better be damn lucky if I wanted to see West Hollywood ever again. And LA. I had a hard time convincing my dad to lend me the money the first time around and now...I leaned back in my seat and started to think about what to say to him this time...

III. THE JOURNEY TO QUEBEC

I ATE THE PIZZA LEFTOVERS FORM JESSICA'S PARENTS' REFRIGERATOR AND thought. I was so preoccupied with what I was going to say to my dad that I barely noticed the taste of stale pizza. I was wondering how I was going to act once I got home. Sitting comfortably in my seat I exchanged a few words with a flying attendant that came by, mentioning that I was going home, and prepared for the flight. I felt quite tired after the food… and I thought once more about my dad before drifting off to sleep.

I looked around myself and realized I was in a cavern illuminated by a faint light. It turned out to be some sort of an antique lamp. The cavern was empty. It was snowing heavily outside. As I stood up I noticed my clothes were wet. I looked downwards and discovered that my clothes were heavily stained with reddish-brown color as if soaked in blood. I got alarmed and lifted my shirt. Underneath my body was unharmed. Outside the wind was sweeping even harder, bringing the cold into the cavern. I felt its freezing grip on my exposed belly and quickly lowered my shirt. I realized I was dressed way too lightly for such cold conditions, even though I didn't feel cold at that moment. As I exhaled, steam rose from my mouth.

»Where the hell am I?« I quietly said to myself.

As I stepped to the entrance I could only see mountains and snow, as far as my eyes could reach. I couldn't remember making any plans for skiing or mountain climbing trips. Especially not in such weather. I heard the sound of pebbles rolling behind me and I turned around. A woman's silhouette stood six feet before me. She had fair, curly, shoulder-length hair, incredibly symmetrical face, full red lips and blue eyes. She was the prettiest creature I had ever seen.

»It's nice to finally see you, Jesse,« she said.

»Who are you?« I asked. She looked like a fairy.

»That's not important right now. What's important is that you've finally arrived...«

Immersed in her eyes I felt no more fear.

»We've arrived, sir, we've arrived!!!« the voice of a flight attendant announced.

I felt being shaken by somebody and the girl with fair hair disappeared. I was on the plane again. We'd already landed and I had a funny feeling in my left ear. It obviously failed to adapt to the pressure changes while I was sleeping. There was nobody around me.

»You've fallen asleep. It's time to leave the plane. Are you all right?«

»Yes, I am. We're already here, ha?«

»For some time now. Do you need help with your luggage?«

»No, no, it's OK,« I answered slightly confused.

It was one of those moments when you're suddenly thrown from one to another, completely different reality. In that moment anybody could tell me anything and I'd believe them. Still slightly confused, I grabbed my bag and stepped quickly out of the plane. Nervously looking around the Quebec City Airport, I was finally convinced I was home. The eternal Los Angeles sunshine and palm trees had been replaced by three feet of snow as far as I could see. I sank even deeper into my winter coat. There was no going back. I deeply inhaled the cold winter air just to calm my nerves. I had to slowly remind myself again of who I was, what I came for and that I didn't have time for silly feelings of confusion. I picked up my suitcase near the exit and headed home.

As I walked along the coast on Champlain Boulevard, I remembered how many times I'd walked those miles, daydreaming that I was in one of the most prestigious neighborhoods of Los Angeles. Instead of old-fashioned houses on the left I'd always imagined prestigious mansions, and instead of French language I'd imagined relaxed American English. Instead of tourist carriages that passed me by I'd imagined polished new Porsches.

With such thoughts on my mind, I'd go home to practice my guitar. I didn't like music school all that much, but I did wear out every single page of the booklet »Learn to play guitar chords« I received for my fourteenth birthday. Now, five years later, that seemed like an entirely different lifetime altogether. Then I couldn't even imagine that freedom could be so sweet – when nobody breathes down your neck; and so difficult – when you actually have to decide what to do with your life to be able to survive – at the same time.

Since I was very near my home and I knew I was early, I sat on a bench near the waterfront. The sound of water made me miss my guitar I'd left in Los Angeles. *I will go back, even if it's just to get the guitar*, I thought. I finally managed to clear my head after the sleep on the train. I stretched my entire body and reminded myself to talk to my dad in proper French. He hated the English language pretty much - he was proud of his roots and his hometown. So: no badmouthing Quebec tourists. And lots of questions regarding his sales. Hmm, this kindness might just give me up!

I slowly got up and headed home with heavy feet. From afar I could already see our brick-colored house with blue garage doors. A couple of cars were parked in front of it. My aunt Monique had obviously already arrived. The spiral staircase on the side still led to the pancake shop run by our neighbor Françoise; luckily it was closed during holidays.

I knocked on the front door and soon my mom's face appeared.

»Mon Dieu,« she cried out in happiness, »you've come, my Jesse baby!« She'd always loved coming up with affectionate nicknames for me, which I always found less and less appropriate. This time I dismissed my ego and smiled at her.

»Hi, mom,« I replied in French. Although I hadn't spoken French for five years (I'd spent four years in New York and one in Los Angeles, where I definitely didn't need it), I quickly realized that you don't forget the language you learned as a child just like that. It came out naturally as I described my journey.

»Our handsome little man has come!« I heard my aunt's voice. Her habits from ten years ago clearly hadn't changed all that much. I listened to her approaching steps sincerely hoping that she won't start pinching my cheeks. God answered my plea – she stopped three feet in front of me.

»Oh, Mon Dieu, he's grown into a handsome big man,« she commented on my figure. Her figure had remained exactly the same: rather stout, with black hair and a double chin. Her pink dress with white dots proved that her fashion sense also hadn't changed at all.

»Where is…Papa?« I asked carefully.

»Oh, he's in the garage fixing a spring in the car. Your mom's gone to get him. Come, let me fix you something to eat!« my aunt's invitation sounded more like an order. Not that I wasn't hungry. But looking at her I was getting less hungry by the moment.

She sat me behind the table and brought out the house specialty: ham and egg omelet with maple syrup. One look at all that fat that I hadn't seen for years, made my stomach turn. The food on the West Coast was much more convenient and less fatty. The streets were full of beautiful girls – most of them were or wanted to be actresses – who probably didn't even know what fat was!

So, not to disappoint my aunt, I carefully started to tackle the omelet. I used the fork to cut it into little pieces, like I was preparing for a feast. I chose the smallest one knowing that the rest will wait for me on the plate anyway. I put it in my mouth and quickly changed the subject.

»And how are things at your house? Is uncle Pierre well?« I asked without any real interest.

»Oh, you know,« she started seriously, thrilled that I asked the question, feeling important because somebody was interested in her life. »His health has always been so-so. He was spearfishing this summer and this winter his back started acting up again...« she spoke with great seriousness and enthusiasm, but I soon stopped listening to her. I gazed somewhere between her eyes and let out the occasional »Aha«. I listened only to the last words in her sentences, so I could ask her an occasional question now and then, giving the impression that I was focused on our conversation. In reality I was thinking about my dad the whole time.

»Well, look who's here! Our little Jesse!« announced mom. It was pointless to point out to her that I was almost two feet taller then her.

»My son,« said my dad seriously. He walked up to me and hugged me. He hadn't changed much. He still had a serious face that could put on a cheerful childlike smile in a moment and then turn serious again, not letting anybody know what was hiding behind the exterior. His mustache danced under his nose making it even harder for me to decipher whether he was actually glad to see me or he expected something more from our reunion. For example...at least part of what I had been predicting a year ago.

»Now we can finally sit down to dinner,« said mom.

We sat around the table and she brought out the food. Dad said grace like he always used to do and the rest of us joined in for responses. I hadn't done that for years. And yet it stayed in me, planted in my childhood, and I could feel that I would carry that imprint for the rest of my life.

The dinner was over almost to quickly. Aunt Monique had enough subjects to discuss to last her a week and she'd still be talking. After the dessert my dad got up.

»Son, would you help me with the car downstairs?« he asked seriously and I could tell that we'd not talk about the thing he'd just announced.

»Go upstairs and change, so your new suit doesn't get dirty,« he emphasized.

»A little bit of male bonding,« he said to my mom and aunt, smiling for the first time.

»Yes, sure, Papa,« I answered, puzzled. I could feel my blood pressure dangerously increasing. I knew that the upcoming conversation could change everything. It could drag me to hell or leave me in purgatory, searching for the road to success again.

I quickly ran to my room – that for some unknown reason had remained untouched for the past six years – opened the bag, and changed into a T-shirt and a pair of jeans. I looked in the mirror and realized that I wasn't completely prepared for what was about to come...

IV. THE CONVERSATION

In spite of the fact that I'd put on a clean T-shirt, it was soaked in sweat as I was halfway down the stairs. What was I going to say to him? What – was I – going to say – to him? I got to the garage door through the house too quickly. The floorboards in front of the door squeaked a bit and he heard me.

»Come on in,« the voice inside the garage invited me.

Damn it, I didn't have even a second to prepare for this. To draw breath or something similar. I'd forgotten about the treacherous floorboards in front of the basement door that squeaked every single time somebody stepped on them. It was too late now. I entered the garage.

Papa was calmly bent over the hood of the car and at first it really seemed that he invited me down there solely because he needed a helper.

»Hand me the pliers, would you?« he said routinely and motioned towards the worktable with tools on it, while his hands were buried deep in the car engine. I silently handed him what he asked for and tried to act normally.

»And,« I started just to break the ice, »how are the sales going?«

»Still going, I've nothing to complain about,« he said like he didn't feel the tension in the air, »the tourists know exactly what they came to fabulous Quebec for. The season starts again in February anyway,« he smiled; he truly loved the Winter City Festival, when visits to the city peaked. In that period it seemed to him that the entire world has come to visit his town. Like everyone was pulsating with him and his art as one; he truly loved tourists and the town he lived in. As I watched his cheerful facial expressions, I thought that it probably wasn't such a bad decision to inquire about his job. Maybe I had a chance.

He got serious in an instant.

»How are you doing...?« he asked, like he completely forgot about everything we'd been talking about five seconds ago.

»I've nothing to complain about,« I quoted his words. I nervously smiled and thought how great it would've been if things had really gone as I'd hoped. My single would've been released, the producers would have fought for me, and I'd have hired a bunch of lawyers to fine-tooth-comb every contract and turned it into my favor. In the end I'd have established my own firm, my own production company, that'd have supported young unrecognized artists like myself...Suddenly it dawned on me. Of course, I would establish my own production company! *That's why* I needed the money! *That's why* my single still hadn't been released! In my head I quickly made a plan to present my newly developed project.

»Actually,« I smiled, »it may not look that good, but it's getting along even better than I had hoped.«

»How's that? I haven't seen a private plane around...« my dad joked.

»Not *yet*,« I quickly responded. »When I had been in these circles for some time, I discovered that these things needed a little longer to take off than I had initially thought, but they pay off significantly better down the line.« I stopped for a while, because I didn't want to lie. Everything I'd said so far was true. I wanted to continue in this way.

»When I started presenting my single to producers, the interest was there,« I said. That was basically true. They were interested, but then they changed their minds and decided to pick somebody else. But initially *they were interested*.

»I've read quite a few contracts.« That was also true. I found a few contracts on the Internet that producers had been offering to their chosen clients. I knew that the combination of my first couple of statements had given a *different impression* from the actual fact: that in reality nobody offered me a contract.

»And in the end I've decided.«

Papa raised his eyebrow. I looked at him and paused. Partly because I wanted to better form the sentence that was coming, and partly because I wanted to create a dramatic effect before presenting my idea. After all, maybe I would establish my own production company sometime in the future for real, so my lie wouldn't really be a lie. Maybe right after my single was released. If my dad lets me and if God allows it, I'd rather die this time than come home again without results! I was truly prepared to die for my dreams!

»Papa, I'm going to establish my own production company!« I declared slowly and proudly.

»How are you going to do that?« he asked in disbelief. His statements had always been brief, but to the point. He always knew how to get to the heart of the problem, which shook my entire world – be it real or fictional – to the ground.

I slowly continued. »Do you remember lending me your savings a year ago?« I asked slowly. »Well, of course you remember,« I answered myself quickly, before he could surprise me again with one of his quick-witted remarks, which would force me to adapt my already shaky plan of what to say to him once more.

»That money was really an investment! Practically all production companies in L.A. know me now!« I said proudly, because it was essentially true. I'd really sent my demo to all of them. It was true that they'd all rejected me in the end, but they did *know me*.

»Now I can go one step higher. And if you help me out now, you won't just double your money, it'll come back to you one hundred fold!« I continued. I was avoiding his eyes on purpose as I was describing my exploits. I was ashamed of not having a more tangible result, but at the same time I didn't want to give an impression of insecurity, which would've certainly happened if my eyes were to meet his.

He slowly put down the pliers. »And how exactly can I do that? I've already helped you out financially, all I can do now is to sit behind a drum kit,« he made an awkward joke. I knew that the time had come for me to muster all my strength if I wanted to survive. I tried to appear calm even though my entire body was shaking.

»Well, maybe you could join me on stage sometime, Papa,« I smiled back, »but I was thinking more about…that first thing.« I was zigzagging towards the heart of the matter. And since he was still looking at me like he didn't understand what I was trying to say, I looked him in the eyes and used much more concrete words: »Papa, I need money.«

»So, that's the real reason,« he said absentmindedly, more to himself than to me.

»Reason for what?«

»Ah, nothing, nothing,« he glanced at me.

»How much?« he asked quietly.

»Ah, you know. Establishing a company is a pretty big thing and at the same time not such a big thing,« I stalled, »it'll be a small company at first, but it'll grow, especially after the first single makes waves. I've really learned a lot about that stuff this past year.« Which was basically true.

»For the equipment, computers, printers, the office, the first down payment on the lease,« I pretended to know what I was talking about, »and the formation of the company, Rodney and me came to the amount of… roughly ten thousand.« I remembered that Rodney had absolutely no clue about my little scheme and realized that it would be rather unpleasant if my dad wanted to discuss this with him over the phone. Luckily, he trusted me too much to come up with such an idea. There was another obstacle, though.

»Son,« he said slowly, »are you aware that you've used the same – or pretty similar – words about an investment when you were describing your last year's project which you still haven't realized? Just the other day I read about how excessive support can spoil and slowly destroy one's child. I'm sorry, son, but my savings aren't unlimited. And anyway, I'm saving that money for rainy days, for the insurance, for the family…«

»But Papa,« I quickly interrupted before he could come up with even more reasonable arguments, »don't you think that your son is one of your life's achievements? Don't you believe that your son is also a sort of – investment? I'm enterprising, I'm young; do you believe in me or not?« I took a step downwards on my morality scale. I painfully *needed* that money, now more than ever. At that moment I couldn't care less about family insurance.

»You already told me that last year,« dad said quietly. Like he had expected my passionate speech. »Of course I believe in you. That's why I also believe that you'll make it without my help.«

I was completely disarmed. I felt how all the pride I still had left slowly drifted away. It was even worse than a week ago in the supermarket. The saleslady knew nothing about me. My father knew everything about my past and I knew that he felt my words were merely bordering on the truth, even though he wanted to believe me. My eyes teared up with anger and humiliation. I swallowed hard. I really didn't need this. Here I couldn't punch the wall. I prayed to God to calm me down. I couldn't remember turning to Him so often ever before, like I had recently. But it worked: dad softened, put down the tool he wanted to use just a minute ago and asked:

»Do you have a clear plan how to execute the whole thing?«

»Of course,« I answered convincingly.

»And the paperwork, how is that coming? Is it a problem you not being a citizen and wanting to establish your own company there? Have you made any inquiries at the municipality, administrative unit or whatever they have over there?«

»Of course I have, Papa,« I continued and tried to be as convincing as possible, »these things are much simpler there than they are here. You just need a few permits and right references. There'll be a lot of those – after my single is released.« There would surely be enough of those. *After* my single was out.

There was a long break in the conversation. Dad leaned against the car and started studying the circuit board. Suddenly he seemed very interested in what was wrong with the car. He reached towards the engine with both hands and unscrewed a screw. Then he carefully took two little wires, pressed them together and joined them using his old soldering tool that miraculously still worked. He shook the circuit board to check how firm the joint was and then tightened the screw he'd unscrewed before. I was impatiently watching his every move, hoping, clumsily moving tools around his toolbox, pretending to be interested in his work on the car. Suddenly, he raised his raised his eyes and looked at me.

»I think I've come to a decision.«

»You have?« I tried to act as unaffected as possible.

»I'd really like to give you my support, but I also feel that I'd indulge you if I gave you everything you asked for. You know, Jesse my boy, it's time you grew up and faced life's trials on your own. Do you think I got my store as a present? Of course not. I decided to have it and I laid each brick with my own hands. That's why I have so much respect for it, even though you might think it's small and insignificant.«

»No, not at all.«

»Well, let me finish,« he continued in a strict voice. »I'll give you… five thousand.«

That wasn't enough. With that amount I was able to go home, but I'd have to be damn lucky and sell the demo right away. Immediately.

»But Papa…«

»The other five you find like I had to, when I was opening my store. You'll see, you'll thank me later,« he reinforced his decision.

»Terry would be proud of you too,« he added. I didn't know why he always had to bring up my twin brother, who'd been dead for more than fifteen years, in such moments. He'd always successfully silenced me with those words since I was a teenager. I simply never knew how to answer that stupid statement. How can a dead person be proud of me?

»Al right, Papa, you don't want to fully help me out,« I quickly blurted out. For the first time in my life I responded to a 'Terry statement', albeit not at a level one would hope for. I felt threatened: like he always, when I was doing less than OK, wanted to tease me or something. I'd had enough of that.

Dad turned away again.

»What do I mean to you?« he suddenly asked.

»What?«

»You heard me: what is my standing in your life, as a person?« he repeated the question. It seemed like a pretty...womanly question. I'd expect something like that from mom and I'd tell her that she meant everything in the world to me, or something similar, and I'd have my peace. But my dad...I didn't know what he meant by that.

I was still leaning against his toolbox. I thought about his support and what his money, should I get it, would mean to me. I looked into the toolbox and thought of the music industry machinery. If I succeeded, I'd be sucked into that system, into that machinery, and its wheels would drive me forward and upward, all the way to the top. That money would represent my tools. My pliers for the mechanism of fame.

»You are like...a wonderful tool I could fulfill my dreams with,« I tried to explain my thoughts in a technical manner.

»Ah, I see...« he said dryly. I haven't thought about how my words could be interpreted differently. For example, that he was nothing more to me than an ordinary ATM machine.

»No, I didn't mean it *like that*,« I tried to correct myself, but it was too late.

»Well, how did you mean it?« he asked quickly.

»I was thinking only about money.«

»Exactly.«

A moment of screaming silence.

»You know that I...I mean that I love you and stuff. Like a father,« I said awkwardly and it seemed that every single word got stuck in my throat.

»Aha,« he was still looking away, and I felt more sorry by the second. How could I be so inconsiderate?

»You can go back up, Jesse, I don't need help anymore,« he said quickly.

I didn't know what to do. I wanted to tell him so much, but I couldn't get the words out of my mouth.

»All right,« was the only thing I managed to utter. I quickly put down the tools and grabbed the doorknob. I inhaled deeply as I stepped through the door and slowly closed it behind me. The floorboards squeaked under me again. It didn't matter anymore what I said to him: regardless of how much money I'd get, I would succeed. And then he would be proud of me. I would show him once and for all that my dreams were real! And that this thing today was just…a misunderstanding. I would apologize to him. Tomorrow.

V. THE RETURN

Mom and Monique stood outside my window at the railway station, competing which one was going to wave at me more noticeably and beautifully. I was looking at them, spending last atoms of strength trying to be as polite to them as I could be. Papa had been pretty much absent the last few days; he spent the entire holidays in his shop due to the increased number of tourists. Even on New Year's Eve he came up to us only to wish us a happy new year and to propose a toast to that effect. Mom was glad that I was with them again and didn't miss him too much. There would be enough time for them to talk when I left.

When the train started moving I began thinking about how easy it was to get the money. I was wondering all through the holidays how that matter was going to unravel. Just before I left, mom came to my room, gave me an envelope and said it was a Christmas gift from Dad. She quickly left the room so I could finish packing, and when I opened the envelope, there was…ten grand inside. I later told her to thank him for me.

I waved at them for the last time and then we were off. I watched the old houses as we were rushing by thinking that I wasn't coming back again without a private plane. My heart was pounding at the thought that God gave me a chance to try again. I was grateful. Really, really grateful. I leaned back in my seat, listening to the train buzzing. Every now and then there was an announcement as we stopped at a new station. This time I had more than enough to eat and the food was fresh. I'd gotten used to full and calorie-rich taste of Quebecois holiday treats during the week and I couldn't wait to bring some of them to sunny LA. I automatically took off my winter coat, which I wouldn't be needing any time soon. Life had regained its meaning and I could breathe again. The thought of being able to afford a can of soup for quite some time now brought a smile to my face, even though I knew I still needed to be careful with money…

I found it interesting how difficult it was for me to leave Quebec the first time. At the time it seemed like I was leaving the only place in the world that I knew and that meant something to me. Like part of me was going to die. And then, when I experienced New York and LA, it was hard to go back. This time it was even easier to leave home; the feeling that I might make it gave me a tremendous uplift, even though I didn't know exactly how to do that.

At the airport I bought a plane ticket and threw my suitcases on the conveyor belt. I bought the cheapest ticket: I needed to make sure that the money lasted for quite some time when I got back and that I…respected it. Since I'd got the taste of »independence« I truly started to respect money. The first ten grand I spend with incredible ease and euphoria, thinking that I was on the way to success anyway…Now, after numerous battles that almost took me to my grave, I respected every cent. And I thanked God for having enough money to buy a can of food.

Before I turned off my phone on the plane I sent a message to Rodney: »Man, I don't know how, but I did it! I'm coming home, with the money. Hope you've taken good care of my baby, ha, ha.« I really loved my guitar and Rodney often teased me, saying that I didn't even need a woman, because this piece of wood would prove to be too much of a competition for her. He was right, for now. I liked girls, but so far none of them reacted to me the way I wanted to. They always wanted me to fall in love with them, to serenade them; they wanted romance…My guitar never asked anything of me. I could obviously simply say that I hadn't met the right one yet.

When we got airborne my thoughts were already someplace else…I was making plans, real plans. This time would be different. It had to be.

Somehow I had to find a gap, a door to get in. There had to be a solution. I checked my envelope again. I knew that I could use that money wisely or I could die. I had only those two options. How was I to use it? I had a demo tape that obviously convinced no one. What did it lack? Bigger arrangement? More instruments?

How was I to attract the attention of producers? Was I to stoop to the level of stalkers and arrange a situation in which I would save life of one of them...? Was I to try auditioning for musical talents once more, even though my music was too precious for me to stoop to that level. There had to be a solution, there simply had to be.

I thought about how I'd really like to know what the truth was in this world. Why I was so driven to become famous and successful. For the money? It's true that I loved money, but I could feel that wasn't it. There had to be something more. Like I could feel I was destined to become great. To be *somebody*. And that a small reality of a small town, a small country, a small body was much too intolerable for me. I felt that I had to have the world, even though I didn't know why. And who was running the whole thing. And was giving me all these wishes, desires and yearnings. It seemed like a good subject for a song. I added a melody that I'd been singing since that morning and I didn't think I'd heard it somewhere before.

I took a pen and started scribbling on the back of the envelope...

> *Am I poor enough to see that I'm sitting on a hill of gold,*
> *am I blind enough to find the path that will never make me fall,*
> *am I dumb enough to be the bravest in the world,*
> *am I good enough for you to show me what's the plan for me?*
>
> *I'm young, yeah, and I'm wild,*
> *like a wild bird in a cage,*
> *please give me one more chance to fly,*
> *please give me the sky and I'll show you why*
> *I'm the right man for you*
> *and you're the one for me.*

I was singing the new song to myself so eagerly that I couldn't wait to show it to Rodney. If I used it for a new demo, they'd *have* to take it, because it was new. And this one was going to be fantastic. Suddenly I heard that we were over Los Angeles, descending.

I couldn't remember ever being happier than now that I could see the ocean and palm trees again. When we got a little closer I could see the familiar dome of the Los Angeles International Airport. I thought I wouldn't see it for a long time. I just wanted to unbuckle my safety belt and jump down there with a parachute.

After agonizingly long twenty minutes we finally heard that we may leave the plane, along with everything else they usually say before one leaves it. *Thank you for flying with us...*

Rodney was waiting for me near the luggage carousels. I spotted him waving at me as soon as I collected my suitcase and I got a strong impression of a new beginning. We went for a drink and discussed which producers we'd already visited and which ones we could visit again with the new demo. We decided to make it really special – with a unique intro, surprising breaks and a hint of madness. I sang the intro for him and he loved it.

When I met Jessica and Jonathan again, I sincerely thanked both of them and returned the suit and the 600 dollars. I really didn't want to owe anything to anybody. I just wasn't used to it. I was actually fed up with people who constantly borrowed money and couldn't return it. I'd never thought I'd have become one of them someday.

Finally, I unpacked my stuff...Back in my room I took the guitar case, quickly opened it and took out the guitar that was waiting for me...I immediately started improvising on the beginning and the ending of the song. In between, I marked the spots for the bridge and the solo. Then I started putting together the most difficult and the most hauntingly beautiful solo I've ever heard...This time it was for real...This demo – would be divine. Nobody would be able to resist it.

VI. PREPARATIONS FOR A NEW LAUNCH!

RODNEY OFTEN SAID THAT WE MIGHT SUCCEED IF WE USED THE right approach. That maybe we ought to disguise as maintenance men or cleaning ladies when knocking on the door. They'd surely let us in, instead of heartlessly taking our demo and slamming the door in our faces. It practically doesn't matter how you get in. Once you're in, you're in. You can talk to the boss and not just to middlemen. There are too many of them anyway and a producer probably doesn't even know that you were at his door. I started wondering how many of them heard my previous demo at all. How many did actually hear it?

We worked two straight weeks on the melody and the arrangement. I'm talking about serious work here; any type of slacking or lounging was simply out of the question. Regardless of where we were and what we were doing, we were constantly thinking or talking about this recording. Where to put the break, which key was right…There wasn't a moment when I wasn't singing a part of the song, I thought about lyrics while I ate, at night I dreamt about singing and playing the guitar in front of a crowd…We took the whole thing really seriously.

Rodney's pal Ritchie helped us make and perfect our demo. Rodney met Ritchie during holidays at Jessica's. He was her distant cousin. I didn't like him too much as a friend – he loved classic debates about women and cars that didn't interest me too much. I thought only about the scenario I wanted to bring to life. But he was a computer whiz. He took care of the mastering and equipped the recording with additional sounds using only a portable hard drive, a UBS key and Ableton software. He would process the sounds on the computer and then we would listen to the song. That's when I knew we were going to make it. The song was simply too good to be turned down by anybody. Even Ritchie liked it.

The time when we had to decide on the action plan came all too soon. The recording was made, even though I was constantly looking for ways to improve it. I had listened to it roughly five hundred times before I decided to take mercy on Ritchie and Rodney, who were already giving me dirty looks. They both wanted the project to succeed, that much was true. But I was...downright obsessed. Then again, the creative process was my home. But the knocking on doors, management, the business side of it...I failed too many times to be able to feel comfortable with it.

After three very busy weeks Rodney and me went for a drink. The newest version of demo recording was resting on the table. I felt this could be it, and the purpose of the meeting was to define who was going where, so we could »process« as many producers as possible, in the shortest possible time, with maximum effect. I felt that the traditional approach was out of the question, we needed to do something much more drastic. But what?

»Man, you'd really be one attractive cleaning lady,« Rodney teased me again.

»Stop with that nonsense,« I quickly interrupted him. I had more important things on my mind.

»I'm serious,« he said with conviction. »It doesn't say anywhere that you can't dress the way you like it. If you prefer the cleaning lady style it's not your fault if people accidentally let you in the building...You're not breaking any laws...«

I thought about that possibility and winced.

»Maybe I could get all the way to the studio...« I realized and the idea didn't seem that bad anymore. Rodney picked up the case with the CD.

»Let's write on the cover: 'Listen urgently, a great demo!' and add your name. Nobody will know who put it there...« he added and burst out laughing. »I'm telling you, Jesse, it's a brilliant idea! When we make it, I'll charge you for it claiming initial promotional activity!«

This time I started laughing too. If it actually worked, I'd be the happiest man in the world. My next thought was where to find a suitable outfit.

»There must be a store with that sort of stuff in this town,« said Rodney with conviction, »Jessica must know somebody«. Recently she had saved our skins so many times that I decided in advance that she was entitled to a few percent of sales when we made it.

We headed home. North Ogden Drive was in bloom like never before. Or maybe I just hadn't noticed that before. When I sent the picture of the street I lived on to my mom, I deliberately failed to describe the real building in the accompanying letter. Roughcast was falling off the fading old apartment building we lived in. It was one of the few buildings that didn't belong to that prestigious neighborhood.

After a few minutes' walk we arrived at Jessica's. When she tied my hair into a ponytail and applied some make-up to my face, I was awarded with hysterical giggling. Then she suggested a few places where we could probably find that type of uniform. But we had to be careful that it was really authentic.

Shopping was fun, but we didn't find the suitable outfit anywhere. Most of them were meant as Halloween costumes anyway, or they simply didn't look professional enough.

»I can't believe that I'm actually doing this,« I sighed as I stepped into the fifteenth changing room – with women's clothes!

Rodney and Jessica stood by me, like a couple of bridesmaids, while I felt like a weird bride looking for her wedding dress. When I threw out the twentieth outfit, Rodney suggested we should check the online offer. Since none of us felt like walking around stores and waiting in front of changing rooms anymore, we went home. I was tired like never before and came to the conclusion that the so-called »retail therapy«, which supposedly helps a lot of people feel better, had a reversed effect on me. Especially because I'd been trying on women's clothes all day.

We ended up at Jessica's and she made us drinks. We were alone; Jonathan was out with his friends and her parents had gone to the movies. We sat behind the computer and opened a bag of chips. It looked like we were about to watch a movie too. A comedy in which my friends would see me in all kinds of cleaning-lady outfits again.

Amazingly, we found the right one very quickly. Jessica had really mastered this type of shopping – it seemed modern women bought most of their wardrobe online. The choice was definitely better. After a few clicks the outfit was ours. At the end of the evening we gave Jessica money for the ordered goods and thanked her for her help.

As we walked home, I got the feeling that my plans were slowly beginning to become reality. I started to consider how I would react if a promising young musician dressed up as a cleaning lady just to make me listen to his demo. I'd probably think: »This one's got the courage.« I'd probably give him a chance purely on account of imaginative approach. But I knew I shouldn't let my imagination run off with me. In most cases such intruders are thrown out with a clear instruction: »And don't come back«! I didn't want that to happen.

My train of thought was interrupted by Rodney saying that we were really going to make it, that I finally had to relax and stop worrying. The outfit was going to arrive in a couple of days and that was that. Yeah, that was that. The demo was recorded, the outfit was ordered…It felt like I was looking at the ocean from a very high cliff. I was ready. All I needed to do was to jump.

VII. KNOCKING ON DOORS

»**M**Y SYMMETRICAL FACE WILL COME IN HANDY AT LEAST ONCE,« I told myself looking at the reflection in a small round mirror that Jessica lent me. If she hadn't enjoyed putting on make-up so much, I'd have done it myself, even though the result wouldn't have been quite the same. Jessica took my make-up very seriously. It couldn't be too glamorous, yet at the same time it had to be feminine enough for me to look convincing. As I was checking myself in the mirror I realized that I looked pretty good. I'd invite such a good-looking babe right in.

I was standing in front of the entrance waiting for somebody to go in. I had a bucket, a pair of cleaning gloves and some other cleaning products; my demo was hidden among them. The last couple of days had gone by in a heartbeat. We burnt quite a few CDs, but we had to be careful that the front cover wasn't too flashy or too average. On each CD we stuck a white piece of paper with an inscription that had to be readable, yet appear as if written in a hurry:

»Musician: Jesse Roy, great demo, LISTEN URGENTLY!!!«.

A couple of musicians came down the street, heading towards the studio.

»Great,« I thought. »I'll be less noticeable if there's more of us.«

They opened the door and walked in. I held the door, waited for a second and then followed them. A receptionist surprised me in the lobby.

»Oh, a new staff member, nice, nice,« he took a good look at me. Before I could tell him to mind his own business, it dawned on me that he was probably being nice to me because I was dressed as a woman. When I saw a lustful look in his eyes I realized that being a woman wasn't all that simple. I felt vulnerable, like some sort of a victim and it felt terrible. Even though I wanted to throw him against the wall, I gathered my thoughts and smiled harmlessly. He became even more enchanted with me and asked: »Can I point you in the right direction, miss?«

It occurred to me that this flirtation might bear fruit.

»The studio please,« I chirped in my best high falsetto. He fell for it.

»Ah, the studio,« he replied seriously, like he was about to tell me a highly guarded secret. »Which one?«

»Well, the biggest one,« I quickly blurted out.

»That'll be studio A. Just go down this corridor, up the stairs, then left to the end. On the right you'll see the door with a glass top part.« I listened carefully because I wanted to leave as soon as possible.

»Aha, great, thanks,« I said, again an octave higher than usual.

»Should you need something else, just let me know,« he said obligingly. Was I really that attractive?

As I walked up the stairs I tried to appear as calm as possible, gently swinging my hips as I saw L.A. women do. I didn't want my cover to be blown. I could feel the receptionist's stare on my back, but I was too close to my dreams to rush up the stairs and destroy everything. When I got to the studio A door, I was covered in sweat. What now?

I peeked through the top glassy part of the door and saw a scenario I'd played in my head countless times: a huge mixing console approximately thirty feet from the door and three people behind it, talking to musicians on the other side of it. I didn't see the musicians, but I could imagine the grandiosity of the studio.

The man sitting closest to the exit suddenly turned his head to the left, looking towards the door. He must've felt somebody was looking at them. I drew back like a woman and waited for the consequences. When nothing happened after a minute, I gathered my courage again and slowly peeked in. Sound engineers were starting to get up and I wasn't sure whether they'd all come and check who was at the door, or they had some kind of a break or something similar. I was lucky: it was the latter.

I quickly retracted down the corridor to the next door. I heard the studio door open.

»I'd die for a sandwich and a beer right now,« said the first one.

»We haven't worked so hard since Britney came here,« grinned the other.

»Well, Sam.I.Am comes in today in person; we better not let him down! And besides, the song's so terrible, it needs improvements badly!«

Thanks to their little chat they failed to notice a shadow holding the door as they left. I stepped into the studio and discovered that they'd left everything switched on. I got to the mixing console and left my demo in the middle of it. It looked even better on such a large piece of equipment: like it had already been accepted. And like one of the producers actually wrote a note to the others telling them how this demo was really something special…

I looked across the console into the isolation booth…My dreams were right in front of me. Behind the glass, there were a couple of different grand pianos, with guitars hanging on the far wall. The instruments used for the present recording were on their stands on the floor. The room also contained several different drum sets, various pieces of equipment for better sound quality, sinfully expensive professional microphones I could only dream about…It was like being in a dream. There was a door on the right leading into the booth. *I had to* open it.

As I stood in the middle of an array of incredibly fine instruments, I went completely numb. I kept looking around in total disbelief. *I belong here, this is my home*, throbbed in my head. I quickly picked up the nearest guitar and told myself: it's now or never. Nobody was supposed to be around for quite some time. I played the song that was already on the demo and some other personal favorites. I was pretty fortunate: as I finished the fifth song, approaching footsteps started echoing through the silent building. I didn't have enough time to sneak out of the studio, but I had the presence of mind to put down the guitar, take a rag and start cleaning one of the pianos. The conversation was getting louder and I realized that the sound engineers weren't alone.

A heavyset man walked in through the door. He wore a worn-out pair of jeans that screamed 'latest fashion'. He also sported a sweat suit top complete with a tie and a pair of sunglasses. I recognized him immediately.

VIII. SHAME

»Mister Sam.I.Am, why don't you sit right here,« one of the sound engineers tried to be extra obliging, with the others trailing behind him. The second one was already bringing coffee, while the third one held the door open.

Musicians also started coming in and soon I wasn't that noticeable anymore. The studio soon became crowded and I wasn't sure anymore what to do: move slowly towards the producer or simply stay in the isolation booth. Then I noticed a small resting area near the producers cabin and started awkwardly moving in that direction with all my buckets, diligently wiping everything I could on the way there. Had somebody taken a closer look though, they would have immediately noticed that I was only pretending.

»Forget the small talk, I didn't come for that,« he said quickly, »play the song for me.« He stayed true to his direct demeanor. When I watched him on television, I always thought he had a big personality. And in the small studio room he wasn't any smaller. He was magnificent.

»Of course, sure, right away,« said one of engineers and it was obvious that they were all very nervous.

Sam.I.Am put on a pair of headphones and listened for a few seconds. Then he took them off, started laughing and said:

»You can turn this piece of garbage off now.«

After the initial glances full of hope the band on the other side of the glass got quiet, and so did their sound engineers. I took a closer look at the band and realized that I didn't know them. So they had to be a bunch of new faces wanting to penetrate the music market. Which wasn't simple at all.

»Are you sure *I* got this band?« he looked from under the sunglasses.

He leaned towards the button that enabled conversation with musicians.

»What do you call yourselves?«

»The Best Rockers,« said the singer timidly.

»Your playing suggests otherwise,« said Sam.I.Am ironically. »No hard feelings.« He sighed deeply.

»I'll give you one day.«

»B-but the contract says…« the singer started stuttering with tears in his eyes, but the producer interrupted him.

»I don't give a damn about the contract. You were obviously a bit too euphoric to read the small print, weren't you?«

He released the button. While »The Best Rockers« licked their wounds in the isolation booth, he turned towards the sound engineers.

»When you call me next time, you better have a really awesome song. Don't make me come down here for some incoherent babbling. I want a song that will uplift people, that will be easy on the ears, that will…« There was a moment of silence, after which he continued in a surprised voice: »…be a 'great demo' at the start! Whose is this?«

Since I was only able to eavesdrop, I didn't notice that he picked up the CD I'd left there. I looked in the direction of the mixing console and got chills all over my body. Sam.I.Am was holding my demo in his hands!

»Well, play me this, since I'm already here. Maybe I didn't come for nothing after all.«

The sound engineers exchanged glances, but didn't say anything. Nobody had a clue how that CD came to be in the room, but they were willing to do anything to improve his mood. The offered CD was a gift from heaven for them. As it was for me.

It seemed like it took them forever to put the CD in the player. When the tray slid back in I heard a slight »click«. Even though there must've been a lot of different everyday sounds around, I heard only that one. I even heard the disc start spinning.

Sam.I.Am remained quiet. He was absolutely serious. Precisely for three minutes and forty-nine seconds. He listened to the entire recording, right to the end. The cleaning-lady outfit was completely soaked in my sweat.

When the song came to an end, he remained quiet for a while with his eyes closed. Then he slowly took off the headphones.

»Now, this is something else,« he said with respect.

»Who suggested this recording?«

Although those present around him wanted to impress him, nobody, but really nobody had an answer. They all stood there in silence.

»Well, who wants a promotion? Did this disc come here by itself or what?« he started to mock them.

»Jesse Roy,« he repeated slowly, turning the casing in his hands. Only then it dawned on me that regardless of how surprised and enraptured I was by the fact that he liked my song, he still didn't have my contact information! I have turned in the demo without any phone number, address, e-mail address... *Bravo, Jesse, you're a born manager,* I steamed with anger. *What now?*

Sam.I.Am was still staring at his subordinates, measuring them with his look, wondering if it might be a hoax.

»Well,« started one of the sound engineers, »we actually...«

»We actually don't really know how this recording came to be here.«

»It doesn't even have our studio mark...«

So many details I should've paid attention to! If I didn't act quickly, my opportunity would slip away regardless of whether Sam.I.Am liked my song or not. I appraised my chances: I took the inserts out of the bra, quickly removed the wig and took off the upper part of the outfit, under which I had a pretty decent T-shirt. I thoroughly wiped off my lips to get at least the pink lipstick off my face. If anybody asked why my eyes were painted, I'd simply say that that was my image. I let my hair down and looked in the glass on the left. I looked…well, pretty decent. Like a slightly deviant rock star.

»Well, if nobody knows who this Jesse Roy is, then unfortunately there's no basis for this recording to…«

»I'm Jesse Roy,« I said loudly. Everybody turned towards me and I was sincerely hoping that I looked at least halfway cool.

»I see,« the producer also turned towards me.

»And what are you doing here? You're probably aware that you're not authorized – except in case that you're one of our performers – to be here?«

I didn't have the right answer to that. I was caught during an unlawful entry. I could at least find solace in the fact that he liked the song; now I could offer it to somebody else, with much more confidence. Next time Rodney and me could both dress up. Suddenly, I didn't care all that much what Sam.I.Am thought of me. I even became bold.

»I'm here because I want to present my music to you. I can go now if you want – I just wanted to see your reaction with my own eyes.«

I headed for the exit with my bucket, my rags and my cleaning gloves.

»Wait a minute, wait a minute, what's the rush?« I heard the producer's voice. I sensed a big change in the atmosphere. Only now that I have recognized the value of my music, truly recognized it within myself, I could negotiate with him. I hadn't had that power before.

»Yes?«

»Interesting look,« he said. I was hoping it would turn out like that.

»Thank you,« I quickly replied.

»The bucket is part of your act, I suppose…?«

I had no ammunition left. I'd have to confess how I got in. I looked at the bucket in my hand and swallowed hard ashamed of being disguised as a woman.

»Actually…this was my only ticket to get in,« I started to laugh to ease the tension. »The receptionist couldn't resist my charms either…«

Sam.I.Am looked at me for a while and then burst into a long laughter.

»Can you believe this kid? He, he, I like him!« He turned towards me again: »You're something else!«

I answered with a smile because I was speechless.

»And now's the time for serious stuff,« he said quickly. »How many songs have you got saved up and how soon can you record them if we give you the opportunity?«

I didn't expect such directness.

»Well, I've got quite a few,« I pretended.

»The sooner we start, the better,« I bluffed some more.

»OK. You're enterprising, I like that. My lawyers will send you a temporary contract. We'll start next week. But you know, if you don't deliver…you may end up like 'The Best Rockers',« he again commented on the band before me. The whole thing seemed a bit cruel to me – but it was a battle for survival anyway. If you were good, you were in. If you were not, you were out.

»It's a deal.«

»You can leave your contact information at the reception,« he told me and indicated that our conversation was over. »I'll keep this,« he didn't let the recording out of his hands.

As I walked through the door I felt an enormous weight being lifted off my shoulders. I did it, I really did it! I'm going to record, I'm going to be a musician, I was in Hollywood and my dreams would come true! I didn't know how to curb myself, to stay at least relatively normal on the way home. I gave my contact information to the receptionist, who was very confused upon seeing me again. He was probably thinking about inviting me to dinner or something like that until he discovered I was a man.

When I came out I started laughing out loud and jumping up and down with the bucket and other things still in my hands. I went down the street applauding to myself; after a while I put the phone to my ear and called my right-hand-man in the band.

IX. THE FALL

»Hey man, guess who's got the contract with Sam.I.Am?« I blurted out directly.

»Don't f…did it work, did it really work!?!« I heard screams on the other side.

»We start recording next week!« I continued sure of myself.

I can't remember the rest of the conversation very well, because we mostly laughed and joked around. Rodney had a few remarks regarding my attractive cleaning-lady look, but at the same time we had nothing meaningful to say. In the end we agreed to meet for a few drinks later that night. This time we went to a real club, not to one of those little watering holes they call a bar, like before.

I went out to buy some new clothes – as Sam.I.Am's new recording artist I had to think about my appearance. In a new pair of jeans, I looked like I'd just stepped out of a Levi's commercial; after a long time I noticed that my figure wasn't bad at all. If I hadn't been devoting so much time to my music recently, I could have probably found a job as a model or something similar. Although it was true that I didn't think that to be too original: almost anybody walking the streets of L.A. was either a model or an actor. I certainly wouldn't stand out.

As Rodney, Jessica and me lined up in front of the club, I noticed two young and very attractive ladies walking past the line, straight towards the entrance.

»Watch this,« I said to Rodney. »Hey, girls!« I yelled after them.

One of them turned around and I waved at her. She said something to her friend and they both approached us.

»Hi ladies, I'm sorry to bother you,« I said gallantly, »but I've just signed a deal with Sam.I.Am, who became my producer, and my band mates and me are here to celebrate. Is there a chance of you helping us get in, so I could buy you ladies a drink?« I said all sweet and smiling.

They looked at me seriously for a few moments and I already thought I'd chosen the wrong approach. Here people were much more relaxed than back home, in good old Quebec. They probably didn't understand that I was asking them for a favor. Maybe I should just walk up to the doorman and say: »We're together«. But when their lips spread into smiles I discovered with great relief that the old-fashioned charm obviously worked here too. They were completely different in appearance (one was blonde and the other had long black hair tied in a ponytail), they both looked like they'd escaped from the cover of a magazine.

They looked at each other. »Of course, why not,« said the blonde.

»Follow us,« said her dark-haired friend.

They didn't have to invite us twice. The doorman removed the red rope for them and as he wanted to close it in front of the three of us, they stopped him with the words: »It's OK, they're with us.«

When we walked in, I thought I was dreaming. A huge space opened up in front of me, with slightly dimmed figures pulsating in the rhythm of the music. Everything was stimulated by throbbing lights and the surround-sound system playing incredible mixes of the latest hits. Since I'd promised drinks to the ladies, I had to be careful not to show my childlike delight at the sight of the crowd. The world was so intensely alive here that it seemed like I'd gone out for the first time.

Rodney and Jessica went closer to the dance floor to check out the scene, while I had other things to do. I took the girls to the bar where we ordered drinks and talked about casual stuff for a while – like where they were from, what they did for a living. They told me their names were Melanie and Naomi. Then they wanted to know the same things about me. I'd always imagined that socializing in such clubs was much more glamorous than it actually was. That first impression of the grandiosity of the place quickly wore off, and soon we were just a group of people hanging out together in a big, colorful, darkened room, trying to impress and like each other. Like in the market, we seemed to be on offer. Actually people offered themselves. The ladies must've noticed that I wasn't in such a partying mood anymore and they started whispering to each other. Then they ordered a couple of glasses of water. As they were giggling, Melanie took a box of TicTacs from her purse. They looked at each other and both took one. I found it curious that they didn't just put the mints in their mouths, but also washed them down with water.

»You want one?« offered Melanie.

I thought it couldn't hurt. Even if mints weren't exactly what it said on the box, they surely couldn't be anything much stronger. They reminded me of ecstasy pills that I saw in New York at a couple of parties, although I didn't try them then. Anyway, I saw that the girls were playing it straight. They both took them, right in front of me. It surely couldn't be anything bad. *Maybe this evening could still be fun*, I thought. And I had to keep up with a couple of girls, anyway.

»All right, sure,« I wanted to remain cool. I took what they offered and washed it down with water. Nothing out of the ordinary happened. Yet.

»Shall we dance?« asked Naomi.

»OK.« Our glasses were empty anyway.

There were several dance floors, mostly round, matching in styles. I'd practiced dancing many times in front of the mirror when I was alone, naturally. I wanted to learn a few dance moves that would look relaxed and attractive; at the same time I didn't want to stand out too much or be too noticeable. I wanted to know just enough so that the ladies would feel relaxed in my company.

I used my technique then and there and I fit right in with the others. It was a group dance anyway. Melanie and Naomi were very attractive – visually. When they danced, they looked like they'd stepped right out of a music video. But I had a nagging feeling that things ended there. They loved shopping (like ninety-nine percent of L.A. women) and attending parties. Their only concern was their best behavior at home, because their freedom during weekends depended on it. They were both models and therefore welcome in the clubs they frequented. And that was it. Nothing more.

I was looking around while we were dancing, because I wanted to see something interesting. I was surprised at how quickly I got bored with the place that made such a strong impression on me just a while ago. All of a sudden everything seemed the same to me. Flashing lights, a crowd of dancing bodies, smoke...

Out of the blue I felt my heart beating faster than before. Was it because of the dancing? I could feel my body being somehow prepared to dance all night, even though I wasn't a professional dancer. Soon the music became louder and clearer. I had the feeling that I could hear it more distinctly. The light added to this sensation because it seemed that I was able to detect laser beams I was blind to before.

DJ started playing truly awesome songs and I felt the rhythm of the music as the rhythm of my heart. I raised my arms and started becoming one with the music. The rhythm took me over completely and it seemed like *I* was creating the music I was dancing to. Like *I* was the creator of this happening. I smiled and looked around the room. Melanie and Naomi were dancing in the flickering light, looking in my direction from time to time. I sensed respect in their eyes – I must've made an impression with my music and my dancing. I looked around the room again and suddenly everything made much more sense than half an hour ago. The large hall throbbed in colors, in *my* colors. All lasers projected the very colors I wanted.

The tempo of the rhythm increased even more and I really started dancing like crazy. I enjoyed the feeling of creating and my every single move made perfect sense. I had never had so much fun. Was it possible that this place turned into a paradise? Into a celebration of my success? I thought about my contract with Sam.I.Am and absolute joy washed over me again. I don't know exactly how long I danced, but it was unforgettable. I had enough energy to dance all night and even longer. A thought throbbed in my head alongside music: I'm successful, I'm a musician, I'm creating this fun, these people know me and they respect me. I looked around the room once more and saw that everybody was rejoicing with me. They were really happy for my success. It was about time.

The music finally changed into a state of rapture in which I listened to intervals between long basses and vocal passages. We calmed down, swaying in some sort of trance. It was really nice.

In the middle of the dance floor I noticed a girl with blonde curls who danced differently from everybody else. Like she knew this old-fashioned dancing style. She looked slightly silly and different, exotic, at the same time. I decided to welcome her to my party.

I was slowly moving towards her since the music was slow to. She noticed me when I was roughly thirty feet away. She smiled at me and I knew that I never saw a prettier smile before. She was different from the other girls. Wilder, much freer. I smiled back. I thought I saw her nod or something. I didn't know what she meant by that.

When she turned away and started dancing towards the exit, I thought that maybe she wanted me to follow her. Maybe she wanted to meet me. I took the hint and started following her. It was pretty difficult keeping up with her through the dancing crowd. On the edge of the crowd she turned around and waited for me. When I got close enough she continued dancing mysteriously towards the exit. She ignored the doormen and stopped when she got to the street.

»Wait!« I shouted after her. I took my jacket and ran out. It was considerably colder outside than when we arrived, which meant that the night was well under way. She was waiting for me on the sidewalk, looking into my eyes.

»Who are you?« I quickly asked. I didn't want to miss this opportunity. I wanted her to at least give me her phone number before she left.

»It's important who *you* are, Jesse,« she said. Then the absolutely unbelievable thing happened: she sank into the ground. She vanished through the asphalt. Just like that.

I tried to follow her and found myself on the ground. I had never seen anything like that ever before. Never. I was shocked.

As I was lying on the sidewalk, I suddenly became very thirsty. I wanted to go back in the club to ask for a glass of water. I walked up to the entrance, where a doorman greeted me. He looked like one of those muscular black guys we usually see in the movies: at least three feet taller and much stronger than me.

»Where to?«

»I need to go inside urgently,« I said.

»That's not going to happen,« he replied, »the place is full.«

»But I was inside a minute ago!« I started getting angry.

»So what,« he contradicted, »you're not inside now. And I don't remember seeing you at all.«

I thought of Rodney and Jessica. Maybe I could mention the girls that took us in with them. »I've got Melanie and Naomi waiting for me inside,« I tried to sound important.

»Anybody could have seen them go in,« he was still immovable.

And I was thirsty. Awfully thirsty.

»C…Can I at least get a glass of water…?« I stuttered.

»Ha, ha, ha, how do I look to you? Like a bartender? Get lost or there'll be consequences for this insult. This is my territory, so my rules apply.«

I didn't have the strength to argue with him anymore. I walked thirty feet away and collapsed on the sidewalk again. How was he able to forget who I was? A short while ago *everybody* knew me. Everybody rejoiced with me. Then I remembered the miracle I witnessed.

Was it possible for a person to sink into the ground in front of your eyes? And to vanish just like that? Did I hallucinate? No, she vanished right here, in the middle of the sidewalk. I could clearly remember what she looked like.

My throat started to burn again. Incredible thirst was followed by a pain in my legs when I wanted to get up. I would have got myself some water if I had been able to stand up. I felt the full weight and tiredness of my body. Suddenly my feelings had changed too. I wasn't the important musician anymore. I heard from the passers-by that I was a »hobo«, a »junkie« and a »boozer«. I felt small and insignificant. There was no trace of my dreams. So what if somebody offered me a contract?

Was that even real Sam.I.Am? Or just somebody that looked like him? In this town you never know what's real and what's not. Anything could happen to you. What if there was a production company where people that looked like celebrities worked, and took care of intruders like myself? I'd heard that movie stars have their own 'doppelgangers', who go places where real movie stars simply don't want to go – to various events, receptions…What if Sam.I.Am had his own doppelganger?

My heart sank just thinking that. How many times will I have to dress up as a cleaning lady before people started taking me seriously? Would they ever? Terry always took me seriously. Even though he was just a few minutes younger than me, he always looked up to me. He was the only one who supported me in everything I came up with. He never blamed me and he wouldn't now…The sadness that used to smolder in my heart now started burning with all its might. If I hadn't sent him across the street after a ball ten years ago, he'd still be alive. Because he looked up to me, he always did what I asked him to do. I didn't feel like going after that stupid ball, that was it. And the driver of that damn van was too busy with his car radio to look at the road.

My throat ached again. I wanted to scream in pain, but no sound came out. I was helplessly opening my mouth like a fish on dry land. I tried to move again without success. My muscles were completely inert. Was it possible that I felt like a ninety-year-old on his deathbed – or sidewalk – just because of one night of dancing…?

I felt my strength completely gone and closed my eyes. Rodney, Jessica…I wondered if they resented me for leaving just like that. I shouldn't have done that. I thought of the evening that was behind me one last time. That girl with blonde curls…How could she have vanished like that? Who did she think she was, Houdini's assistant? Was all this just a weird TV reality show? I leaned my head back on the asphalt and the rhythm of the music still echoed in my mind...

»Jesse! Jesse! Oh, my God, Jesse!«

I'd have answered if I'd had something to answer with. I felt a tight grip as somebody strongly pulled me by the arm. I looked up and saw Rodney by my side, while Jessica talked to the doorman.

»How long has he been here?!« she asked in tears.

»I don't know, a couple of hours,« he answered calmly.

»A couple of hours?!? And you didn't think of calling an ambulance?«

»Miss, these things happen regularly around here. If I called an ambulance for everybody that's feeling a bit sick, there'd be even more crowded here than it already is. Everybody is responsible for themselves. It's not my problem if your friend's a drug addict.«

»You don't know who you're talking to!« she snapped at him angrily. »And Jesse isn't...the thing you said. He's a bit inexperienced when it comes to partying, but that's not your business.«

Rodney slowly dragged me to the car.

»The boy did say something when he came out,« the doorman remembered, slightly touched by Jessica's concern. It's obviously helpful if people find out that you have friends. Maybe I wasn't such scum after all.

»At first it seemed like he was following somebody, but I didn't see a soul. He kept yelling in the air for somebody to wait for him – he must've been hallucinating, what do I know. Then he fell to the ground, face forward. When he came to again – and I'm not allowed to negotiate with people who are high – he asked for a glass of water. I thought he was messing with me. Anyhow, I couldn't go in to bring him one.«

»Hey, Rodney, wait up!« she yelled after us.

She briefly, but clearly, explained to the doorman to get out of her way, went back in and quickly came back out with a large glass of water.

»Drink, quickly,« she said. After a couple of not too successful attempts

– my face was also disobedient – I slowly started drinking. The feeling was divine and the water tasted like real spring water. The fire that burned in my throat, and almost destroyed my respiratory system, slowly started to die down.

I let out a sigh of relief.

»More, please,« I heard my own hoarse voice. She brought me two more glasses and I gulped them down. When I was able to speak again, I described briefly what had happened and then tried to direct them towards the car. When Rodney realized that I didn't know what I was talking about and that I didn't even remotely know where I was, he took charge. We soon found the car. Then I lost consciousness again.

It was nighttime when I woke up. I wanted to get out of the bed, but my body still hurt too much. I had to get to the bathroom somehow. I rolled off the bed and got to the toilet on all fours. When I was done, I slowly washed – having regained some of my strength – and brushed my teeth. As I stumbled out I bumped into Rodney.

»Hey, Sleeping Beauty,« he teased me. »I thought that was you.«

»Rodney, what's going on, how long was I asleep?«

»Just one day,« he smiled. »It's Saturday night and tomorrow's Sunday. Go and rest, and tomorrow we'll make a recording plan.«

I remembered the week ahead of me and my mood improved immediately.

»Yes, yes, great,« I smiled.

I stumbled to my bed and quickly fell asleep for the next twelve hours.

X. WHAT NOW?

WHEN I WOKE UP, I COULD STILL FEEL ALL THE PAIN THAT TORMENTED me the day before; luckily it was slightly more bearable. Rodney brought me breakfast, which in spite of all my effort, I couldn't even look at. Just one look at it made me sick to my stomach.

»Hey man, it'll pass,« he encouraged me. It seemed like he was my only friend in this cold world. Which was basically true. Without him I'd have died on that sidewalk.

»Thanks for breakfast,« I said, »although I'll have to get to it later.«

»Alright.«

He put the tray away.

»Big day tomorrow, isn't it?« he said and I could sense anxiety and pressure in his voice.

»I don't want to upset you in your condition, but…the matter is serious. Sam.I.Am probably couldn't care less about us partying all weekend, but we don't have the songs because of that. Besides, we need a drummer and a keyboard player.«

He reminded me of reality and my greatest fear: that Sam.I.Am changed his mind after a day and sent me home like he did »The Best Rockers« the day before yesterday.

»No, no, we'll make it, we have to make it,« I was optimistic. »For a start we can use their session musicians, anyway.«

»What about the songs?«

»We can start now!« I tried to act encouragingly.

After half an hour of scribbling on the paper I was less optimistic. And after an hour and a couple of doodles I made because I didn't have an inspiration, even less. After five hours I had to admit that I didn't have the slightest idea what to write about. Rodney held his bass guitar awkwardly in his hands and I could see that he was very anxious about the next day.

The day went by very quickly. Since I'd completely lost my appetite, I was able to devote the entire Sunday to my worries. My inspiration was simply gone; I was confused and indecisive. My thoughts were vaguely circling above my head and I was unable to catch them and turn them into something tangible.

When I started to despair, it occurred to me that I could write about my party experience. Yet everything I wrote made no sense at all. At ten p.m. I had to admit my absolute defeat. Even if I stayed up well into the night I wouldn't find the solution.

Rodney calmed me down by saying that we'd probably just record the demo tomorrow. And we already knew how to play that. But I felt the weight of promise I gave to the producer: »I've got quite a few songs. The sooner we start, the better.«

We decided to try again early the next morning. If that didn't work, we could still come up with an excuse for not having the songs. Maybe we could say that we had left them at home. However, that might sound a bit strange: every musician knows his work and can play it by heart.

I went to bed but sleep eluded me. I was haunted by the shadows of the day approaching so fast that I was terrified of the very thought of failure. Every time I closed my eyes I saw myself sweating in front of the microphone, while sound engineers on the other side of the glass exchange glances as if saying: »Well, another one bites the dust...«

I sat on the bed watching the Moon shining through the little hole that was supposed to be a window. It illuminated our messy room filled with stuff that meant everything to us: my guitar and amplifier, his bass guitar, cables, notepads for writing lyrics, a few items of clothes (among them the cleaning-lady outfit), the box of demo recordings (on which I'd yet to add my phone number, regardless of whether I ever distributed them or not)...All those things, all that effort...Everything that led us to this moment. Like all the paths I'd taken and thought reasonable and right led into the abyss.

I lay down again, because I knew I needed the rest. On the other side of the room Rodney happily snorted on his mattress. I counted his breaths, but it didn't help. I tried to think of something interesting that might inspire me to write at least a romantic ballad, but couldn't come up with anything.

Again I felt the pain of pressure under which I found myself. All my efforts, conversations with dad…Was I really going to disappoint him again? Was I really going to return to Quebec once more, this time for good? The very thought gave me the shivers. Don't get me wrong, I love my hometown, but I'd much rather perform there than sell souvenirs…

I started crying in this agony. I don't do that very often. Yet lately I'd found myself in a desperate situation so many times that I become sensitive like a woman. Mom was always telling me that God was absolutely good and that he loved all his children.

Yeah, right, I thought. *If that were true, I'd be on the top of the Billboard chart right now…*

OK, I came back down to earth. *Maybe annoying the Big Brother wasn't the smartest thing to do.* If He was perfect and I was not, then obviously I was doing something wrong. Lying in the dark room I suddenly realized that He, She or It was the only one that could help me in that moment…

I put my hands together like people do in church.

»Hey, God?« I whispered so Rodney wouldn't hear me. But even if I said that out loud, I probably wouldn't wake him from his sound sleep.

»Please, I really need you.«

Well, if I was in His place, I wouldn't listen to such a weak plea. I needed to try harder. I was nervous, like I was really talking to Him.

»What do you want from me? What am I doing wrong? What should I do for you to inspire me?«

But seriously: what did He expect of me? What could I, an insignificant little person, give Him?

»If you inspire me to write one single song, I swear I'll act like You want me to.«

What did I mean by that? Even I didn't know. Wind blew through our little window. Rodney must've left it open.

I separated my hands and wiped my cheeks. I moaned again as I tried to turn around in bed. Physical pain was still vivid in my mind and I remembered the previous night.

The girl with blonde curls…This was the second time that I'd seen her. Once in my dreams and once in real life. Well, the doorman talked about a hallucination, but she was so real to me! I wondered what kind of a sweet Melanie and Naomi gave me. After all the torment I went through over the weekend, I'd still gladly take one if that meant seeing her again. She was like a goddess. Wearing some sort of white dress that didn't exactly stand out, but didn't really belong in that club. Like she emerged from another world…

> *From another world…*
> *From the edge of eternity…*
> *Out of the darkness you came into my heart…*

A clear thought started circling in my mind, clear enough to overshadow all the others. A melody also appeared. I grabbed a piece of paper without hesitation and started writing. Soon I grabbed my guitar too. Not even my singing woke Rodney up.

> *From another world,*
> *from the edge of eternity,*
> *out of the darkness you came into my heart.*
>
> *So what if I'm stoned,*
> *so what if once more,*
> *I've followed a dream and a vision,*
> *that reminded me of whom I really was.*
>
> *Will I ever be with you?*
> *Will I ever get to feel,*
> *what your plan is?*
> *Will I ever know how it feels to be great?*
> *Or will I always fall to the ground,*
> *small, frightened and alone?*

XI. MORNING

I WOKE UP WITH A PIECE OF PAPER AND MY GUITAR NEXT TO ME. Finally the breakfast, that Rodney cooked for me again, smelled really tempting. I almost felt like his little wife.

»Hey, this looks alright,« he was surprised. »Can you play it for me?«

»Sure,« I was wide awake immediately.

I played the song for him and he was thrilled.

»It doesn't sound familiar, yet it's catching. Do you know what that means, man?«

»What?«

»THAT YOU RULE! We're going recording!« Rodney shouted euphorically, but I knew whom to thank for my inspiration. Well…maybe that prayer from the previous night fell on fertile ground.

When we were getting ready I couldn't help feeling slightly euphoric myself, especially after Rodney's outbursts.

»Do you hear this? I'm already humming it,« he said and started singing the chorus. »This is going to be a hit, I'm telling you.«

His enthusiasm wasn't exactly helpful. The last time I gave in to emotions I ended up in a ditch. I didn't want that to happen again.

»Please calm down, it's just a song,« I tried, but he wouldn't listen. He was obviously pretty much convinced that we weren't going to make it, so the song he found on a piece of paper in the morning, was quite a shock for him. I concluded that euphoria was basically a good indicator of how little one believed in success. Otherwise one wouldn't be so surprised when things worked out.

But who could blame him? I was pretty much the same: did I really believe it to be possible, really possible that a crowd of ten thousand could experience enlightenment bellow my stage?

When we got to the car I felt ready. I hadn't felt that calm for a long time. Although it seemed like any word of agreement I might offer to Rodney, could immediately throw me off balance. That's why I decided to leave the talking to him, while I tried to compose myself and focus on the recording day in front of us.

We arrived a bit too early, which I liked. It made us look professional on the very first day. As I got out of the car I couldn't help but feel self-confident. A young girl was waiting for us at the entrance.

»Jesse Roy and Rodney Kirk?« she asked with a bored voice. She was obviously sent out to escort us to the studio, although she had much more creative work.

»We'll be recording in studio D,« she continued, »you'll familiarize yourselves with the rest of the place with time if you stay, that is,« she measured us from top to toe.

»We've changed seven young bands in the past couple of weeks. There's no need for you to imagine that you'll stay more than a couple of days. If the boss doesn't like your music…«

»Don't worry, honey,« Rodney put on a brave face, »we'll stay, we'll record and we'll tour until we get a better offer.«

Better offer than Sam.I.Am's? I poked Rodney to get a hold of himself. Who knew who she was involved with. But she obviously didn't care: she probably heard such arrogant statements every other day from each new performer.

»Here,« she motioned when we finally arrived to the mentioned studio through a maze of corridors.

»And lots of enthusiasm, boys,« she said slightly sarcastically as she opened the door for us. It was obvious that she'd seen a lot of young musicians like us come and go. That's why she didn't believe we were any different. The recording of a song was just finished when we arrived at the studio. I wasn't paying too much attention to the band performing, because I wanted to concentrate on my song.

Finally the song itself drew my attention. It spoke of a boy who didn't know whether the girl, he was constantly dreaming about, was just an illusion or not. It made me remember my experiences of the past few days and it really touched me. Not so much that I would cry, though. But it made me take a closer look at the isolation booth.

»Hey man, do you realize who this is?!?« Rodney poked me.

»'The Exceptional Nation', unreal!« he couldn't believe his eyes.

They had an interesting name, undoubtedly, but The Exceptional Nation had already been filling halls and stadiums all over the world for a few years. They were one of the most recognizable young bands of our time.

A sound engineer looked at us for a moment as if he wanted to tell us to shut up. He said: »We're already a bit behind schedule, could we have silence, please.«

He pressed the button for communication with the isolation booth.

»Sammy, could you please reduce distortion on the second verse, because I can't hear the lyrics clearly? Tom – excellent!«

So, it was true. It really was them. Right in front of us. In the very studio we were going to record in. I already felt famous. Just because my predecessors were so remarkable. Although they didn't look too imposing behind the glass of the recording studio. They acted completely normally. Rodney, on the other hand, was nearly ready to be committed to an asylum.

»Would you please calm down?« I tried to get him in order. He was completely euphoric. I could feel, though that I'd be the same if I didn't have such a tiring week behind me.

He subdued his hysterical laughter and kept it within him. I'd never seen him like that before.

They finally finished with the recording. I realized that we were probably the first people from the outside world to hear their new single and that entranced me again. The musicians started to put away their instruments. »Well, you two,« one of the sound engineers turned towards us again. This time I had enough time to recognize him. He was also here on Friday, with Sam.I.Am. »Now it's your turn. My name is Jim,« he offered us his hand and we introduced ourselves. Besides a tattoo on his right arm which made him look a little bit rougher, he didn't have any other distinguishing marks. Just a guy, wearing a pair of jeans and a T-shirt, with a slightly stubbly chin. Not too glamorous, considering who he was working with.

»Wait, there's two of you,« he quickly summed up, »are you the ones needing a drummer and a keyboard player?!«

»Yes, that's right,« I confirmed.

»Why doesn't anybody tell me these things?« he protested. »I should've been reminded!«

He immediately pressed the red button for the communication with the isolation booth. The Exceptional Nation were on their way out.

»Johnny, Max, could you do me a favor?«

Rodney and me looked at each other. Was it possible that we'd record with the guys from The Exceptional Nation? Just thinking that made the blood rush to my face. I was going to play with the drummer and the keyboard player from The Exceptional Nation! I was slowly becoming euphoric myself, and at the same time I started worrying about my own performance.

After a brief discussion we reached an understanding. Tom the singer and Sammy the guitarist said goodbye to the rest of the band. And I had no idea they were coming to us! Two seconds later they entered the room with the mixing console. I couldn't believe my eyes. They were of roughly the same build as Rodney and me. Just two ordinary guys like hundreds in the street.

»Hi, I'm Tom,« singer started the conversation, »you don't mind if we wait here, do you?«

XII. RECORDING

»HAVE YOU BROUGHT THE LIST OF SONGS WITH YOU?« I heard Jim asking, pulling me out of the trance caused by the fact that Tom from The Exceptional Nation knew who I was.

»Excuse me?«

»The list of songs, pieces, tracks, whatever you call them. You've said you had quite a few. I need the list for the recording plan. To divide them over the week when Sam.I.Am. gets here. Then, later, we'll polish them.«

I knew it was too early to count my chickens. Where was I to find a list of songs that *didn't exist*? From euphoria I bounced right back into anxiety.

»Yeah, yeah, sure, in a minute. Can I get a piece of paper, or maybe two?« I decided to simply make up the titles. I also thought it would be good to make the same list for myself, so I would know what topics to cover in my homework – namely the songs that still didn't exist.

I was looking at the piece of paper, deciding. I wrote down the first ten words that came to mind: »From Another World« (this was the easy one), »Piece of Paper«, »She«, »Contract«, »Sun«, »Desert«, »Car«, »Suit«, »Map« and »Guitar«.

»For now, I've selected the best ten,« I handed over the paper, evading discussion. He was pleased.

»Oh, great, thanks.« It crossed my mind that I might've written down too many and thus added additional pressure on myself. Because now, I really had to write ten songs in a week. The pressure made my muscles tense up all over my body. I couldn't even be sure how this first day of recording would end.

»Let's start with the first two today,« said Jim. »So:« he took my piece of paper – »'From Another World' and 'Piece of Paper'.« I swallowed hard and tried not to reveal my nervousness.

»So, two a day, huh? Isn't that a bit much?« I tried to remain calm.

»If we want to give the boss the best possible insight into your work, that's the only good option. You do wish to stay here, don't you?«

Yes, I wanted that more than anything else.

»Well, yes, of course, alright,« I mumbled. Maybe a miracle was about to happen. I did my best to calmly walk to the isolation booth, being careful of where I was walking, so I wouldn't give away my nervousness. Rodney started tugging at my sleeve as we were walking there and when we got to the passage where they couldn't see us, he snapped at me: »How are we going to do that?!?«

»I have no idea,« I said calmly like a death row inmate considering his last wishes. »I just know that I want to stay here. Just so you know: 'Piece of Paper' will be in G-major and as far as the rest of it goes, just try to follow my lead. And another thing: when we record 'From Another World', try teaching the others; that way we may buy ourselves some time so I can write the lyrics. Maybe we'll get away with it after all.« I handed him the lyrics and chords for the first song.

Rodney nodded silently and we entered the isolation booth where the drummer and the keyboard player were already waiting.

»So, here are the lyrics with chords,« said Rodney, trying to be as convincing as possible. He put them in front of Johnny, behind the keyboards, directing Max the drummer at the same time. On the other side of the glass Jim noticed that we needed more time to adjust to each other.

»Take 15 minutes, guys,« we heard over the speaker.

Rodney started instructing Johnny and Max, and I grabbed a blank piece of paper. I scribbled the title on it. What now? »Pleasehelpme, pleasehelpme, pleasehelpme...« echoed in my head. I was thinking with superhuman speed. Piece of Paper, Piece of Paper, Piece of Paper...

Minutes went by like seconds.

After five minutes I still had nothing. It seemed like my life was passing in front of my eyes. I felt strong pressure and my hands started to shake. I knew I couldn't give way to my emotions. Not now, in front of all these people.

»Great job, guys,« enthused Rodney. As professional musicians, guys from The Exceptional Nation absorbed new material immediately. Nevertheless, their instructor could've been a bit more demanding and that way buy me some additional time. I gave him a harsh look and motioned that he should think of something else.

»Well, on the other hand, maybe we could ease a bit on the tempo in the second verse. Johnny, are you sure about D-minor in the third line?« Rodney tried to stall some more.

And I was stuck with 'Piece of Paper' and three minutes I had left. »I'm not going to make it,« kept pecking in my head. »It's impossible…I can kiss my music career goodbye…« I started writing down random sentences that came to my mind, even though I knew that made no sense whatsoever.

White sheet of paper…
Horrible white sheet.
I'd like to write you a letter,
must be pure enough to do it.

Why don't I have inspiration?
Don't I love you enough?
So many times I tried!
Why am I so powerless?
Against a white sheet; powerless – like a child?

White sheet of paper…
Horrible white sheet.

When will I be strong enough?
Pure enough to do it?

I read my scribbles once again and in haste it seemed they made some kind of sense. I strummed a few passages in G-minor and started experimenting by moving my left hand across the frets. It didn't seemed familiar, but it sounded pretty good. If the previous song was more of a ballad, this one was a bit rougher, rawer. Like the time in which it was written. A squeak from the speaker ended my improvisation.

»Sorry, guys,« I heard Jim on the other side, »sometimes this thing squeaks. Are you ready?«

I looked at Rodney, who proudly gave me a thumbs-up. He saw me scribbling on the paper which could only have been a good sign.
»Yes,« I sighed into the microphone with relief.

We recorded the first song and then Jim gave us an equal amount of time to practice the second one. It was simpler than I'd expected. While I was showing chords to Max and Johnny, Rodney picked up on things automatically. We finished the recording ahead of schedule.

»Like I said, these are just basic tracks. Detailed processing and additional recording is planned for next month. For now we only need to know that the boss likes what he hears, so we can move forward. Considering the stuff we recorded today,« a little smile escaped him, »I think you've got nothing to worry about.« I thought he was genuinely satisfied.

My adrenaline rush subsided and I finally felt peaceful and happy. I did it, I really did it!!

Tom entered the isolation booth. I automatically stepped away. I wasn't used to hanging out with rock stars.

»Great music, guys,« he said. »Want to join me for a drink?«

Rodney answered enthusiastically without even asking me for an opinion: »Of course, why not!«

XIII. DEVIATION FROM THE PLAN

I SILENTLY PUT MY GUITAR IN ITS BAG AND ONTO MY BACK. When the guys from the band were far enough, I quietly asked him:

»What's the matter with you? We haven't got a second to celebrate – tomorrow we're recording two new songs, and I don't have a clue where they're coming from!«

»Don't worry, man, you're the band's inspiration,« said Rodney with a phony smile. »You'll put something together. We may never get an opportunity to have a drink and a chat with The Exceptional Nation again!«

»If we manage to stay here, another one will surely come,« I sneered at him. »And if we end up in the street because you want to be recognized in public, then it's really better that we enjoy every possible moment with them right now – because we're not going to be here much longer anyway,« I continued.

He got serious. »Sorry, man,« he said and I could see, that I got through to him. »But what was I supposed to say? I mean, The Exceptional Nation invite you for a drink. You can't say no just like that...«

»Okay,« I quickly concluded, because I didn't have an answer to that. »Let's try and do it as quickly as possible.«

He agreed. We got to a bar and pushed a couple of smaller tables together, because there were too many of us for a single one. We ordered – I decided to have something non-alcoholic just in case, because I wanted a clear head later – and then Tom leaned back in his chair and started the conversation.

»I've got a good feeling about you two,« he said seriously. »Your songs are full of energy, lyrics are original, music is innovative. You'll get far, at least in my opinion.«

I didn't know what to say to that. I took a deep breath to say »Thanks«, but Rodney was faster.

»Oh, it's not worth mentioning. The music you play, ours can hide in comparison.«

We looked at each other and an awkward silence set in. Rodney realized that he didn't make the best possible impression and immediately tried to rectify the mistake.

»I guess I'm not that good in the company of famous people, so I apologize. I wanted to say that I'm glad that you like it.«

»He meant to say: thank you,« I quickly summed up.

Tom smiled – he probably recognized himself from a few years ago. A couple of young, inexperienced and overly euphoric guys with good ideas that wanted to conquer the world – it usually starts that way. Soon we relaxed and the conversation turned much more lively. The guys talked a lot about their experiences on tours. There were quite a few amusing anecdotes. I couldn't decide whether all were real or not, but it did seem that everything was possible in the crazy world of rock'n'roll.

Soon we drank beer, as befits the telling of such stories. I was surprised at how much they chose to share with us. We could have sold that information to any L.A. tabloid. Then I came to a conclusion that, in all probability, nobody would've believed a couple of anonymous nobodies anyway. The Exceptional Nation must've counted on that. It seemed like we'd just started with the debate, when I realized it was eight p.m.

»This is on the house,« announced Tom.

»Are you sure?« I was being polite.

»'Course, we invited you, remember,« he replied.

We said goodbye and then I realized again what trouble I was in. I'd been immersed in the life of the famous so much that I forgot to live *my own* life. I'd been so enthralled with the journeys Tom had been talking about that I completely forgot about the journey that awaited me if I didn't record ten songs by Friday: the journey home.

I felt slightly dizzy after half a dozen beers I'd had. My noble abstinence didn't last long. And my dear friend Rodney forgot completely that neither one of us had the songs we needed the next day, anyway. I walked him to the car and tried to focus. Before we drove off in our old piece of junk I reached in my pocket for the piece of paper with song titles. I pulled out a bunch of papers and, to my great surprise, a hundred-dollar bill. I must've had it since Friday's party…I put the money away and looked at the paper with song titles. The next two were »She« and »Contract«. I put it back in my pocket and sighed deeply. I had a long night in front of me…

XIV. SHOCK

AFTER I DROPPED RODNEY OFF, I PARKED THE CAR NEAR OUR apartment building. It was already dark. I was overwhelmed by a strong need to clear my head.

I got out of the car and started walking down North Ogden Drive. Mostly prestigious houses in company of two low-rise apartment buildings that didn't belong there. In one of them – the white one with heavily worn eaves and cracked and flaking plaster – the two of us lived. At least they looked a little better in the dark, when the ugly details couldn't be seen. Thus I was able to pretend to be living in a prominent neighborhood, side by side with those beautiful homes…Someday I would live a prestigious life. And maybe that someday wasn't that far off anymore. If I could only find inspiration for new songs.

I started running. The street was peaceful and quiet. Sounds of people talking, having fun, or just sitting in front of their TV sets were coming from the houses. The smell of hot asphalt was in the air, rising from the ground, mixing with the scent of flowers.

As I was listening to the echo of my steady footsteps on the road, I started thinking about the next title…»She«. I knew immediately who I was going to write about. That much was certain. The smell of hot asphalt made me think about how she disappeared into the ground. The memory of that incident was so vivid in my mind that it seemed impossible it was just a figment of my imagination…Is it possible for a human mind to go astray so much that creates an image real to the eyes and yet completely fabricated?

I was still running. I was so immersed in my thoughts that I ran into somebody.

»Hey, man, watch it,« he roughly pushed me away.

»I'm sorry, I didn't see you,« I apologized. I was certain that I didn't run into him on purpose. But I realized that it was the other way around: he was looking for an opportunity to run into me. I also noticed that he wasn't alone.

Five robust figures stepped out of the dark. I couldn't believe my eyes. Such a peaceful neighborhood – and I was about to be involved in a street fight...? Now I was sincerely sorry that I didn't stick to karate lessons in the third grade. As a young kid I wanted to try everything and karate was popular for about six months. When the popularity wore off, so did my interest. My parents had tried, but…I didn't persevere. Unfortunately. Now I was obviously facing the consequences. Other gang members started to comment on our little collision. I knew they were together, a part of the team.

»What's wrong, man?«

»Hey, what's happening?«

»Is there a problem here?«

»Why are you bumping into innocent people?«

They surrounded me and I couldn't get away. Even if I knew how to fight, there were simply too many of them.

»I'm sorry, I really didn't do it on purpose,« I tried to apologize again. That was the only thing I had left.

»I saw you,« said the biggest one of them, »it didn't look like you pushed him so hard – by accident!«

»And I think,« added another one of the tall shadows, »that you bumped him on purpose!« These words were followed by a sudden punch to my stomach, which I really didn't expect. Suddenly I was left breathless and I didn't know how long I'd be able to endure that. I was on the ground in a second. A few moments later I was able to breath again, albeit shallowly, and it seemed that I'd pull through. When my gasping calmed down a little, two shadows grabbed me by my arms and lifted me up. The biggest one came closer and I noticed that he didn't care in the least about his appearance: that must've been a part of his image.

»Well, did you strike him by accident or on purpose?« he asked me again from up close, while they still had me in a lock.

»By accident, truly,« I apologized yet again. Another unexpected punch followed, this time in the face.

Watching movies, fighting in the night always seemed absolutely masculine to me. I found it cool when the main character had a few drops of blood in the corner of his mouth. The sound of a punch also always sounded cool to me. But now, as I was experiencing it myself, it wasn't in the least like in the movies. The punch didn't sound like I had expected; it was much harder and I felt my entire skull. It sounded more like an earthquake and the clash of my jawbones. In addition to that I felt a squirt of blood from my nose – a special effect, obviously, like a bonus. When the punch ended, my nerve endings transmitted the information to the brain, and it hurt a lot more than I ever could imagine. This feeling definitely greatly exceeded my pain threshold. I sighed as deeply as I still could.

»How's that, please?« the man faked politeness. »By accident or on purpose?«

It became crystal clear to me that I already answered incorrectly twice. And since I didn't want to receive another blow, I changed my press release.

»On purpose, on purpose,« I uttered through a gush of blood, »I definitely bumped into him on purpose. I apologize for my rudeness…«

The whole gang started to laugh. Well, nothing seemed funny to me. That's probably why I received another blow to the stomach. Why did it hurt so damn much? I wished I wasn't left breathless again!

»I think this requires more that an apology,« said the biggest one.

»Did we bring any money with us?« wanted to know another one.

I remembered the one hundred dollars. If they left my hands intact, so I could play the next day, this one hundred dollar bill might represent an investment – the insurance for my future in music...

»Of course, guys,« I said quickly. I reached in my pocket and offered them the money.

They were more than satisfied.

»Only rich boys live in these houses,« said the first one.

»Such a kid and he takes out a hundred-dollar bill like it was change,« thought the third one.

»Where do you live...?« the biggest one turned to me again.

Damn, I made another mistake. I offered them money so fast that they concluded I was rich. I didn't have any choice left. I could either lie, point them in the wrong direction and stay away from home entirely, or try to run. These five guys would probably catch me, though.

»Far away actually,« I lied.

»I came to visit my cousin. And I'm not as rich as you think. I got that from my grandmother for my birthday...« I was hoping that customs in L.A. and Quebec were similar, because back home I received money for my birthdays from my relatives. The gang sighed like they just heard something romantic.

»Ah, from your grandmother...? And where does your grandmother live?« they made fun of me. Since I was pretty broken up, I decided for diplomacy.

»Pretty far away, as I said. She sent the money to my cousin and I went to visit her today. I decided to go for a run before I returned home...«

They started considering what to do with me. My story was pretty complicated and I was hoping that it sounded genuine. The gang leader was walking around me, sizing me up from head to foot. I was praying. *Please God, let me live through this. It doesn't matter if I record another song in my life or not. If I make it through this, I'll live completely differently. I'll be happy, really happy and creative! I won't care if the entire crème de la crème of music invites me for a drink! I'll do what I have to do and I'll be truly happy. And also this: I'll probably enroll in a self-defense course. Just help me survive this!!!*

The gang leader must've made a decision, because he stopped directly in front of me.

»OK, then go ahead and exercise some more,« he said to me like talking to a five-year-old. I felt completely humiliated, even though that wasn't important anymore. I sincerely hoped for a positive outcome.

»Have a nice evening,« he said kindly and then suddenly kicked me in the shin so hard I bent down screaming in pain. Then I felt a strong blow hit my back and I fell to the ground. After a minute the pain spread all over my beaten body. When I eventually opened my eyes, the gang was gone. I just lay there without moving for a few minutes and held the parts of my body that hurt the most. For the first time in my life I was involved in a fight where me and only me got hurt. There were simply too many of them. I was writhing on the sidewalk, sighing from time to time. Even though my face was grimaced in pain, I was happy to be alive.

I considered crawling home, but I didn't know whether the gang hid somewhere, where they could watch me. They could've been hidden waiting for me to go home. So I decided not to go home, at least not while it was still dark. I had to protect Rodney. And the rest of the money. And my dreams.

I slowly got up and limped away in the same direction I was running earlier. Every time I stepped on my right leg it hurt like I was shot through the shin. I was breathing shallowly and I knew that I couldn't go into the studio in such a condition. After half an hour of limping I stopped and with some difficulty sat on the grass next to the asphalt. Even though it was already midnight, I was still hoping for inspiration. I curled up in a ball and shook. The grass on my face softly soothed the pain from the punch. Lying on the soft ground, I slowly lost the sense of time.

XV. MORNING

I WAS AWAKENED BY THE SOUND OF THE CELL PHONE RINGING IN MY jacket. I'd completely forgotten that I had it with me! I'd have called Rodney last night and he'd have come and got me. It was already daytime. I couldn't tell exactly what was ringing louder, my head or the device in my pocket. I didn't feel quite like myself. Like I'd actually won the most important battle of my life the night before…I remembered all the promises I made just before a group of shadows decided to finally leave me alone. The morning sun was shining upon me and I was glad to be alive. Even though I was still half dead. The cell phone kept ringing.

I found the device and leaned it against my ear.

»Where are you, man? You didn't go to another party without me, did you?« Rodney joked.

»Actually,« I summed up in a hoarse voice while listening to the loud ringing in my head, »I got robbed yesterday…and beat up.« I must have sounded pretty helpless. Rodney knew from the sound of my voice that I was telling the truth.

»What? Where are you, man? Should I come and get you? So you can clean up before the recording!« He obviously still believed that we were able to show up for the recording without the songs we were supposed to record.

»No hard feelings,« I said, »but I don't know what to do about the songs today.«

»No problem, man. I've already written them!« he said confidently.

»What? How?« Rodney hadn't written a song in his life, and now two at once?

»Yeah, I woke up and simply started singing to myself. Then Jessica surprised me earlier this morning and we've finished them both together. I knew about the titles, because you kept repeating them on the way home. They're great!« I wasn't even aware of the fact that I'd been repeating the titles out loud.

»Yeah, alright,« I said surprised, »please come get me, then.«

I explained to him where I was and he arrived in a few minutes. When he saw me, he stopped the car and came running to me with a horrified look on his face. I obviously looked much worse than I realized.

»Are you alright, I mean, really? Can you play?«

I wiggled my fingers. Thank God they were left unharmed. I smiled and unknowingly revealed a bloody coating on my teeth, which made Rodney jump back. Life force filled my body again and I knew that this time I was *really* going to live. As I had promised to myself.

»I'm great, man. Just get me home, so I can clean myself up.«

I got in the car and Rodney simply couldn't believe that somebody whose life was hanging by a thread a short time ago, could be in such a good mood. If he had been in my place, he'd have understood. I was given another chance and *that's* why I was so happy.

At home I quickly cleaned myself up and when Rodney played me the songs I was even happier. But not jumping-in-the-air, screaming-from-joy happy. I was sort of…at peace with myself. I could feel that there was nothing worth killing myself over, because this life clearly wasn't mine anyway. A gang of thugs could – regardless of how much I struggled – come from behind the first corner and destroy me. That's is why I needed to *live*, regardless of everything. That's why I needed to create. And not so that a crowd of people could scream below my stage. Well, maybe it was a little bit about that too.

The songs were really good.

»Shall we?« I said calmly.

»Let's go. We're a bit late already. You did a pretty good job,« he said when he saw that I managed to remove all the blood from my face. Considering what I'd been through, I looked rather decent. If I didn't limp, nobody could guess that merely twelve hours ago I was saying – my almost final – Our Father.

We hit the road. On the way he sang both songs to me a few times. The first one was about Jessica and it was really beautiful. I could feel that whatever had been happening between the two of them over the past year, was real and genuine. »Contract« was more of an amusing song, describing how God and the Devil reached an agreement in some other dimension, consequently ruling us, insignificant little earthlings. I was impressed with such an imaginative idea that also seemed really fresh. Soon after that we arrived at the studio. I'd never felt such a profound peace before.

XVI. A WEEK FOR HOPE

AFTER A SUCCESSFUL DAY OF RECORDING – MAX AND JOHNNY HAD become a permanent fixture in the studio, while the other two The Exceptional Nation members also liked watching us work – we headed home. This time we politely turned down the invitation for drinks and I could tell that Rodney didn't mind it that much. He knew we had to work.

Soon Jessica and the two of us became a pretty good team. We started writing songs together and things slowly began to turn around. On Wednesday we wrote four songs (»Sun«, »Desert«, »Car« and »Suit«) and they all had some sort of special, personal note about them. Since Jessica had taken piano lessons in elementary school, it occurred to me that she might, with a bit of practice, play keyboards for us.

»Oh, my God,« she was ecstatic, »is this an invitation? What do you think Rodney, would you like that?«

Rodney looked at me seriously and said: »Well, there is one thing that really bothers me about this!«

»And that is…?« she asked uncertainly.

»That I didn't think of that!!!« he said with a smile and hugged her. »I'd love that. I'd be thrilled! Of course!« he kissed her. I was a bit jealous. But nevertheless happy for them.

»Well, lovebirds, shall we practice?« I joked.

Later we went out and bought a keyboard for Jessica, who was ecstatic. She loved our type of music and I could tell that she might've come up with the same proposition herself, had she dared. It seemed that she was somewhat intimidated by male company. Maybe she had thought that we wanted an all-male band. It made no difference to me, in a way. The important thing was that we played.

On Thursday she joined us for recording and replaced Johnny. Even though he was a bit disappointed, seeing her enthusiasm and happiness quickly calmed him down, and he watched the recording with Tom and Sammy. Jessica's playing was very good and confident. I didn't think you could master the rock scene after studying Bach and Mozart.

The recording continued on Friday. Sam.I.Am came to visit us on our last day. After five days of constant creating I was pretty calm, considering the fact that not that long ago I trembled in front of famous people.

»What's up, team? Are you cooperating now, or what?« he was surprised by the crowd at the mixing desk. »Have they asked for useful advice so I wouldn't throw them out, or are they just learning technique from you?«

»Actually, we're learning from them,« replied Tom, »I have to admit that the scene hasn't seen such a refreshing band in a long time.« He didn't have to say that. My ego suddenly rose to the sky and I had a hard time taming it. Then I remembered the fight in the street and that immediately changed my perspective. *I could lose all of this in a moment*, I thought. *Keep your head clear.*

»Well, I'll be the judge of that,« the producer smiled vehemently. »Take half an hour off while I listen to the songs.«

We stepped out. I didn't know what to think. Tom was assuring us the whole time that there was no question about whether we'd stay here or not. Sam.I.Am supposedly held on to good bands no matter what. He even said we should carefully read the provisions of the new contract, so we wouldn't be tied to Sam.I.Am's projects too tightly. I was honored that somebody had such a high opinion of my music. Although I wasn't even sure it *was mine*, regardless of the effort I put into it.

Tom also asked us if we wanted to join their next tour as an opening act.

»Isn't it a bit too early…?« I tried to remain levelheaded.

»You need to book a good band early enough,« he asserted. Somehow I wasn't sure why he was being so nice. Did we really make such an impression?

Half an hour flew by incredibly quickly and soon we were in front of the studio doors again. *Now it's going to be serious*, I thought and knocked. There was nothing but silence. We peeked inside and saw Jim signaling us that Sam.I.Am was listening to the last song. After a minute or so he slowly took the headphones off – he would always do that like some sort of a ritual – and put them on the desk. He looked towards the door and saw us through the glass.

»Come on in, kids,« he said and I couldn't tell whether he was in a good or bad mood.

»I'll say this, straight out and without exaggerating.«

A few seconds of rhetorical silence followed, while the producer positioned his hands in some sort of speaker's poise.

»The songs really are pretty original. If you have the time, I'd like to book you for the next month. Let's get this clear: we'll sign a new contract first thing Monday, without any unnecessary bullshit like you signed five days ago. This is serious business now. You will be appropriately paid for your work – whether inside or outside the studio. But be careful: I won't tolerate any slacking or rock star excuses. You'll have to stick to your guitars now. And drumsticks. By the way, do your have a drummer or should I get you one?«

After half a second break he continued: »I'll send you one.« It was obvious that this was business as usual around here.

»After a month we'll release a few of the best songs, one by one. As singles. And finally the whole product. Promotion will be huge; I hope you're aware of that. After that comes a tour, CD signings, videos, interviews. Sometimes all of that may be a bit unpleasant. Are you ready for this kind of life, do you really want that?« It sounded like somebody

had just informed us that we'd be going to the Moon and asked us if we really wanted that. I didn't know, I'd never tried it before. In any case, everything that the producer had offered us was exactly what I had been dreaming about my whole life. So now I couldn't say no. I was too close to realizing my dreams. So what if things turned a bit harder every now and then? I'd survive.

»Of course we do,« I answered on behalf of the three of us.

»Good,« said the producer quickly. He was hoping for such a quick reaction. Once you've said »Yes« and signed things, you can't change your mind anymore. »I'll need a signature from parents or guardians for everybody that's under 21 – a pure formality,« he distributed a few sheets of paper. It was like school all over again, when our parents had to sign invitations to PTA meetings.

»Well, this is it. Actually, I'd like to congratulate you on a job well done. Really good music. I'm wondering what'd have happened if that cleaning lady hadn't charmed the receptionist that directed her towards my door...« he said and burst into laughter. We laughed to.

»Have a nice weekend, guys,« he added. »See you on Monday. Try not to party too hard.« He was obviously familiar with the habits of young people that made it. In their euphoria they reached for every possible substance to prolong and intensify that state. But they refused to see the side effects that followed once chemical effects subsided. Well, he didn't have to worry about me. I'd already shad my share of experiences.

We left the studio relieved. Before we said goodbye to The Exceptional Nation, we went for a quick drink with them and exchanged contact information. They insisted on having us as their opening act.

»It doesn't matter if you have your own independent career going, we'll convince him somehow,« said Tom. We said goodbye at six p.m.

Rodney and Jessica soon started talking about going to the movies and I could see that they wanted to have the evening to themselves. That was perfectly understandable after a whole week of hanging out together.

»I don't know, I don't know,« said Jessica and then asked carefully, »would you like to go, Jesse?«

»No, you guys go ahead,« I quickly turned her down. »I've got my own plans.« Which was true. I really had something planned.

»OK, man,« Rodney patted me on the shoulder, »try not to get in any fights. And be home early,« he said in a patronizing tone of voice.

»Yes, yes,« I said impatiently and couldn't wait for them to leave.

When they finally said goodbye, I took a piece of paper from my pocket that I'd been carrying around for several days. For the time being I was carefully hiding my secret research from my band mates, because I didn't know what exactly they would think of me. Even so the situation was awkward enough. And in view of my upcoming regularly paying job, I decided to spend some money this evening and called a taxi.

XVII. FULFILLING THE PROMISE

I ASKED THE DRIVER TO DROP ME OFF QUITE CLOSE TO THE ENTRANCE. It was getting dark and although evenings in this town were warm, pleasant and mostly peaceful, I didn't want to run into some unexpected trouble. I also asked him to pick me up in the same place in couple of hours.

I took the bag I'd prepared a couple of days ago and clumsily got out the narrow car door. Even though I was now able to spend more on my transportation, I was still being thrifty. Once you have experienced poverty like Rodney and me lived in a month ago, you tended to become careful with money. I planned to relax only when there was a million dollars or more in my bank account. I could never imagine how much money average rock stars were actually making. It simply seemed too abstract to think about such large numbers. One apple, two apples, that made sense. But five million apples…That was unimaginable.

I paid the driver for my ride and to wait for me, because I wanted him to really be there in two hours' time. Then I vanished through the entrance of the dark building. Had I not made inquiries over the phone the day before, I'd surely get lost in the building's dark corridors. Luckily for me, some parts of the way as well as turns were marked with arrows. I looked back from time to time, so I could find the way out more easily later on.

Soon I heard sounds emanating from the gym: the sound of protective leather gloves hitting punching bags and men shouting. I was about to fulfill the last promise I made to myself before those gang gorillas let me live. I opened the door and walked into a locker room with endless rows of lockers. Straight ahead was the entrance to the main gym. Soon tall and muscular guys started coming out of the gym, drenched with sweat from the workout. Their sweat seemed almost like a fashion accessory – a proud proof of their workout.

Soon a man came through the door that appeared to be their leader. Although he was a little shorter and somewhat older than the rest of them, he nevertheless seemed tough and in a really good shape. *You won't knock this one to the ground that easily,* I thought. He moved gracefully and was wearing a robe.

I was so preoccupied with checking out the new place that I didn't even notice a few guys that had joined me at the entrance, checking out the place for themselves. I noticed them only when one of the muscular guys turned towards us.

»Oh, rookies,« he grinned. »Come on in girls, we don't bite,« he teased us.

»And that's the only thing we don't do,« said another one. He had a darker, Hispanic complexion. As he watched us motionless, he smacked one fist against the other like he wanted to say: "soon it'll be your turn to fight".

»Look at them, how frightened they are,« continued the first one.

I didn't feel afraid. Although it was true that during the five days at the studio I wasn't exposed to such quantity of testosterone.

»Well, boys, what did we say, a bit of respect, please,« calmly, but firmly said the instructor in the robe. »Don't let me start telling stories about how you looked on your first day of practice.«

They all stopped speaking immediately. I could only hear the sound of water dripping in the showers. The man in the robe really had the authority. I had a feeling that he wouldn't even have to fight his opponent. He had some sort of…inner power. Nevertheless, his physical strength was also more than evident.

»Well, fresh blood, if you've seen enough,« he finally addressed us, »I'd like to invite you to choose your space in the locker room.«

I turned around and finally saw that there were approximately ten young guys standing behind me, of roughly the same size as me. So, there were more of us in need of self-defense lessons. Most of us weren't here to pump up our muscles – that much was clear – but exclusively to learn how to stay in one piece.

I followed the others and changed in the locker room. I was considering all possible outcomes of my secret training. How Rodney, Jessica and me could find ourselves in trouble one day, and I'd chase away the bad guys and surprise my friends with my skills. Or how I could protect a beautiful girl. And of course, how I could by pure chance run into *them* again. Only this time I'd give them the surprise of their lives. Like Jean-Claude Van Damme. Or Arnold Schwarzenegger. My head was full of these self-grandiose thoughts as I stepped into the gym. There, our teacher was waiting for us.

»Hello again, my name is Adam and I am your self-defense instructor,« he said quickly. »By deciding to take this class you've made a big step towards self-respect, respecting others and the world. I must warn you that this is not a school for Rambos,« a little smile escaped him. I tried not to be surprised by how quickly and simply he'd read my thoughts. »Every result will be a product of hard work and practice. Any questions?«

We looked at him in silence, not ready for his call – concerning questions. Every one of us was entangled in his own thoughts and expectations. Each one hoping to get rid of his fears and become some sort of hero. Or at least a safer person.

»Well, if there are no questions, I'll present to you the schedule for our daily practices. We'll always start with warm-up exercises. I'll later explain why. Be persistent. Those persisting will be richly rewarded. You won't need any equipment today; for the next practices you can order it with me. I presume none of you have any chronic diseases, inflammations or serious illnesses that would require a medical certificate permitting you to attend this type of class?«

We looked at each other and sat in silence.

»Excellent. As I've already said, for a start we need to warm up and get in shape.«

I was glad that we were finally going to start with serious workout. But I didn't have a clue what exactly he meant by 'getting in shape'. I imagined we were going to hit some punching bags or something similar. But something completely different happened: he led us to the running track that encircled the gym and told us to run.

So, we ran. At first, it was rather interesting, and every now and then there was an amusing comment. After the third lap most of us were pretty exhausted. New instructions followed, telling us to include our arms. We were supposed to stretch them out in front of us as if attacking an opponent.

Over the next three laps we gritted our teeth and tried to follow the instructions as best as we could. I wanted to impress our instructor and so did my classmates. I was slightly embarrassed, though, when my body started shaking from exertion after the sixth lap. When I looked around the group I noticed that everybody was minding their own business. I recognized fake smiles: we all wanted to look normal and rested, even though we were already dead tired.

When he instructed us to run even faster, somebody protested by saying that his whole body hurt. The rest of us took advantage of that and the group slowly came to a stop. I was slightly disappointed. Half an hour of practice had already passed and we did nothing but run. If I wanted to jog, I'd go jogging and wouldn't spend additional money on a self-defense class. Or maybe our instructor was trying to suggest that the best way to protect yourself was to quickly run away. How simple. Now why didn't I think of that!?

Adam finally stopped us and gave us instructions for stretching exercises. That actually resembled a real training or a fight. Another half an hour later, when we were properly stretched, he addressed us again.

»Fighting is actually a mere checking of the combined concentration of our mind, body and spirit.« It sounded like a line from a kung fu documentary.

»In reality you *don't want* to start with the fighting today. Not really. You are not ready yet. If I challenged you with punches and kicks today, while you're still panting and gasping for air, it wouldn't do any good to anybody. That's why running is so important during the warm-up phase.«

That was his only explanation why we spent the rest of the training running. In the end I was really angry with the world, and especially with him, for pushing us like cattle. I'd like nothing more that to quit the class, but then I remembered what would happen the next time I ran into a group of people that wanted my money. *Calm down, Jesse*, I consoled myself with a thought that could barely travel through my tired nervous system, *at least you'll be able to run fast.*

After we completed the final part (exercises for cooling down the body), he concluded the training by reminding us of the next one on Monday.

We didn't have to hide our tiredness anymore. As we got to the locker room, each one of us immediately sat or even lied down for a few moments. We didn't even have enough energy for a conversation.

I remembered that I had a taxi waiting for me outside and was consequently the first one to leave the locker room. I mumbled something like: »See you,« and – miraculously – found my way out. As I sat in the yellow car I wondered whether Jessica and Rodney were already home. Even though I was really tired, I was actually satisfied I did this. I actually took a class. I sat back in the upholstered seat and enjoyed the simple feeling of sitting down…

XVIII. A MONTH FOR FULFILLMENT OF DREAMS

WHEN I GOT HOME THAT EVENING ALL SWEATY, RODNEY AND Jessica were already in the room. As I opened the door they quickly switched from lying on the bed to a more discreet sitting position. I smiled.

»I apologize for interrupting. How was the movie?«

»Great, thanks,« answered Jessica and took a closer look at me. Women obviously had a knack for paying attention to a man when they didn't have to.

»Hey, where have you been? You're all wet!« she exclaimed.

I was hoping to be able to hide this for at least a while, but I obviously wasn't going to.

»You didn't have a date of your own today, did you?« asked Rodney with insinuating smile. Well, I did have a date, just not the sort he imagined. I decided to tell them openly; I was planning on going there to train intensively at least for a month anyway. They should know.

When I was finished with the explanation they were both very pleased and happy for me.

»At least we won't have to pay for bodyguards,« Rodney grinned.

»Well, maybe for one or two,« I added.

The weekend that followed went by extremely quickly. We practiced the bunch of songs we wrote during the week and worked on our respective solo parts. Interestingly enough, I didn't feel the need to go out or do something similar. I had my music, I had the life I had been dreaming about and I was perfectly satisfied. On Sunday I even phoned home – got mom – and told her we were doing great. I was being truthful for a change this time and hoped that the news would reach my dad.

Before we started recording on Monday, we were shown the recording contract we were supposed to sign by the end of the week. Jessica suggested that we have the contract looked over by some friends of her parents that had a law firm. I was happy and satisfied that things were going smoothly and without any unnecessary emotional distress for a change. I was totally fed up with my emotional swings between euphoria and depression. This time I just wanted to live and create. Just that.

The recording went on without interruptions and our new – somewhat timid, yet excellent – drummer Tim fit right in with our little group. The interesting thing about him was that he was the smallest of the four of us, yet he was the shyest. He would always wait for other people to finish what they were saying before he spoke. He would politely open doors when people were behind him and he would always ask to go to the bathroom, which I found a bit strange. He had short brown hair and I'd never guess he was a rock musician. I'd probably think he was into math or something like that. But never music.

It was also interesting that he would manage to completely relax only behind his drum kit. He became another person behind his drums. His body would relax from his usual upright and often-uptight posture, and his hands would relax while holding drumsticks. I realized very soon that Sam.I.Am gave us one of his best session musicians.

When we were out one time having a drink, and I mentioned to him that I couldn't help but notice these little quirks of his, he started to laugh.

»Is it that obvious?« he said like he knew immediately what I was trying to say.

»Actually…yes.«

»It's an interesting story, really. I haven't been here that long. And I'm here purely because of the luck I've had in my life. Even though I was born and raised in England, in an aristocratic families, I've always known that I was somehow different from everybody else.« It was only now that I realized that he occasionally pronounced words differently than other Americans. But I didn't pay too much attention to that.

»My parents wanted me to continue the family tradition, but I rebelled against it. I know that sounds simplistic, but tradition is everything where I come from. To follow the tradition means more than life to some people. Well, I didn't think it was that important. I renounced my nobility and they renounced me, in a way. Don't get me wrong, I haven't severed all ties. The only thing my mother asked for when I was leaving was: 'Don't come home until you've stopped wearing scruffy cotton T-shirts and worn-out jeans.' And that's it,« he simply concluded.

»Your family don't like rock music too much, do they?«

»They support it, actually. But I'd have to be a really big star to be accepted in their ranks again. They sometimes organize charity concerts and similar events. All invited musicians must be dressed elegantly for those, of course, regardless of their usual image,« he said absent-mindedly.

»Well, maybe they'll invite us some day – but for a fat fee, of course,« I tried to get him in a better mood. I discovered that we were alike, in a way. I was far from being an aristocrat – I didn't even know that people still took these things seriously – but I could relate to that stuff about tradition. Suddenly his behavior seemed much more familiar.

Jessica quickly found her musical feet too. Her solos were exactly what our music often lacked. She had a distinct feeling for what belonged together and what didn't. That's why she often found herself on the other side of the glass giving the guys instructions.

When Sam.I.Am decided after a couple of weeks that the time had come to release our first single, he asked us what our band's name was. That question left us speechless. We'd been so busy creating music that we didn't consider that at all.

»Can we have a day or two?« asked Rodney. By then we had become completely relaxed in Sam.I.Am's company. That was, actually, even one of his conditions for working with us. »From now on no more kid gloves, please,« he said to us upon signing the contract we all thought was pretty fair.

So, we took a day to think about it. Each of us wrote a few suggestions on a piece of paper. Later on we met to discuss them and choose the right one. This time we met in Tim's apartment, which he shared with a couple of roommates.

He even prepared snacks and drinks; it was obvious that he took this search for a name absolutely seriously, like everything else in life. We sat around the coffee table that was the only slightly loosened thing in his otherwise impeccable tidy little apartment.

»What about…Wild Souls?«

»Crazy Looks?«

»New Blows!«

»Hidden Souls.«

»The Magnificent.«

»Famous Bastards.«

»No. Let's get serious. We have to find something really catchy,« Rodney interrupted us after an hour of similar suggestions.

»Any ideas, Jesse Roy?« he looked at me.

»That's not bad at all,« said Jessica, like she had just realized something important.

»What's not bad?« I asked her.

»Jesse Roy,« she answered. The other guys smiled in relief, but I wasn't so sure that it was such a good idea.

»Come on, Bon Jovi's stage name is also the name of his band. You're our frontman, anyway,« said Rodney with conviction. »How are you going to prove to your father that you've made it if you sing under the name

Wild Souls? No offence, Tim,« he quickly apologized to the drummer, who suggested that name.

»Those who agree with this name,« solemnly said Jessica, »raise your right hand and say: 'I'«.

Everybody raised their right hands in oath, and simultaneously said what the leader ordered them to say. Everybody except me.

»Are you sure…?« I continued in doubt. »Are you really all for this…?« I looked at Tim, who sported a peaceful and satisfied smile. It was painfully obvious that they all really loved that suggestion. The next day we met the designer of our CD cover, gave him our new name and picked one of his suggestions.

»This is going pretty fast, isn't it, Rodney?« I remarked at the end of the meeting. I remembered how we were trying to come up with the money for my plane ticket to Quebec barely a month ago, and now we were about to release our first single.

»Very fast, and that is very good,« calmly concluded Rodney.

The month started passing by even more quickly and when we finished recording all the songs, two more singles were released: »From Another World« and »Piece of Paper«.

I tried to remain calm the first time I heard myself sing on the radio. It happened while I was on my way to my self-defense class, which I still attended regularly (fortunately after a week of running we started practicing punches and blocks). I just sat into the taxi when the radio anchor announced a new song in the charts. I didn't really listen to the radio; it served more for background music. Only when the anchor said my name I snapped out of my thoughts and started listening to it. I couldn't believe my ears. I wanted to scream from happiness. And when the anchor said that that young band had already started climbing the Billboard chart, I simply couldn't remain calm anymore. I called Rodney immediately. And so the taxi driver found out who I was.

XIX. PREPARATIONS

SOON THE SHOOTING OF VIDEOS FOLLOWED. It was usually very abstract: most of the time I had to stare at the camera and »look sexy«, with a fluorescent green screen behind my back. The others had to pretend to play their instruments – also in front of the screen. All that was »enriched« with long breaks and preparations for the shooting, but we slowly had to get used to it. Often I was exhausted simply because of the waiting for all the cables to be in place and the scene to be ready. The most interesting part came at the end when I had to put on a tight jumpsuit (because I turn into a piece of paper myself at the end of the video). They drew a few dots on my face, and I had some sort of outgrowth on the top of my head – an additional camera that recorded my facial expressions or something. Interesting experience.

When we saw the finished video a few days later, I was elated. I couldn't have even imagined that someday I would be a part of such a mini science-fiction movie. The video too became an instant hit. And when Sam.I.Am then struck again with the video for »From Another World«, we really became recognizable. That way the public had two songs, two versions of the Jesse Roy band: the rougher and the softer side.

Then the first interviews started. In a few meetings the producer explained to us exactly how to act in front of the media – for a start we had to be »cool«, not talk too much about personal things and avoid scandals – what we could talk about and what we couldn't. He hired designers so we could put together a visual image of the band. In the end – after countless experiments – we decided to go with jeans and T-shirts, which we completed with slightly more sophisticated jackets. That was actually Tim's idea and it seemed very appropriate to me too. I did like the fact that we stood out from the crowd.

We also decided to have a few rules of our own that applied exclusively to us, the band members. We would never disclose anything going on behind the stage. We would never talk about any conflicts or crises. That was purely our business. Whatever we told about ourselves to each other, had to stay inside the band. We would never get upset in public or on the road. Soon people were starting to recognize us in the street, which was a good sign, but we couldn't know whether there were photographers or reporters around, hidden in bushes. We opted for unity. And we sealed it with our internal, secret contract.

Sam.I.Am soon announced our first tour and we were thrilled. He too took his work with us extremely seriously. Even though The Exceptional Nation with Tom at the helm still insisted that they wanted us on their approaching tour as an opening act, he turned them down. It even seemed that he set our tour dates to roughly match theirs on purpose. We had to adjust.

Two months after the first recording we already started with the preparations for the tour. Sam.I.Am – who obviously didn't want to wait that a good band that could make him a lot of money, would find another producer – thoroughly acquainted us with the touring schedule, our obligations and rights. We were elated and could hardly wait for our first shows. It was true that we were scheduled to start out in smaller venues, but they were bigger than any event I ever performed at.

»The first part of the tour is for warming up,« he smiled, »and we'll finish it in stadiums.«

I could hardly imagine how somebody could fill out a stadium after only three months of work. Obviously managerial work represented a challenge to Sam.I.Am and he took it up with passion. It seemed like he was playing with numbers. Like he simply loved his work so much that he was prepared to set himself goals the others would think impossible to achieve. After an additional month of preparations – we got a few special effects experts, and for some songs Sam.I.Am decided to hire dancers and pyrotechnics – we were really ready.

The producer truly didn't mind the expenses when it came to our appearance or reputation: we found ourselves on quite a few magazine covers. Naturally, we had to invite our viewers to our upcoming tour during each and every interview. He even hired a psychologist who coached us for TV interviews and taught us a few relaxation techniques. That reminded me of my high school years when two of my classmates taught a similar course…Besides, I didn't pay too much attention to it: it seemed that I'd be equally good in interviews – with a relaxation technique or without one. With abdominal breathing or without it. And for the time being – I was right. Up until the tour.

XX. PRESS CONFERENCE BEFORE THE TOUR

ALTHOUGH THE FOURTH MONTH OF OUR COOPERATION WAS APPRO-aching, the tour dates started being postponed. Sam.I.Am called it the strategy of postponement. The more we would postpone the dates, the more people would know our music. And it actually worked! More and more interviews showed that we were really becoming recognizable. That was the reason he would still not allow us to open shows for The Exceptional Nation.

I eventually had to drop self-defense classes, because it soon became public knowledge that I was going there. Even though my increased income and luxury hotels might suggest I had more freedom, in reality I was less free. Soon I started missing lonely walks where a gang of thieves could attack me. Such outings simply weren't possible anymore.

On the other hand, I did enjoy the attention. I came up with a few stories for the press about how the songs came into being. I did, however – because I didn't want to set any bad examples for young people – leave out certain details, like taking ecstasy, for instance. And I also kept quiet about the fight during which I was robbed. I didn't want to give the impression of a drug user or a coward. Besides, I had protection – a couple of men in black were watching over me. I'd never expected being that protected someday. And even if somebody did outsmart them, I had the basic knowledge of self-defense that I got from Adam.

The other band members were experiencing the same things. When they realized what it meant to be famous, they instinctively kept pushing me to the forefront, saying that I was the head of the band anyway.

They wanted to protect and enjoy their privacy and I was their sacrificial lamb of sorts. I can't say whether that was good or bad. It certainly had its advantages and disadvantages. I had to laugh when I saw myself on the covers of various girly magazines that were declaring me the most desirable bachelor in Hollywood. Sam.I.Am really worked hard on the publicity. We were being invited to all types of events.

Private therapist, Dr Ian Keller, hired by the producer for the band, kept breathing down my neck. He wanted to make sure I was »down-to-earth« enough to have enough energy for the demanding interviews…Of course I had it! This was exactly what I came to Los Angels for!

Then the first fan letters started to arrive. At first we thought it was fun, but after a while it became boring, because most of the letters sounded almost the same. Soon the producer had to hire a few people to deal with the mail; they'd send back our signed photographs.

I also had to change my phone number. The producer informed us that, except for the »JesseRoy.com« website that was set up for us by computer experts, we could forget about using all the other social networks. So I waved goodbye to Facebook, Twitter, Badoo,…I was protected like I was inside aluminum foil. Nobody could touch me – which seemed absurd.

Sam.I.Am was becoming more and more rigorous: »I've told you that it won't be always easy. Now you're climbing to the top and you have to obey the rules! You could fall on your faces in a heartbeat!«. And so we obeyed his rules. Every day.

Finally in May the time had come for the tour. The masses were excited and so were we. On the day we hit the road, our producer organized an event, where fans could buy tickets to accompany us from the press conference to the tour bus. I felt like a parade monkey. It seemed absurd to me that someone would pay for a ticket, just to *escort* me to the bus. But our producer knew very well what he was doing. People could see almost every move we made – for a proper compensation, of course.

The press conference was a routine affair. Nothing out of the ordinary happened, except fans escorting us to the tour bus afterwards. I enjoyed it in a way, because it was packed with reporters. Most of them I knew already; I had spent the last few months almost entirely in their company. Or in my therapist's. I even saw the members of my own band less.

After approximately ten questions that were directed merely at me – the rest of the band insisted that I was the one who knew all the answers for so long that reporters gradually left them alone and focused entirely on me – something interesting happened.

I noticed a blonde female reporter in the last row. Her curls were shoulder-length, she had a symmetrical face and an interesting white dress. Once again she looked slightly archaic, even though she didn't stand out from the mass of reporters. She wore exactly the same dress as she did the last time I saw her...on the dance floor... In that club... Months ago. I was surprised: so it turned out that she did exist. Working as a reporter. I wasn't mistaken. I thought about possibly inviting her to a dinner; I had quite enough of invitations from girls that thought I was god. I really hated that.

I'd never have thought that this business could be so lonely. It always seemed to me that stars had countless friends. In reality they only had *fans*; true friends were rare and far between. I could really talk only to my band members if I could see them at all in between interviews and various events.

Be that as it may, she was standing there. I didn't even know how to address her in front of the crowd. And since they were about to escort us to the tour bus at the end of the conference, I wouldn't be able to approach her and ask her for her phone number or something similar.

Luckily, she helped me out by raising her hand. *Excellent*, I thought, *she has a question. I'll gladly answer her.* Even though several reporters simultaneously raised their hands when I finished answering the previous question, I pointed at her.

»The lady at the back, in the white dress.« Some reporters looked back, but most of them just waited for the question.

She looked downwards and appeared to be a bit embarrassed.

»Well, don't be afraid,« I gently encouraged her. I really wanted her to feel as relaxed as possible in this crowd. People started looking towards the last row, but I didn't mind. *Let them see the possible future Mrs. Roy.* She smiled and I did the same. It seemed like those few seconds lasted forever. I was enjoying her presence and it seemed that she somehow understood me. Inside. The world made sense again.

»Jesse?« Rodney looked at me.

»Jesse, who are you talking to…?« asked Sam.I.Am, who was sitting on my right. I looked at him. Didn't he see the pretty blonde?

»Who am I…« I looked in her direction again. She wasn't there. I looked up and down the hall, but she was nowhere to be seen.

The questions poured in, but Sam.I.Am cut them short.

»The members of the band are quite tired, as you can see, and we haven't even started the tour yet.« Laughter spread through the crowd and I noticed that the producer always managed to find the right words to calm down those present, even in moments of crisis, usually with a healthy dose of humor. Long years of practice in the music industry we evident.

He gave us a sign to get up and unnoticeably started directing and almost pushing us towards the exit. We had to smile and act »normally« the whole time, naturally. The smile was stuck to my face like somebody glued it there. I didn't feel like smiling at all. Just a few moments ago I saw the girl with my own eyes. She was really there and nobody could convince me otherwise. So what if she was a hologram or Houdini's daughter? She was good at disappearing, that's all. Or, I was seriously going out of my mind. Maybe I'd had a few screws loose from the very beginning and didn't know it. Funny, because I didn't take any illegal substances before the interview. And I had been leading a healthy lifestyle all these months, just like the producer had ordered us.

I climbed the tour bus with mixed feelings. When the order came to look relaxed and wave, I waved. Pure farce.

It seemed like it took forever for the bus doors to finally close. We weren't alone on the bus, though. Our team was traveling with us: two bodyguards, our therapist and Sam.I.Am, who didn't want to let us out of his sight on our first tour. In the second, less colorful bus, driving behind us, were technicians, electricians and dancers.

The producer asked Dr Keller to join him. They sat behind the red curtain in the back and I could hear angry whispering. It sounded like a serious argument. The others took their seats, while I stepped closer to the back of the bus.

»Why have I been paying you? So the kid can hallucinate, or what? He's the frontman, for God's sake – do you realize how much he's worth? What are you treating him with?«

»Well, I haven't prescribed him anything yet. We're mostly talking…« Dr Keller defended himself.

»Talking?! You haven't given him any sedatives or whatever? Can you even begin to imagine how stressful the life of a rock star can be? And you're 'talking' to him. Had I known that, I'd have hired somebody else a long time ago…«

»OK, OK, I'll talk to him…«

»I don't want you to talk to him, how many times do I have to tell you that!! I want you to *cure* him, do you understand? The tour hasn't even started yet and the kid's already hallucinating. Have you ever asked yourself if he's maybe on something you don't know about? No, because you're just talking to him. Have you checked his blood? No, because you're just talking to him. Do you maybe know what's he doing in the toilet? No, because you're just talking to him. We've agreed that you'd follow his every step, but no. You're just TALKING TO HIM!«

Sam.I.Am was so angry that I began to feel sorry for Ian. At least now I knew why he was following me all the time.

»Alright, I'll start with medications,« said the therapist in a low voice.

»You make sure you do that,« threatened the producer. »Start today.«

»But I can't do it that quickly. I have to find out what type of hallucination we're dealing with. I can't just start prescribing everything at once…«

»I said: TODAY! PERIOD!« Sam.I.Am ended the conversation. I heard him get up and I quickly withdrew. I didn't want to be caught that near the curtain that hid them. I sat somewhere in the middle of the bus and took out my cell phone. When the producer walked by, he looked in my direction with the corner of his eye and saw me surfing the net. I was hoping that he'd keep walking. He stopped and looked at me.

»Are you OK?«

»Yeah, I'm great,« I lied.

»You're scheduled to talk some more to Ian today. Pure formality.«

»OK, alright.«

So, they'll start feeding me pills today. *Excellent, Jesse.* I really, but really didn't expect this to happen. I didn't think my dreams would re-semble...a prison. Or an asylum. Or both.

I leaned back and watched the landscape. Every now and then a car would pass us by and honk, people inside waving at us. That wasn't surprising, because our entire bus was covered with our logos and pho-tographs. So everybody knew who was in it, everybody knew we were on tour and where we were going. They could even follow our journey over the satellite. But I gradually stopped caring. I was looking forward only to being able to play again. I was fed up with the interviews, TV shows, press conferences...I just wanted to play my music. That was all.

XXI. TRUST

NOTHING MUCH ELSE HAPPENED THAT DAY. I had a conversation with Ian, who kept digging deeper: he was asking questions about my childhood, my parents…I really didn't think I needed therapy, but at the same time I knew that Sam.I.Am's instructions were final. If we wanted to succeed, we had to listen to him, regardless of what his instructions were. If I needed to take medications, then I was going to take them. Maybe I really was crazy.

At the end of the evening he asked me to tell him truthfully whether I was on something he didn't know about. I looked at him.

»You know, Ian,« we had been on a first name basis for quite some time, »my dream is to become famous. Do I look to you like someone who'd waste his dreams for a few imaginary illusions under the influence of illegal substances…?«

»No, of course not.«

»Then please trust me. Everything I've told you is true.«

He sighed and I could see that he believed me. I didn't want to tell him that I overheard his conversation with Sam.I.Am, but I understood the pressure he was under. We all were. I was going crazy too – never before had I performed in front of so many people, who expected me to be perfect. We also discussed that and it seemed like I was gaining a new true friend.

Rodney was much too preoccupied with Jessica; now they were constantly together. It seemed unnatural to me. Being together with your girlfriend all the time sounds romantic when you're in love. But when you have problems that make you want to scream your lungs out, and you're surrounded with people you're traveling with all the time…Then things tend to get less romantic. Sometimes I saw them quietly biting their lips in anger, not knowing where to go to yell at each other in peace. That too I mentioned to Ian and he smiled in agreement.

»I've noticed that to,« he said. »That is a powerful test for young people. Often people have many wishes, but they don't know what the side effects of those wishes will be. Is that why you don't have a girlfriend?« he asked carefully.

»Look who's talking,« I replied with a smile. Judging by the silence, it seemed that I probably went too far with my teasing.

»Ashley…My wife died a year ago. Somehow I'm still not ready…But, maybe you're right. Maybe I should start dating again,« he replied calmly, while I wished the ground would open and swallow me up.

»I'm sorry, I didn't know…« I said quickly. I thought it was strange that he had all the time in the world to travel around with us. Being in his thirties, he could've had a normal job and a family. I didn't have a faintest idea why he was such a workaholic. In a way, I had a talent for finding the right moment in a conversation when people could totally misunderstand me. At the same time I knew how to say the most stupid thing in exactly the wrong moment. While writing a prescription for me he should add something that would prevent me from expressing stupidity.

»It's OK,« he waved his hand. I saw that he was uncomfortable with this subject and wanted to steer the conversation in a more cheerful direction. »You still haven't answered my question. Since I've answered yours, you owe me an answer.«

»Yes, of course,« I said. »I obviously…haven't found the right one yet.«

»That's kind of a girlish excuse,« he teased me. »You know that women usually say: 'I haven't met the right one'. You're old enough to think about that. It's something else, isn't it?«

He was right, as usual.

»Well, I was involved with girls before,« I quickly corrected myself, »I used to date a lot in high school and all that. But one thing always bothered me: it seemed that they liked me because of the stuff that wasn't mine. For example: I knew how to play the guitar and they thought I was attractive. What if I didn't know? What if somebody cut my hands off? I had the feeling that they wouldn't find me as interesting anymore.«

»Keep talking.«

»And my looks. I know that I looked good. What if I didn't? What if my face was disfigured in a traffic accident? I always thought that the girls were so smitten by me because they saw some kind of perfection in my face, some kind of model ideal, which I'm not. I didn't want to disappoint them, so I withdrew before it was too late. And then they'd be beside themselves, telling everybody how I broke their hearts…But in reality I did them a favor.«

»You're a complicated person, Jesse Roy,« he said thoughtfully. »And none of them ever made you feel like they might understand, really understand who you were? That they could love you regardless of your looks and abilities?«

I was silent for a moment. We came dangerously close to the topic of hallucination. After the long conversation we had just had, I started to feel that I could trust him.

»As a matter of fact, I…I dreamt of a girl once.«

»Yes?« he listened with interest.

I told him everything about her, the curly blonde. He was discreet; he explained that he wouldn't tell anything to anybody, because he'd be violating the code of his profession.

»Do you think she's real?« he asked me.

»You tell me,« I teased him, »you're the expert.«

»Judging from my experience, she represents the image of a perfect girl that in reality doesn't exist. You can establish that based on several facts: she's always dressed the same, the same hair length…And she doesn't age.«

»Well, I haven't been seeing her that long…«

»I'm just telling you what my experience tells me,« he explained.

»Do you think I need medication…?« I asked carefully.

»Yes…and no,« he said absorbed in thoughts. »Yes, because you'll be calmer that way. Although it's a really nice hallucination, it's still just a hallucination. We can't prove that this girl is real. Maybe she is the one preventing you from living a real life with a real person. And that's the only thing on account of which I can tell you that you are…ill. Don't be afraid, this is nothing more than a cold or a flu in my book. Illness like any other illness. Once you admit that to yourself, you're much more at peace with yourself.« That made sense.

»And why *not*?« I was curious.

»That's because you're not showing any other dangerous symptoms. None of the creations in your mind is trying to persuade you to commit mass murder or something like that. You seem totally fine, just a bit absent-minded. If you didn't carry such a responsibility and weren't a public figure, I'd probably send you home with the instructions to take more walks in the nature or something similar. And now…I must follow the rules. You'll also have to give blood for testing soon.«

»But I've already told you that…«

»And I believe you,« he asserted. »But there are people that don't.« I knew who he meant.

He wrote a prescription and gave it to me.

»As soon as we hit the town, send somebody to the pharmacy to get it,« he said. »I deliberately didn't write the name on the prescription.« Of course: it wouldn't be very practical if the word got out that Jesse Roy was on the verge of a nervous breakdown and at the beginning of the tour at that.

I glanced at the paper and it looked like it was written in Chinese.

»What is that?« I asked openly. I really wanted to know what I was going to put into my body.

»A mild antipsychotic, nothing stronger.«

»OK.«

I didn't know what else to ask. I looked at my watch and realized that we had had a really long therapy session.

»Well, since it's time to go to bed and there's a tiring day in front of us, I recommend that you get some rest,« he said smiling, »you mustn't disappoint the crowds that can't wait to see you play.«

»Hey, Ian?« I stopped him. »Thank you, you know. I know that talking to me is actually a part of your job, but anyway…It's really precious to have someone to talk to in this lonely world that I currently live in, even though you're getting paid for it. Thanks.«

»Believe me, I'd do it even if I wasn't paid for it,« he said on his way out of the therapy booth. »As a matter of fact, some people are against me talking to you.« Since I'd heard his conversation with Sam.I.Am, I knew who he meant.

He softly punched me in the shoulder and said: »Well, you go now, rock star.«

I went to bed and I did feel better because now at least somebody else new about her. About my feelings. I didn't know whether therapists were supposed to take care of their clients' emotional wellbeing at all times, but this one did a pretty good job today. And tomorrow…I'll be finally playing again. Just me, my guitar and my band. And as far as my beautiful hallucinations were concerned…They were nice until they lasted. It was time for them to go. Like a fall cold.

XXII. THE LAST ADVICE

WHEN I WOKE UP THE FIRST MORNING ON A STANDSTILL BUS, our road crew was already preparing the stage in the Philadelphia Civic Center. We arrived in Philadelphia extremely quickly. Our road crew had a busy morning. They even got the permission to bring a few vehicles into the arena, to unload the sound system. The stage also needed to be additionally modified for various parts of the show we've been diligently practicing in the past few months. The producer let us eat our breakfast in peace and then preparations and the soundcheck followed.

It wasn't even noon yet when one of the dancers returned from the pharmacy with my bag of pills. Sam.I.Am immediately came to me, holding a glass of water in his hand. He really thought of everything. He asked me how I felt and I said that I was feeling great. I didn't want to cause him any additional worries. Since he still seemed a bit suspicious, I asserted that I felt reborn after the therapy the day before (I deliberately avoided the word »conversation«). That – and the fact that he saw me swallowing the sedative – seemed to work and he left me alone.

I also managed to reconnect with the other band members. The simple fact that we could pick up our respective instruments and play together again, was the biggest help. I was very glad when I saw how good we could be together. When you are connected with your band, sometimes a single look is needed and the flow of thoughts is already in motion. Like telepathy. I've always loved that feeling. It seemed like I was operating on a different frequency. After the soundcheck that flew by incredibly quickly – I didn't even notice when the dancers joined us – we went to lunch, during which time our opening acts had their own soundchecks.

I found it unbelievable that we had three bands opening for us. I always thought I was going to start that way…But my entrepreneurial side and crazy persistence bore fruit: we succeeded incredibly quickly. That was the only solution for me, really.

After lunch we hid in our dressing room and went through the preparation process. The stylist brought our stage clothes, we all had appointments with the hairdresser, the make-up artist…About an hour before the concert – the first opening act had already started warming up the audience – I became slightly nervous. I listened to them playing, trying to imagine what the huge arena looked like when it was full.

Ten thousand people…Never before had I performed in front of such a crowd. Well, maybe on TV, but studio experience was a totally different matter: we only had to mime for the cameras. It was stupid, that's true, but there was no danger of things turning out unprofessionally. And here…Seats everywhere you looked. A huge arena…I admit, I had stage fright. When I started pacing around the dressing room to relax, I heard Sam.I.Am knocking on the door.

There are animals that can sense your fear. Like snakes and bears, for example. Their reactions can vary: they can either leave you alone or attack you even quicker. The important fact is that the sense of fear always triggers a reaction. Our producer had such a sense. He twitched at my slightest move. This time was no different and he caught me in the worst possible moment.

»Am I disturbing you?« he asked after helping himself to open the door. I could see his delight when he realized it wasn't locked.

»Not at all, come on in.«

»You know, as I already said, the life of stars can be – like you've noticed yourself – pretty stressful.«

I've noticed that, yes.

»And I've warned you that it won't always be easy.«

That was true; only then he didn't exactly go into details…

»And today is your first show.«

I noticed that he was nervous too. Maybe even more than I was.

»You know, I've learned something in my ten years of working professionally with musicians…« He took my pack of pills.

»…And that is that little additional stimulation never hurts.«

»But I've already taken today's dose.«

»I know, I know,« he calmed me down, »but today is your first show and in front of ten thousand people at that. I've been thinking and I talked to Ian. Maybe it wouldn't be that bad if you slightly…enhanced your first dose.«

He took another pill from the pack. I knew what was in store for me. If he ordered me to take it, I'd take it. There was obviously nothing wrong with that. And even Ian, who I started to trust, was in agreement with him.

He put a napkin on the table, placed a pale green pill on it and a glass of water next to it: »Well…?«

»Should I take it?«

»Maybe it'll get easier now for you…«

I decided to put an end to his mind games. I took the pill, put it in my mouth and washed it down with the glass of water. Sam.I.Am relaxed.

»Excellent,« he said as though a huge weight had been lifted off his shoulders. »Now relax for a while, you know, like you've practiced with Ian,« he started faking deep breathing like he was present at childbirth or something.

»Yeah, inhale slowly, exhale by pulling your belly in,« I added, »I know.« I wanted him to leave as soon as possible.

»Well, OK, you just get ready,« he said while still exhaling, and then he left. The second band was already playing, with crowd roaring in the background.

In order to perform my duties as best as I could, I actually sat on a chair and started breathing. I was imagining how well I was doing on the stage and how good the other members of the band felt because of me. How we played as one finely tuned unit and ignited the crowd below the stage...Ian called that visualization. And I'd like to call that extreme-effort-to-stop-being-scared-to-death.

Rodney interrupted my breathing.

»Are you ready, Jesse? You could come over to us too.«

I really did miss them. In the last few minutes before we walked onto the stage, we went through the setlist one last time and I felt that we'd do great. That we knew how, and we still had a great rapport. And if something should go wrong...improvisation. Like in practice. We'd do it. We knew how.

I heard the announcement and my name. We put our hands on top of one another and broke the stack with a loud: »Let's go!«. As we walked towards the stage I tried to remain focused as much as possible. Like when you're walking across a narrow bridge with a deep canyon beneath you – when you simply mustn't look down. Now I could see just the stage and nothing else. I preferred not to see how many people there were in the arena, because I didn't want to risk a dizzy spell at the sight of the crowd...

XXIII. THE FIRST SHOW OF THE TOUR

WE REACHED THE STAGE AND ALL I COULD THINK ABOUT WAS: *look down, look down, not at the people, it's all right, it'll be great…* As I came to the microphone, I somehow managed to relax. Like a huge weight had been lifted off my shoulders. The crowd began roaring when they saw us coming, but I was in a completely different world. I didn't hear them. My attention was focused completely on the show ahead of us. I checked the tuning of my guitar one last time. I heard the delicate intro to »From Another World« played by Jessica and then Rodney joining in.

The silver microphone glimmered in front of me. I remembered for whom I wrote this song. I knew that *she* was the illness I had to be cured of. And at the same time I could think only about her at that moment. I decided to sing to her just this one time, even though she didn't exist. I felt completely relaxed when I thought of our brief, yet intense encounters. Funny thing, being in love with a hallucination…A beam of light shined at me and I couldn't see anybody anymore. As I started to sing, I saw only white light in front of me…

Before I could take everything in the song was already over. The crowd went wild and I looked towards the band. Rodney gave me a thumbs up – I evidently sang well. I didn't notice any significant improvement – but I knew I sang sincerely. Tim's drumming intro to »Map« snapped me out of my thoughts. That was one of our last recorded, less recognizable songs. The setlist was put together in such a manner that interest in what was about to come could only increase.

I could remember that that song was one of my favorites from the very beginning. It's about a boy and a girl that are separated – they have a long-distance relationship and live on their respective sides of the world. Each night they meet in their dreams and together they celebrate every second of life. The idea for lyrics came from me, while Jessica and Rodney came up with actual words.

When I heard how the audience was enjoying our show, I finally managed to raise my eyes. When I saw the audience, I suddenly felt profound happiness. Huge amount of their energy poured into me and I was fulfilled like never before. I knew and I felt that everything I had had to endure so far in the form of Sam.I.Am's instructions and near-orders, had finally paid off. All of my dreams rolled into one couldn't compare with that feeling. I was playing, I was singing, people were dancing to my rhythm and feeding off my music. The happiness of ten thousand people was circulating around the room and I knew that if there was heaven on Earth, *this* was it. I looked again towards my band members and I could feel that we were in the same flow. They were all…absolutely happy.

When the song ended Rodney nodded at me. Before the show we'd agreed that I should say a few words at this point. I boldly took the microphone and put my other hand on top of its stand.

»Good evening, Philadelphia!« I said and a crushing applause followed. I looked at my band members and they were thrilled. What a response!

»I have to tell you that we are very happy that we could open our first tour in your city…you're awesome!« I shouted and fired them up even more. A few flowers and a teddy bear landed on the stage. I picked it up. It was just right for the next song.

»And thank you for this,« I smiled while the crowd was enthusiastically approving my every move. »We'll name him…« I looked at the others and we all laughed.

Jessica spoke into her own microphone: »He could be Ned. Or Neddy.«

The crowd applauded and I joined them.

»Well, Neddy, are you going to help me sing the next song?« I asked him.

»Well, all right,« Rodney assumed the role of Neddy, raising his voice by an octave. When I saw him do that, I shook the teddy bear like he was really talking to me. Even though it was pure improvisation, it turned out great and once again I had the feeling that we could read each other's minds.

I put Neddy on the music stand with lyrics, six feet from my microphone and placed him so that everybody could see him. I began playing intro to »Guitar«. That song was also done near the end of the recording sessions. It tells a story about how an ordinary guitar can make a person's dreams come true or burn down his entire world of reality. The boy in the story is called Iggy – and I changed that to teddy bear's name, Neddy. Every time I pointed at him while I was singing, the audience laughed. During my solo spot Rodney had a few »bear moments« of his own. The crowd were enthusiastically raising their hands and I was very surprised to see that the majority of them knew our lyrics by heart. Our CD had been in the stores for barely a month and a half – was it possible that everything was developing that quickly?

Three songs later I addressed the audience again and introduced the members of the band, although they already knew them. I realized that while we were playing – I could see people holding placards over their heads, with our names, pictures, words of encouragement and even witty remarks on them: »We love you, Jesse«, »Jessica is the head of the band!«, »Rodney rules!« and »Rock us, Tim!«.

After an hour of performing, while we were playing »Piece of Paper«, I got an interesting feeling in my left hand. My index finger, which was holding a part of the chord on the guitar neck, went slightly numb. I wouldn't think much about it, if that tingling sensation didn't start recurring more and more frequently. It spread to my middle and ring fingers. Pretty soon I couldn't feel my left hand at all and I had to stop playing. The band kept on going without me. The lack of my playing wouldn't be that problematic, if it wasn't for my approaching solo part. I desperately looked at Rodney, who couldn't understand why I stopped playing. I started to shake my left hand and he realized that I must've had some sort of a problem with it. He took a few steps forward and tried to play something simple instead of my solo.

»I'm playing the solo today!« he quickly improvised and took over the microphone before he started playing. Although concocted at the last moment, his joke was still funny and the audience loved it. I didn't know what was wrong with me. I was wondering if I'd have to see a doctor or something like that. Behind the stage Sam.I.Am was holding his head in his hands, directing me towards the microphone to sing. Maybe I could redeem myself that way. I only had to sing the last verse and once more repeat the chorus, which usually ended with my sigh. That was my favorite part. I stepped up to the microphone.

»Whi...te...p-piece...« I felt the tingling sensation in my lips and tongue. *Oh, no. I evidently can't sing or speak anymore either!* I panicked. Rodney saved me again by singing the rest of the song himself. I withdrew. I slowly turned away, while Rodney did his best to sing the song as correctly as he could. I took my guitar off since I couldn't play it anyway.

As the crowd applauded, Sam.I.Am signaled to Rodney to start bidding farewell on behalf of the band.

»As you can see, our frontman is already a bit tired, aren't you Jesse,« Rodney looked at me and I smiled weakly. I couldn't answer anyway.

»Maybe he started turning into a piece of paper,« he continued. The crowd, familiar with the video, burst into laughter.

»Thank you for a beautiful evening, we had a great time,« he quickly summed up, »we salute you: Rodney on bass guitar, Jessica on keyboards, Tim on drums, and of course...our frontman, Jesse Roy!«

During the thunderous applause that aggressively demanded »more«, we went back to the stage to bow at least ten times. We didn't have a plan B:

what to do if I became a mute invalid in the middle of the show. Then Jessica suddenly came up with the idea that Rodney could sing »She« while she accompanied him on keyboards. After all, he did write the song. I nodded. They went back on the stage and started performing the song. As I was watching them from the backstage area, I started thinking that, after all, it had to be nice to work like this with a person you loved. I felt lonely again. At the same time I could feel that the tingling sensation managed to spread to the other parts of my body...I couldn't actually remember any of this, but...they said I was completely soft when I dropped to the ground.

XXIV. THE WEAKEST LINK

I WAS AWAKENED BY VOICES. Some sort of hushed arguing again. I couldn't recognize the voices yet, but I thought that one of them was the producer's. The only surprising thing was that his voice seemed much more…meek this time. I didn't know the man that was angry with him. I didn't want to open my eyes yet, because it seemed that I might find out more that way…Sam.I.Am's meek voice slowly continued.

»I'm sorry, I really didn't know…«

»Didn't know…what exactly? That only a professional may prescribe drugs? That you can't swallow antipsychotics like candy – to change the taste in your mouth? That the fate of the band depends on what you tell them to do? Have you ever asked yourself what they wanted? *Truly wanted*? You don't even know them!«

»Well, I wanted them to succeed…« carefully continued the producer. I really wanted to know who he was talking to…He must've have had a supervisor or something. I didn't know that before.

»And you wanted to fulfill your wishes by force. I know this business. I know how it starts and how it ends. Do you think I was enjoying myself while Ashley was swallowing all those pills? Of course not, but I didn't have a choice. She wanted to succeed so badly that I let her do that. Now I've had enough of this. It makes no difference to me if the guys never play again. I don't care what happens with the tour. I know I have a month's notice, I'm not stupid. But I like the guys too much. I'm leaving. Go and sue me if you want. I'm not prescribing him anything anymore. As a matter of fact, I'm leaving psychiatry, because everyone's exploiting it. Human psyche is not a machine that you take for repair, fill with pills and it's suddenly all right again. You write his prescriptions if you think it's that simple. I think the guys need more freedom. There is much more to life than just pleasing the crowds.«

I recognized his voice during this agitated speech. I heard footsteps walking away.

»Ian, wait,« shouted Sam.I.Am fearfully. He was completely unrecognizable. Never before had he sounded that helpless.

»Have a nice tour, *doctor*,« ironically retorted Ian. »Why don't you treat him yourself, now that you think you know what dosage of medication is appropriate for him.«

I heard the door open and close behind him. Too bad. I'd miss him. At least I knew – felt – he was on my side. I've had enough of fictitious »sleep«, so I coughed a little. Sam.I.Am took my hand and I knew that he did that in smaller part because he was sincerely sorry for what happened. In addition to the fact, that in that moment I represented a million dollar investment for him.

»Are you all right?« he asked anxiously.

»Where am I?« I answered with a question. When I opened my eyes, I discovered that I was in a fairly bright room.

»In a Philadelphia hospital. Don't worry, everything is rigorously guarded and the bus already drove away. Nobody is going to find you.« I had a feeling that he was more consoling himself than me.

»And where are the others...?«

»I'm glad you asked,« he continued proudly, like it was a surprise, »the others are in a hotel. The bus is headed towards LA, but they're not on it. Great plan, isn't it? You'll travel by plane. I've arranged luxurious transportation, so you can spend time together in peace and quiet...«

So, that was the big surprise.

»Where's Ian?« I played dumb.

»Ian? Ha, ha, why do you want to know that now...?« he tried to avoid the answer.

Because I wanted to know if he'd answer me truthfully. »Just so.«

»Well, Ian...had some...things to attend to. I'm afraid he won't be back,« he confessed quietly. Well, at least the bigger part of the answer was true.

»So, another happy news: no more therapists! Isn't that great?« he tried to cheer me up again. I had a feeling that, in addition to ordinary medical care, I was also given a clown with balloons, to entertain me and teach me that life was great. I was waiting for him to pull out juggler's balls or something like that.

»Really? What about the medication?«

»Hmm, hmm, well...« he looked at me helplessly. He reminded me of a lost cat on the side of the road. He obviously wanted to apologize.

»I owe you an apology for that,« it sounded almost impossible. Sam.I.Am, whom all of us had to obey in the last few months, regardless of the nature of his instructions, was actually willing to subdue his ego to that extent. I could tell that he was in a difficult position. He had already lost one link in the chain and he couldn't afford to lose the others too.

»Actually...I didn't consult Ian before I advised you to take another pill before the show...I just wanted to make sure that you'd be able to do it. I don't know you enough to know how you react under pressure. And I wanted to help.«

He actually wanted to help himself. Now I became brave.

»You wanted to make sure that the band you represented played very well...«

He started to confirm that: »Yes, that's right, that's right,« when he realized, what I said: »No, no, I mean – no. I just wanted to help.«

»And why did I pass out?«

»Because...this medication – especially when you first start taking it and in too large doses – might produce side effects...Honestly, I didn't know.«

I was looking straight ahead and didn't know what to say to him. 'That's all right'?

»I did realize something, though,« he said quickly, before I managed to decide what my answer would be.

»I realized that you are very good when it comes to controlling stage fright and such. The audience ate out of your hand, everything went down smoothly and spontaneously, up until…the additional pill started working…I'm really sorry.«

His kindness started to annoy me. I had to say something.

»It won't happen again, right?« I asked in a conciliatory voice.

»No, no, absolutely not. You can take the medication exactly like Ian prescribed it: one pill a day, every day at the same time.« It sounded like he had just offered me something very generous.

»And you'll have much more time…and freedom.« I thought that he said the last word to cleanse himself of the guilt that Ian planted in him before he left.

»You'll also have more freedom to go out – maybe you'll meet a girl-friend, who knows.«

I could feel that he suggested that more out of a desire for bigger publicity than because he wanted to help me deal with my emotional needs. Regardless of the effort he made he was still primarily my manager and producer. For him a person as an individual didn't exist – only his qualities existed and those could be traded with.

»Yes, yes, okay,« I said fed up with him. »How long do I have to stay here?«

»That depends on how you're feeling,« he said invitingly. »You could leave in a few minutes.«

I sat up in my bed and moved my left arm around. Thankfully, the tingling sensation has gone. The other parts of my body also responded well…I felt…completely reconnected with my body.

»It seems that I'm quite all right,« I replied. I thought that he wanted such an answer, and at the same time I wanted to get out of there too.

»I'll be ready in half an hour.«

I wasn't used to discharging myself from the hospital; doctors usually did that. But when you're a star, you can obviously do that too. I was really happy when I remembered that I was going to LA by plane. In the first class. Whenever we'd traveled by plane – even to interviews – for some reason I always felt safer. And it seemed that I had more peace that way. And I also liked the view.

I got slowly out of the bed and made a few steps to the window. I saw green surroundings and hospital staff with patients outside. I was glad that I didn't catch anything serious. At least I hoped I didn't…

XXV. AN INTERESTING FLIGHT

IT WAS NICE TO SEE MY BAND MEMBERS AGAIN. It seemed that we could once again be more relaxed than usual. Sam.I.Am had kept his promise: the entire crew was traveling by bus. We only had one bodyguard with us. For better feeling.

Our section of the plane was completely tranquil. If it hadn't been for occasional turbulence and the view from the window, I'd have thought that I was in a five-star hotel somewhere and not on the flight to LA. After a couple of hours – when I managed to explain to everybody how I was and what actually happened to me the day before – we turned on the TV. We were pretty surprised when we saw ourselves.

»A new young band led by guitarist Jesse Roy took over young hearts in Philadelphia with their first live concert,« said the anchorwoman. They showed the footage of me pressing the teddy bear against my cheek and saying: »And thank you for this!« while the crowd went frantic. I felt like I was watching some rock star's concert and not my own. It didn't seem plausible that was me. It looked great, though.

»What a charmer,« openly said Tim. I could feel that he was a bit jealous. But he too received a lot of letters from his female fans.

The anchorwoman continued: »It seems that the band chose to conclude the concert in an interesting manner. Jesse Roy suddenly became silent, while bassist Rodney took over the microphone. It's still unknown today whether that was part of the script or not.«

»He, he, pure improvisation, my dear,« self-confidently said Rodney.

»The reporters managed to film the singer of the band passing out backstage.«

I saw the footage shot from some distance showing my shadow dropping to the ground. »Is the young singer using illegal substances? Stay with us.«

Suddenly we stopped laughing. Everybody knew what had happened, but we weren't prepared for such a response.

»Sam.I.Am will surely know what we should do,« said Jessica convincingly. »This can't be anything serious. Or we could wait for commercials to be over.«

For the first time in my life I decided not to change the channel during commercials. I watched each and every one, waiting for possible additional news. I wanted to know what reporters knew and didn't know. Rodney got slightly upset too.

»Damn, I already thought that we've made it,« he raged.

»You were great, darling,« Jessica tried to calm him down, »but you know how these things work. You'd have to be James Bond to cover all tracks and lead them to you...«

In the meantime there was an interesting commercial on TV.

»Hey guys,« said Tim, »look at this!«

I wasn't even sure what the commercial was about. The people were happy, like they always are in commercials, and the advertised product looked like a small rectangular memory card for a cell phone.

»And everything is one-hundred-percent hygienic,« continued the commercial hostess. »Let's hear what our consumers think.«

»When they were finished with the procedure I told myself: that was rather quick!« a middle-aged lady was thrilled. »Following my husband's death I suffered from a severe depression. You know how it is. Today I can gladly say that thanks to the Happy&Contact memory card I'm happier than ever before. I wasn't this calm even on my wedding day. And the best thing is: it's connected to my nervous system. I can call anybody that has such a card anytime I want. All I can say is: miraculous!« She was sitting in an armchair, smiling contently. The idea seemed a bit abstract to me. Memory card in the head. To be used as a phone or merely as an antidepressant. Amusing.

Three more satisfied comments followed, while we were already discussing what was about to follow.

After a few minutes the news report about our concert continued, but it didn't show anything more than we've already seen. They must've been trying to achieve higher ratings or something by repeating the information. Soon we turned the TV off, I leaned back in my seat and started thinking about the shows ahead of us. Knowing that I was going to have a bit more freedom filled me with a sense of peace. And we'd be able to play again. I didn't even realize that I liked performing so much. Actually, I couldn't wait for our next show.

XXVI. A SHOCKING PART OF THE TOUR

WITH SIXTEEN SHOWS IN A SINGLE MONTH SAM.I.AM REALLY made sure that we were fully busy, albeit mostly with traveling and waiting for our shows to start. But, in truth, from the moment we walked on the stage to the moment that we played the last note, we were completely fulfilled. I was really enjoying myself.

It's also true, that I quickly developed a sort of an inner feeling of being *somebody*. On the one hand I was enjoying it; on the other hand it made me feel cornered and trapped. Every time the crowd below the stage gave us an ovation, I'd feel more and more that they were giving it to me personally…Sometimes I would laugh differently than I used to before I became famous. That was an unpleasant feeling, but it got a hold of me and it wouldn't let go. *I am somebody, I did it…*These people admire *me…*

Jessica and Rodney also started to change. Jessica changed her dressing style and everywhere we went she had to buy something new. Rodney started to enjoy meeting celebrities – he acquired some secret knowledge that enabled him to conduct himself in a way that didn't appear so spaced out anymore. Tim was the only one maintaining his usual image of a humble Brit; drums were the one and only thing that interested him. He didn't even care about the girls.

During the tour I finally settled my debt to my father. While our crew was preparing the stage for the show – one of my wishes was to perform in my native Quebec during the tour – I paid a visit to my family. Unfortunately once again without a 'private plane' like I had solemnly promised my father – although this time because I didn't want to be too conspicuous. I actually drove there in a very inconspicuous old red Renault, which had tinted windows, though.

I rang the doorbell and my mom came to the door. She was totally surprised.

»Hi, mom,« I said with a smile. »Surprise!«

»Jesse, my boy,« she gasped and then the emotions overwhelmed her. She was really surprised, but I didn't think she was crying because of that.

After a brief conversation about my trip and an invitation to the show (with VIP tickets and backstage access, naturally) I asked her where Papa was. Her face became serious and slightly distorted again.

»Ah, your Papa is…in hospital. You haven't received my letter, have you? When I couldn't get you on the phone, I wrote you a letter and explained everything in it. It came back a few times, because the address was supposedly wrong. Then I found your new address in some magazine. I sent the letter to that address and, luckily, it didn't come back. I was certain you've read it…until I received your signed photograph…«

I was completely disarmed. It hurt even more that my mom, in all her love, didn't resent me because of that. She was just sad. And I just wanted to succeed. To really succeed before I went home again. Maybe that's why I hadn't called since I left. I wanted to prove to them that I was capable of succeeding. I wanted to wait until my face saturated the entire world and then come home as a winner. I'd been selfish.

»How is he? What's he got?«

She sighed quietly. »Cancer. In his brain.«

We sat in silence.

»There's this memory card, you know. It's the latest thing. They could cure him, but he's against it. He's determined not to allow them to insert anything in him; 'I'm not a robot', he says. The doctors estimate he's got a month to live…«

I was completely crushed. In that moment it seemed that I had to talk to him no matter what. I called the producer and he arranged a safe visit to the hospital. I too needed to take care of my family's privacy and safety. Mom and I soon sat in the old Renault and headed for the hospital…

XXVII. ANOTHER CONVERSATION

I WORE A HAT AND A PAIR OF SUNGLASSES. And I'd have put on more stuff, if I could. I didn't want anybody to see me like this. Distressed and upset I marched with my mom – who I made wear a scarf around her head as well as sunglasses – down the halls until she brought me to the right door. I opened it and saw him lying on the middle bed. Fortunately, the others were empty.

»He's not conscious much, you know,« mom warned me, »it's quite possible that you won't be able to talk to him. Besides, he doesn't speak anymore. He smiles from time to time, though. If his nervous system allows him. The doctors are trying their best…« she was overcome with tears again. »I'm so glad you're finally here, Jesse baby.«

Once again her diminutives didn't bother me. Quite on the contrary. I felt so small and insignificant that the sound of the word »baby« gave me a sense of safety…It also protected me from guilt that was telling me my dad got sick because of me. What nonsense. He just got sick. I didn't care why. Nobody had ever died because of the stupid things I said. And nobody ever will.

I entered the room and mom asked me if I wanted to be alone with him for a moment. I gladly agreed because I really wanted to talk to him. He would surely hear me, somehow. Surely.

I squeezed the envelope that I brought with me. I had always imagined this scene totally differently…

My father, still repairing the car that means so much to him. He sits in the garage and when I walk in, he stands up and hugs me.

»I've listened to your music, son. Seriously, it's not bad,« he says. He laughs aloud through his moustache.

»I've had it with you now, having to watch you every day on TV,« he says with a smile. I know, I feel that he's proud of me with every fiber of his being. And that he understands me, that he supports me.

»I brought you twenty grand Papa, and some interest on top,« I say with a smile and hand him the envelope. »Thank you for believing in me. Thank you for the support.«

»I've always believed that you'd make it, Jesse my boy,« he's smiling. He hugs me and I smell the motor oil again, mixing with the smell of sawdust from the wood he uses to make souvenirs. I really love him.

»I love you, Papa,« I say openly. »Please forgive me for the things I said that time. I didn't mean that.«

»I know you didn't. I love you too, infinitely. I forgive you.«…

I blinked and awoke from a daydream. My father was lying on the bed, much paler than I ever remembered seeing him. His moustache, which had adorned his face as long as I could remember, was gone. I almost didn't recognize him…

The door behind me was closed. I was alone in the room with my sleeping father. I cleared my throat.

»Papa?« I began with my script. I stepped closer and saw that he was sleeping truly peacefully. The machines around him were showing his heartbeat and other vital signs.

»I brought you…twenty…thousand…with…interest…« I said through tears. I couldn't care less about the damn money. I wished he would wake up.

»And I'm sorry…for everything, you know. I love you, I always have. Obviously…I was just mouthing off…Sometimes…I think you know. You're definitely not just my tool…You're my friend, my confidant, you played football with me when I was little. And hockey. You're the best Papa in the world to me,« I said and handed him the envelope.

He opened his eyes. The machine by the bed started beeping faster.
»Papa?«

»Jes…Jess…« he struggled to speak. And not just that, he even recognized me.

»Papa, did you hear what I said?« I asked ardently.

He nodded with his eyes.

»Look, Papa, envelope with money, for you!« I quickly summed up.

»And music, have you listened to my music…?«

He nodded.

»And I love you. To me you're the best!« I smiled widely through tears and hugged him. His arms also reached out into a hug.

»Believe…in…« he started to stutter. »In-you.« He said slowly.

I looked at him and truly felt happy. I truly felt that he knew that I really loved him.

Mom walked in through the door and was totally taken aback.

»Jesse, Papa's speaking!« she was exhilarated.

»Can you hear me darling? Oh, how I've been missing you!« she also hugged him. The doctor came into the room.

»Well, what's going on here?«

»He's speaking, he's speaking,« said mom excitedly.

»And you're just upsetting him with your euphoria,« he said. »You better leave now.«

We looked at him and thought it'd right to let him rest.

I thought about how the tour would end in a couple of weeks.

»I'll be back soon, Papa, and I'll stay longer,« I told him.

He nodded again.

»Take care of yourself, Eugene,« sighed mom. »I love you, my darling.«

»Me…too,« he stuttered. She kissed him.

Using the hand he could move more easily, he took the envelope and gave it to mom smiling.

As we got to the door we waved at him one last time.

See you soon, Papa, I thought. Back in the hallway mom and I discussed what he said to me. Mom told me that he kept my CD in the garage, listening to it every time he repaired or cleaned the car.

I decided to give my best possible performance that day. Should it get recorded I could give it as a present to my father. I felt relieved – a huge burden was lifted off of my shoulders. Once again I knew who I was. And I could breathe again.

XXVIII. THE TOUR

OUR PRODUCER OFFICIALLY DECLARED THE SHOW IN QUEBEC OUR best ever. The dancers had long since been perfectly attuned to our songs and accustomed to the tricks we liked performing live. The other effects were also impeccable and we played like never before. I was enjoying every second on the stage. Rodney, Jessica and Tim also managed to connect with me on a higher level and once again we played like one tight unit, like one.

Sam.I.Am, who initially objected to my suggestion that we should officially record the show, had to admit that he hadn't seen a better live performance yet.

»We'll release this on DVD with special behind-the-scenes footage! This'll be a big project!« he was thrilled.

I was pleased too, because I knew that this new gift would definitely make my father happy. I wouldn't let him get rid of me that easily, let him leave us just like that. Mom enthusiastically applauded throughout the show and I saw her secretly wiping away a tear or two every now and then. When I said at the end of the show that this was my hometown, the crowd erupted into enthusiastic applause. I thanked my family and especially my mom for support – while the spotlight was directed at her and she was quite embarrassed. After the show I took her backstage and showed her how everything worked.

»What do you think, mom?« I asked in French and flapped my arms around like I just showed her my kingdom. I actually did, in a way.

»Beautiful,« she said. »But take care of yourself, Jesse darling. I've read…
that…« here she became silent. I didn't know what she meant by that,
but I suspected that she might have been paying a bit more attention to
the yellow press since I was featured in it.

»What did you read?« I asked with a smile. I knew that she must've
read some stupid thing about me.

»That you're taking illegal substances.« I could see that she had a hard
time saying it.

»I'm not taking anything, mom. Look at me,« I turned her face to-
wards mine, »do I look like a junkie to you? No, because I'm healthy. I've
got no needles, no powders of any kind, no sunglasses to hide my pupils.
Tabloids were created to suggest such things, so they can make money.
Don't worry. If something were wrong, you'd be the first to know anyway.
Sam.I.Am has got your number. I've warned him about that.«

That was true.

»But they showed on TV how you collapsed to the ground…« she
said with concern in her voice and I could see that it was difficult for her
to watch such things. And then she couldn't get me on the phone. I felt
sorry for not giving her my number sooner.

»And don't watch TV anymore, mom,« I smiled, »I was a bit tired
that day and they blew it out of proportion. Surely there are times when
at the end of the day you feel like just dropping into an armchair and
staring into the air. Well, that's how I felt that day. And if you feel like
watching TV, I'll give you a DVD to brighten your day. They just need
to complete it first. Till the end of the tour.«

»Well, all right,« she said reassured.

»Now I'll give you my number, so you can reach me anytime. And
please forgive me for not giving it to you sooner.«

I gave her my phone number, sensing again that I was doing the right
thing. My life started rearranging itself exactly the way I always wanted it
to be – except for my father's illness, of course. I was calm and happy. I also
made sure that mom got a safe and discreet ride home – the red Renault.

I could hardly wait for the tour to end. I couldn't remember when was the last time I wanted to go back to Quebec that much. I slowly stopped taking the medication for schizophrenia and Sam.I.Am consented to that. But not until he saw me perform even better than before. Or saw that I was even calmer. My hallucinations had – thankfully – disappeared for the time being. Although I had to confess that I missed her a little bit.

The rest of the tour dates were sold out too. The news about our faultless performances spread like wildfire, making us more recognizable than ever before. In that regard we became even bigger than some bands I used to listen to and admire in the past.

After the last show, which was once again excellent, Sam.I.Am stopped us backstage. The audience that had squeezed into the Lakefront Arena was absolutely thrilled and kept demanding *more*.

»Dear Jesse and the gang,« he said solemnly. »I'd like to tell you that you've done your job excellently. That's why I decided to slightly change your contractual fees. I'd like to round them up…by three percent in terms of profit for each one of you!« That was an extremely generous offer. Three percent means an awful lot when it comes to the multi-million dollar business. We smiled completely astonished.

»Hmm, sir,« one of the technicians interrupted us. »The audience simply refuses to go home. Could they play at least one more song…«

»They'll wait,« he replied.

»There's another important matter: I'm inviting you to a ceremony where you could really shine. Dear Jesse Roy Band, you've been nominated for a Grammy!«

We all cried out in excitement.

»When are we going?« Tim couldn't curb his enthusiasm.

»We've got important preparations coming up, starting tomorrow,« announced the producer. I could hear the audience still demanding *more*. But I was confused.

»Does this mean that I won't have the time to visit my family?« I quickly demanded to know. »My father is sick...«

»You were there a couple of weeks ago,« he refused my request. »This is once-in-a-lifetime opportunity. Besides, your contract obliges you to attend all important musical events and the Grammys are definitely one of those.«

I remembered reading that in the contract. I especially liked that article at the time. It represented socializing with the famous, being at the heart of the musical community...I didn't realize that would be the thing I'd want the least in the days after the tour.

»Think Jesse, the Grammys,« enthusiastically said Rodney. Yes, the Grammys. A gold-plated trophy in exchange for freedom...

Finally Sam.I.Am let us back on the stage. The crowd was thrilled when we said our goodbyes by playing »From Another World« once more.

XXIX. PREPARATIONS FOR THE BIG EVENING

As Sam.I.Am already explained to us, we had to prepare psychologically for the Grammys. He booked us into a very expensive spa, where we were supposed to relax and bond as a band. We had three days at our disposal to look as refreshed and healthy as possible – which was no mean feat after a month of switching buses and planes. He kept telling us over and over again:

»And don't forget guys, the important thing is not to win but to participate!« At the same time he incessantly kept asking me if I had my speech ready.

Of course I had it. It certainly contained his name, but I also wanted to thank Ian and my family. That is, if we won the Grammy at all.

It seemed to me that Sam.I.Am was the one wanting it the most, anyway. I had other things on my mind: I spent a lot of time on the phone with my mom, who was keeping me informed about my dad's condition. She told me he hadn't spoken since I left, but that he did see the Quebec show footage and smiled. The doctors thought he did it intentionally and that it wasn't just a muscle reflex. She kept asking me when I was going to come home and I kept truthfully answering her that I didn't know, but that I would as soon as I could.

Jessica and Rodney finally found some time for themselves, which helped alleviate the tension between them that was so obvious during the tour. They obviously found the way to deal with things that had been bothering them – once they weren't constantly trapped among the same people on a few square feet inside a bus or a plane anymore.

And Tim realized that he had been slightly missing the life of luxury he was accustomed to before he became a professional musician. Consequently he managed to relax completely in the spa. He also managed to curb his kindness a bit more and he became…almost unnoticeable.

After a few days our evening had finally arrived. I knew that our chances of winning a Grammy were almost non-existent – also because we really hadn't been on the scene that long. Less than six months had passed since Sam.I.Am took us under his wing. But I was honored we were considered for an award at all. For me this nomination was an incentive to work harder in the future.

Our producer supervised the preparations for the appearance on the red carpet. Since we were supposed to look as blooming and sophisticated as possible, everybody had their hands full with us. We had to try on at least a couple of dress suits, everybody's hair was done by a recognized hair stylist and there were make-up artists present (devoting their attention mostly to Jessica and her evening make-up), as well as other members of the crew. A limousine was waiting for us in front of the hotel to take us to the big event.

When I was ready, I decided to call mom once more, to make sure she would watch the event on TV and tape it (she stayed at home to be close to dad). I had to let the phone ring for quite some time, before she finally answered.

»Jesse, it's you,« she said absently and I could hear hesitation in her voice. Like she was trying to hide something.

»Hi, mom. You are going to watch the ceremony, aren't you?« I asked her and tried not to worry too much about the tone of her voice. She must've had a reason for that.

»Ah, yes, sure,« she said and I could hear that her nose was stuffed-up. I couldn't stand that any longer.

»What's wrong, mom?« I stressed the question. She started to breathe deeply, until I heard sobbing on the other side of the line.

»Eugene…Papa…They're resuscitating him right now…«

I turned white as a sheet. In that moment I couldn't care less if the producer wanted me on that ceremony; somebody else would have to read that speech instead of me.

»Hang on, mom, I'm coming,« I said with conviction.

Suddenly the phone was snatched from my hand and before I could react, it landed in the pool under my window. Sam.I.Am was standing in front of me.

»Where are you going?« he asked in a harsh voice. I could see that the ceremony meant way too much to him.

»My father…I need to go home. They're resuscitating him. He might not make it.« I replied. »Somebody else can read the speech…«

»Do you realize, Jesse,« he started solemnly, »that if you leave now, before the ceremony, you'll attract a whole swarm of reporters – like bees after honey? Did you ask yourself how that could affect your family? Your mom?«

»It doesn't matter…«

»Oh, but I think it does. Your every move would be recorded, your every emotion. And we don't want that, do we? Besides, wouldn't your father be proud seeing you accepting a Grammy…«

»So what…«

»And thirdly: you've signed the contract, stating that you'd attend this event.«

I remembered the exceptions: »Except in exceptional circumstances!«

He looked at me: »Define exceptional circumstances!«

»Death of a parent?« I asked helplessly. In truth, he was way more familiar with business and legal matters than I was.

»Your father is not dead now and he won't be after the ceremony. They're resuscitating him, so what. My mother has been resuscitated fifteen times and she's still alive. That's the purpose of resuscitation.«

It sounded reasonable and unreasonable at the same time. Like a squabble between two kindergarten kids, both wanting the same toy truck…

»I don't like reminding you that I could sue you…« he had already said that to me several times when we disagreed about something. And then I would always let him know that I was the one making him a lot of money and the disagreement would be over. This time that same threat sounded differently, more seriously. Like he didn't care about how much money he was making because of me and would go through with it if necessary.

I'd obviously have to wait until the end of the ceremony and hope for the best…

»Are you ready?« I heard the chauffeur's voice at the door.

»Yes, yes, of course,« Sam.I.Am replied and took me under my arm.

»I can walk, you know,« I said roughly and withdrew my elbow.

»I'm just checking whether you are going in the right direction,« he laughed.

I walked rigidly, sensing that my place wasn't at that ceremony. But I also felt that I didn't have any choice. I was hoping that I'd be able to jump into a taxi immediately after the ceremony and catch a night flight to Quebec…

XXX. THE GRAMMYS

WHEN THE DOORS OF THE LIMOUSINE OPENED IN FRONT OF THE RED carpet I felt like in a dream. Only I couldn't decide whether it was a good one or a bad one. On the one hand I was surrounded by the people I enjoyed working with (Rodney, Jessica and Tim were thrilled by the response from the fans tightly packed behind the barrier), while on the other hand my thoughts were in the Quebec hospital all the time. I found the world of music awards to be very similar to some sort of illusion. If you play good music, your award should be the fact that you're helping people. Why do you have to give hundreds of interviews, while at the same time watching not to soil your ten-thousand-dollar worth suit, you got for free anyway...?

After a few routine statements I had to give to some reporters (which designer made my suit, how I was feeling, whether I was honored by the nomination...) and a few short discussions with people I had to talk to, we finally sat down for the opening of the ceremony. There were a lot of famous people around that I had never thought I would actually meet in real life. Rodney just couldn't stop his head from continuously rotating in all directions. He couldn't believe his eyes. Ian once explained to me that there was a difference between being one of the famous and being their fan. You couldn't be both and I tried to explain that to Rodney from time to time. But he still rotated his head like an owl. I realized, though that six months ago I'd be much more excited by the fact where I was than I was now. I somehow got used to it.

Finally, the time had come – after all the glamorous performances and presentations – for the Grammy Award for the Breakthrough Act. When the nominees were introduced, it became more than clear to me that we didn't stand a chance to win – although Sam.I.Am kept trembling in his seat next to us. I actually felt sorry for him – in advance. He was going to be in a pretty bad mood when we didn't get what he came here for... The thought occurred to me that it might be good to have a plan how to react if he went berserk in the middle of this crowd. But he seemed to be professional enough to wait until he got to his hotel room.

We were introduced as the last nominees; they played a short segment of the »Piece of Paper« video. I remembered the stressful circumstances in which the song was written and smiled. I also remembered how Rodney sweated while he waited for me to start writing...That song was our last chance to survive as musicians and keep living the life we worked so hard for. I'd never have thought that it'd become a hit, much less such a huge one! Now those events from six months ago seemed so distant...

Before I could register what was going on, I received a powerful punch in the right shoulder. Rodney was tugging me at my sleeve and on the other side Sam.I.Am, reduced to tears, was euphorically trying to indicate to me to head towards the stage. As incredible as it may sound, we won a Grammy!

I staggered for a moment and then slowly headed towards the stage with my band. I felt wobbly all over; I didn't expect this at all. My band members had already told me that they would accompany me to the stage, but merely for support – in case we did win by some accident, but none of them wanted to speak. The bad side of such a decision is that you're in the background all the time. The good side is that you don't have to assume the enormous responsibility like the person who has to thank everybody...whose names will appear in tabloids the next day.

I stepped to the microphone and looked around. Although I was used to performing in front of thousands of people, I'd always had enough freedom to say at least roughly what I meant. This time it was serious: I had to stay focused on everything I wanted to say in my acknowledgements...A small gold-plated gramophone was staring at me and I knew that my time was limited and that it would be smart to start reciting all the names immediately...As I stepped closer, I forgot everything I had memorized. I could only think about dad and pray that he would be saved somehow…

I cleared my throat.

»Err, thank you for this,« I started slightly embarrassed. »I think I should share with you who is responsible for me being here on this stage today.« I could see from afar Sam.I.Am's surprise, because the speech we had practiced definitely didn't begin this way. I didn't care.

»Six months ago I visited my father in Quebec and asked him for financial support. If he hadn't given me that initial amount of money, which I used to record the demo that I would later send around to producers, I'd be carving wooden statues now somewhere by the sea. It's because of him that I am here today,« and I added in French: »thank you for everything, Papa.«

People started applauding and my eyes filled with tears. *Pull yourself together, Jesse, this is a public ceremony,* I kept repeating to myself. I quickly concluded my speech. »I'd like to thank my band for standing by me this entire time: Rodney – you're the best, Jessica – his beloved and Tim – our most royal part of the band!« he knew what I was talking about and he smiled. He had revealed his family background in the interviews a long time ago and his family started to treat him with a lot more respect.

The music indicated that our time ran out and the presenters escorted us off the stage. I was still walking like I was in a dream. While everybody else was raving about the Grammy I asked Rodney to lend me his phone.

»Sure, why not,« he said. I quickly dialed mom's number.

»Jesse?« she said tearfully.

»Yes?«

»Eugene…I mean your Papa…didn't…make it…«

What started accumulating in my eyes on the stage now regained its strength. I collapsed on a chair backstage.

»What!? How!?« I howled in pain.

»They tried as best as they could…« said mom, »but they failed…«

The sound of her sobbing cut into my soul again.

»I'll c…call you about the funeral…« she said and hung up.

I screamed out loud. The happening on the stage was loud enough for my scream to go unnoticed: a young pop singer was performing at that moment, gliding easily among her sexy dance crew and nobody could know that a life had just ended. A small life, but so terribly important to me…Could I have gotten there in time, had I left a few hours ago? Probably. Would I've been able to stop time, to enable my father to live longer, at least a little bit longer? After all, when I was at his side, I made him speak. I'd surely have been able to help somehow, I'd surely have been able to prevent some little thing! A heavy sense of guilt washed over me, eating away at me much more than deep mourning. The guilt I had been subconsciously carrying with me since my childhood – that I was responsible for Terry's death – mixed with the feeling that my father could have lived longer had I not pushed forward with this ceremony! It was more than sadness, much more. I felt that it would've been better if I had never been born. I was sinking into the abyss and I could feel splinters of guilt piercing my heart on the way down…

»This surely must've been the most emotional and euphoric response to such an important award as the Grammy!« I heard Sam.I.Am's voice. »It's a shame that you completely forgot to mention the person who actually made all the sacrifices and organized all those months of shows…« Indeed, I forgot to mention *his* name.

Incredible anger washed over me. Everything that felt like sadness a moment ago, turned into anger. I attacked him furiously, punched him in the face and pushed him to the ground. It was fortunate that I wasn't alone, because I'd have ground him into dust. One of the technicians who saw what was happening, held me back and said with emphasis: »Get a grip, man! The ceremony is still going on!«.

I withdrew and said to the piece of garbage on the floor: »My father's just died. And thank you so much for the useful instructions before the ceremony. You're fired. I'm going to Quebec.«

I vanished in the crowd of music stars waiting for their performances before Sam.I.Am could catch his breath.

XXXI. THE BREAKDOWN

IN THE FOLLOWING MONTHS I CONSCIOUSLY THREW MYSELF INTO experiencing mourning and depression. While I was distancing myself from the band, Sam.I.Am tried to sue me. I discovered that he set the provisions of the contract so that I would be heavily indebted to him, should I quit the band. I'd have to pay an enormous amount – we're talking about millions – for him to let me go. He hadn't told me that until the conflict arose, naturally. I couldn't get away from him or maybe I simply didn't want to. He withdrew the lawsuit under the condition that we continue our cooperation.

I continued with the shows, but they weren't nearly as good as before. It was at the Grammy ceremony itself that I'd heard about the Breakthrough Act Grammy curse:

»Once you win it, you start sinking into oblivion and suddenly you're not on the scene anymore,« I heard some of the artists whisper. And that's exactly what started happening to us.

Our audience started to disperse, in a way. Our fans simply started to disappear. There were fewer people at our concerts – we signed the contract for the new tour, in accordance with Sam.I.Am's wishes, of course – and the interviews became increasingly less inspiring. I preferred not to turn on my TV set. When I occasionally, purely by accident, caught sight of my face on the cover of a tabloid newspaper, it was always accompanied by comments such as: »The fall«, »Depression«, »Where's the energy gone, Jesse?« and similar.

Relationships between the band members started crumbling too. The tension was only increasing during the long hours spent on buses and planes, and I often wanted to simply break a window and escape. But at the same time I had a strong feeling that our manager would find me regardless of my hiding place. I barely managed to convince him to let me visit my mom when we were in Quebec. This time we didn't have a concert there, because we didn't sell enough tickets. My career really started to sink with lightning speed. I was glad that my dad didn't live to see that and hoped that there wasn't an afterlife, because I'd die of shame if he saw me like this…

I stopped at my mom's house and there was absolutely no need to hide. Nobody cared that I was there. Like the world had suddenly forgotten about me. It was a rather cold afternoon, even though it was July. I was cold in a T-shirt when the wind blew around me as I knocked on the door. It soon opened and my mom gave me a warm welcome.

»Jesse, my baby,« she said smiling. Like her husband didn't die a month and a half ago. I was surprised by her good mood.

»Hi, mom,« I said surprised, »how are you?«

»Excellent, thank you. Actually, I'm baking croissants right now. You want one? They'll be done in a few minutes.«

That was all fine, but I came to visit her for completely different reasons, not to chat like at a tea party. I decided to ask her as directly as possible why she was in such a good mood. Had she already met somebody? So quickly after thirty years of marriage to her previous husband? Had she joined a self-help group? Was she reading books?

»You're in a very good mood, mom,« I said slowly. »I have nothing against that, but I'd like to know anyway how did you do it that quickly… get over dad.«

I emphasized that so she'd see I was shocked by that.

»Do you like it?« she asked with satisfaction, like she was talking about a new dress or something. I was disappointed because I obviously couldn't make her feel guilty.

»I don't – know…« I answered slowly. I really didn't know how to answer such a bizarre question. Luckily she helped me with her answer.

»You know, I have to tell you something, Jesse,« she continued cheerfully, like she wanted to tell me a secret.

»I'm listening.«

»Do you remember me telling you how I couldn't recover by myself if your Papa wasn't gone…?«

»Of course I do. That's why…«

»Well, that's exactly what happened!«

I didn't understand anything anymore.

»What happened?!« I asked totally confused.

»There's no need for yelling. The real truth lies in happiness…« she explained calmly. How could she be so calm when she lost her husband a month and a half ago?!

»Explain it to me, then,« I pretended to have calmed down, »what happened, please.« I sugarcoated my request with a phony smile, which she got completely wrong again.

»Well, that's better,« she continued proudly. »You know, when Eugene died, I couldn't think about anything else except how nice my life with him was. And how attached I was to him. After all those years I felt like he had somehow…grown into me. And that I would – if I ever lost him – die of sadness too.«

That seemed reasonable.

»That's perfectly normal,« I said with conviction. »That's called mourning.«

»That's not normal, Jesse my baby,« she interrupted me. »When somebody is so dependent on another person that they would follow them in the grave – that really isn't right. And I did – how interesting – start contemplating suicide…«

I had no reasonable answer to that. On some level I knew that she had to mourn anyway she knew how – and I'd support her and help her go through that sadness as easily as possible. But if she considered things that destructive that obviously also wasn't right...She saw that I was absorbed in thoughts.

»Don't be afraid, Jesse my baby, I knew that I mustn't do that – because of you. And because of myself. And also because life is actually beautiful.« I couldn't help but notice the change in the tone of her voice again. My mom was always very emotional. Any word could make her cry. And now she was talking calmly and with conviction. On the one hand she still resembled my mom and on the other hand...I didn't know where this huge change came from.

»And so I decided to do something I should've tried a long time ago!« she said with conviction.

»What's that?« I asked in expressionless voice.

»A friend had recommended it. Now you can get them at such an affordable price – almost everybody can get it! And I had some savings. The best part is – the procedure is quick and painless, and it absolves you from pains for the rest of your life!« These words sounded so familiar... Where had I heard them before?

»What did you buy?« I asked.

»A memory card,« she announced formally, like the introduction wasn't pompous enough. I hung my head. Of course I heard about it. On that trip, in a TV commercial! They offered it to my dad too, because it could supposedly cure him, but he turned them down, saying he wasn't a robot. Well, he wasn't but my mom obviously was! Was there something worse than that? I lost my mom and my dad, and the prison I worked in gave me no satisfaction at all.

Soon I'll be suitable for a head implant too, I thought. I shivered and looked at my mom again with tears in my eyes. She looked like a phony robot. *No, never, never*, I screamed in my head. Treacherous tears ran down my cheeks by themselves.

»You mustn't cry, Jesse,« she wanted to reassure me, »There's no truth in crying. Crying prevents you from fulfilling your life's dreams. Besides, I can show you a small trick that'll make you feel better,« she smiled. She closed her eyes. In a few seconds my phone started to ring.

»Neat, isn't it? It's me – my card, I mean. It's already so sophisticated that allows me to make calls to somewhat obsolete networks like the one your phone is in. Although the reception would be much better if you also had…«

»Stop with this nonsense, okay? I'm not a robot and I never will be!!« I burst into tears.

»Jesse, I didn't mean to insult you…« she said ignorantly.

»YOU DIDN'T INSULT ME! You don't understand anything! You don't understand my feelings, my emotions! You don't know who I am, because you act like some stupid microprocessor in your head dictates you to! Get out of my sight!« I yelled. I couldn't hurt her feelings anyway.

»I don't know how to disappear,« she explained benevolently.

I turned away and tried to calm myself down. After all, my mom's body was still alive, even though I'd never see *her* again, not the way she used to be. Maybe some small part of her did remain inside. I decided to say goodbye to her in a dignified manner.

»I'm sorry for getting mad,« I said calmly and wiped off my tears. I turned towards her again.

»It's all right, Jesse my baby,« she said softly.

»Please know that I really loved you, mom.« Another tear rolled down my cheek. I felt that this was a final goodbye. I didn't want to visit her ever again. It didn't matter if I was talking to an artificial intelligence or a robot that looked like my mom. It was unacceptable – and she wasn't aware of that.

»I love you to, Jesse,« she said surprised, like she really couldn't understand where all my emotions came from.

I hugged her and hoped to wake her from this dream with something. From this falsity. I'd do anything to get her back. I looked her in eye again.

»Your card…Can it be removed…?«

»You see, I forgot to ask that,« she said thinking about that. »But why would I want to have it removed? I like it, I'm pleased with it.«

And I'm not, not at all, I thought. But I didn't want to start a discussion with a robot again.

»Have a nice time, mom,« I said and rushed towards the front door. »Try to socialize with someone, find some friends or something.«

»I will, I will, don't worry,« she said and I had a feeling that she was already doing that.

Before I closed the door she shouted after me: »Oh yes, do you want a croissant?«

How could she think about pastry at a time like this?

»No, I'm okay,« I pretended. If I wanted artificially made pastry I could always get it from a vending machine.

»Bye, mom.«

»Bye, Jesse my baby.« Those were the only words that she managed to remember and would remind me at least a little of her. That thought made me grimace with pain again as I closed the door behind me.

XXXII. THE INVITATION

ODDLY ENOUGH, OUR SECOND TOUR THAT SEEMED TO TAKE FOREVER finally came to an end. Sam.I.Am came to his senses and realized that blackmail wouldn't get him very far, because bad relationships eventually resulted in his artists performing worse and worse. And such performances drove our audience away. He changed his approach and decided to leave us in peace for a while.

»You just need a break, really,« he encouraged us. I wanted that to be true. Our relationships were far from what they used to be.

»Take some space for yourselves, go on separate vacations or something. I'll pay out everybody's share. Take…six months off. And think about what you *really want* in life.« He put a special emphasis on those last words. I knew what outcome he was hoping for, of course. He wanted an eager, young rock band full of energy he used to know months ago. I suspected that he even knew or felt that he was the one who managed to »wear us out«. That he was the one who sucked the life out of us, which he now regretted very much, but didn't know how to fix it.

After eight months of torment his offer seemed fair, but I thought it was too late to fix anything. Even though he wanted to.

And we did walk away in our separate directions. Before Rodney said goodbye to me, he shoved an envelope in my hands.

»I found this the other day by accident,« he said. »We get less and less mail. Actually, its amount is pretty much down to the usual number of letters we used to receive before we became famous,« he smiled.

»It's written in distinct handwriting and it caught my eye. One letter was addressed to me and the other to you.«

I spun the envelope in my hands. My name, my address…The sender's address was missing. I opened it while Rodney stared at my face with anticipation. He obviously already read his letter and wanted to see my response.

I unfolded the old-fashioned piece of paper with neatly singed edges.

Dear classmate of class 2011!
Two years have gone by quickly and we haven't seen each other for quite some time. Therefore I am inviting you, dear Jesse, to attend the high school reunion scheduled to take place on September 15th 2013, at 6 p.m., at Rigoletto's Pizza in New York. The pizzas are still wonderful and crunchy, only the restaurant's location has changed. The new address is 141 West 72nd Street. You'll come, won't you?
Best regards,
Ravi R. Davies

XXXIII. THE REUNION

»I'LL SEE YOU THERE, RIGHT?« he said from afar. The taxi was already waiting for him and Jessica in it was getting increasingly impatient. »Of-of course,« I said confused. He surprised me with the question and I had to say something.

I did go to New York and spent the following couple of weeks roaming the Central Park all alone. I wasn't quite sure yet whether I really wanted to go to the reunion. How could I show my face in front of all the people that must've been following my life through the pages of the yellow press for the past eight months? I felt stripped and embarrassed. Especially because the majority of that nonsense wasn't even true.

On the day that we were supposed to meet I made a decision. I went to a hairdresser and then went to buy some new clothes. I shaved, which I haven't done for quite some time. I cleaned myself up, so I looked younger than I really was. Suddenly I felt refreshed – looking at myself in the mirror in my hotel room.

And it also struck me that I was on vacation after all and I smiled. *I've got nothing to be angry about, I've got no reason to be in a bad mood. It's going to be a good evening. Really.*

I realized that sullen facial expression had become a sort of my trademark in the past couple of months. When I tried to smile at myself in the mirror, I could feel that I hadn't used my facial muscles for a long time – like they had atrophied. After two years I didn't want people to see me depressed. Especially not them.

I put only my phone, a credit card and some cash in my jacket pockets. I really looked good. I set out for the restaurant with a spring in my step…

As I was walking along the Central Park I deeply inhaled the sweet scent of greenery overhanging the street. The evening was beautiful, just perfect for a good party. Maybe even for romance? I started walking faster at the thought that I had been unnecessarily neglecting that part of my life too much. Now, that I wasn't that popular anymore, maybe I could make something normal with some girl. I involuntarily thought of the mysterious blonde as I crossed the 71st Street.

I spotted the pizzeria front window from afar and saw the lights in it. I sensed that the place had been reserved just for us. I had a lot of stories to tell them: what a superstar's life was like, what I've been through… Surely none of them had such a rich history like me!

When I came to the door I saw my classmates inside. Ravi and Ina were sitting at the table in the middle of the room. They noticed me and I walked in.

As I walked up to their table Ina stood up and greeted me. She quickly said she needed to go to the ladies' room and ran towards its door. I found that to be a little odd. But I didn't dwell too much on it.

»Hi, Ravi,« I said and hold out my hand.

»Hey, musician – I'm glad you could come,« he replied with a smile.

I sat down and took a quick look around the place.

»And – what's up? Have they all turned up?«

»More or less,« he smiled. »After all, we were a pretty…close-knit class,« he said thoughtfully.

I had a pretty good idea what he meant by that, of course. I too remembered our gatherings in the Central Park during our senior year of high school. We would sit on the grass and talk about frequencies, the universe…Some would stay on and meditate. I liked the first part better. I would debate with the girls and…sometimes such meetings would end very pleasantly in the dorm.

I smiled at that memory and Ravi too couldn't suppress a smile.

»What are you smiling about?« I asked.

»I'm thinking about the different aspects of comprehension of the world,« he said. He was still good with words.

»Aspects?«

He looked at me like he could read my thoughts. »Something might represent the meaning of life to somebody, and somebody else might not notice that at all. Or they might interpret that wrongly.«

I wanted to ask him what exactly he meant by that when I noticed Ina returning from the ladies' room. She wasn't alone, though. She was talking to a friend. I was about to look away when her friend became familiar to me. Her blonde curls swayed as she walked; she wore a white dress that was slightly old-fashioned, yet contemporary enough for her to fit in with the crowd…I jumped to my feet.

»What is it?« asked Ravi.

»That girl! The one talking to Ina! Can you see her?«

He looked in their direction.

»Can you see her!?« I asked desperately. It was true that I was off the medication, but it started to feel like I'd have to start taking it again. *Oh, Ian, where are you when I need you!?*

»Of course I can see her,« he answered calmly.

He could see her! So she *is* real! After so much speculation who was crazy – who was overworked and who was hallucinating! I needed answers urgently. I started to approach them slowly, so I wouldn't scare them. And then they noticed me. They were obviously just saying goodbye. Ina escorted the girl to the exit. I started running towards her. The door just closed as I got to it. Ina asked me completely surprised: »Where are you speeding off to?« I didn't have the time to answer her.

»Hey, you!« I shouted as I opened the restaurant door.

There was nothing but an empty street outside. A few people on the other side of the street looked at me. »Hey, you!« could refer to any one of them. They all looked at me in surprise, expecting me to show who I meant. She was nowhere to be seen. Like she had vanished again.

I smiled embarrassed and decided to go back in. I wanted to turn around, but for some reason I couldn't. My legs were stiff. As I was walking away from the restaurant my legs were working normally. But back…I couldn't move. At all.

I couldn't be sure whether this place was bewitched or I just found myself in the middle of a slightly terrible dream. I couldn't go back in. Quite a lot of people had gathered in the restaurant, but it seemed that they hadn't noticed me. Like I wasn't there. I was looking at them, waving my arms. Nobody noticed me!

After a few minutes of ridiculous moving, turning and waving I decided to let the whole thing go. After all, the people in the street could see me and they couldn't understand what I was doing.

I was angry even though that wasn't helpful at all. I headed back towards my hotel, unable to say goodbye to anybody. I felt excluded and started wondering why this was happening to me. A malicious disease. I was obviously really nuts. My nerves had obviously been sending completely wrong signals to my muscles. I started searching for Ian's number in my phone. I gave him a call and got his voicemail.

»Hi, you've reached Ian. Currently I'm not available. Please, leave your message after the beep.«

»Hi, Ian. I can't talk to you over the…voicemail. I'd like you to call me when you find the time. Have a nice day,« I answered to the recording.

I walked into the warm night and I could hardly wait to clear my thoughts in my room…

XXXIV. THE PHONE CALL

THE RINGING OF THE PHONE WOKE ME FROM MY SLEEP AT HALF past one at night. I turned over in my bed, remembering that I called Ian the previous evening. I assumed he was returning my call, not knowing that I was in New York. I picked up the phone.

»Ian?« I made a guess.

»Actually...No. It's Ina.«

»Ina?« I was surprised. Why was she calling this late? Have they just noticed that I was gone or what?

»Please forgive me because you couldn't come back to the reunion...« she started. I was shocked. So she knew?

»What? How do you know...what happened?« I was surprised. I didn't know what to say. I obviously wasn't meant to.

»Let's leave that for now,« she said quickly, but still friendly enough. »I was wondering if you'd like to – in exchange for a lost evening with friends – meet us again? Well, some of us. My friend will also be there,« she summed up. She must've noticed how I was looking at her and rushed after her. Of course, she was like an apparition! I urgently wanted to come to the bottom of this – there was no going back now.

»Of...Of course I'll come. Where, when?«

»In one week, on the Prince Edward Island. Do you know where that is?«

I thought it was interesting that they picked out precisely that location. Of course I knew where it was, I was Canadian. Prince Edward Island was one of the most visited and most popular tourist destinations in the vicinity. And full of tradition, like Quebec.

»I know where the island is. Which town?«

»I'll send you the invitation tomorrow and explain everything in it,« she said kindly.

»Thanks…«

»It's OK. I can't wait for us to meet,« she said quickly and hung up the phone.

As I put down the phone I didn't know whether I was dreaming or not. It was one of those moments when you realize that you must've just talked to someone, yet you're not sure whether you talked to a voice in your dream or you actually heard someone.

I put the phone back on the dresser and realized that in spite of talking to her I didn't have any answers. Who was the blonde girl? Why didn't somebody come and get me in the street when obviously everybody knew that I wasn't able to move. And most importantly: *why* wasn't I able to move?! What was wrong with me? My phone silently sat on the dresser and I seriously started doubting that I talked to somebody.

But wait, she said she was going to send me an invitation. I'd know whether I was crazy or not when I received it. If I received it, then everything was real. Ina, the girl in the white dress, my inability to move… it all really happened! And if I didn't get the invitation…my therapist had better call me back as soon as possible…

XXXV. THE VERIFICATION

I WOKE UP IN THE MORNING WITH A HEADACHE. My head had been turned away from the window the entire night and I slept on my stomach. My neck hurt and I was wondering if it was possible for a person's head to »fall asleep«, like an arm when the circulation is hindered for a while due to the incorrect position. My entire head felt like pins and needles and I there obviously was something to my thesis. I felt like I had a hangover, although I didn't drink anything that could cause it. I didn't get the chance.

I got up slowly and yawned. The sun had already been in the sky for a few hours, and I had forgotten to close the curtains. I wanted to check the time on my phone. Still sleepy I reached out my hand towards the dresser and got hold of a smooth envelope. I flinched and was wide-awake in a moment.

In front of me I held a slightly glittering envelope with my name written on it. »Jesse Roy« was written in some sort of archaic style. I opened it immediately.

> »Hello, Jesse. I'm inviting you, as agreed, to join us on Prince Edward Island. Exactly one week from now, on 22nd of September 2013, at noon, we'll be glad to meet you at Cape Tryon, which is the northernmost point of the island. There is a lighthouse there you can't miss. Best regards,
> Ina Davies.«

Hah, so I learned two things. First of all, Ina and Ravi were obviously married. And second of all, they obviously liked visiting typical romantic tourist destinations…

But I forgot to mention the third finding! *Everything I had experienced so far actually happened!* I held that piece of paper in my hands, feeling it with my fingertips to make sure it really existed. I had to make sure of that. I quickly put on a pair of jeans and headed out. I didn't care if people thought I was nuts.

A receptionist was waiting at the reception and I thought of something innovative. I would simply ask for directions like a real tourist.

»I apologize for bothering you. Can you tell me what it says here?« I made an excuse and pointed to the place on the paper where it said Cape Tryon. If the receptionist was to read the name of the place I was pointing to then the thing was real.

»C-ape Tryon?« he asked surprised.

»Yes, yes, that's right!« I exclaimed in delight. A bit *too* enthusiastically for the poor man to know why. »Do you know how I could get there?« I played my part.

»Sir, this is New York. Maybe you should consider the option of flying to Prince Edward Island first and make your inquiries there…?« he reminded me kindly.

Of course, I was in New York, asking stupid questions. If he was in my place, having had five nervous breakdowns on account of a stupid blonde, he'd know why I was like this.

»Ha, ha, that's right. Yes, of course, yes. Thank you so much,« I backed away towards my room.

But I did know something. Everything *really* happened. Well, maybe not every little thing. That somebody evaporates in the middle of a sidewalk…? And vanishes during the press conference? Based on the true logic of laws of gravitation and mass, the dreams I had about her were

closer to the truth – how ironic. I couldn't wait for the week to be over. And I decided to leave right away that same day. I had to find out where that mentioned point was. I could still wait once I was there.

I quickly grabbed my phone, booked a plane ticket to Prince Edward Island and started packing. Nothing else in my life mattered anymore: not playing my guitar, not performing…I was drawn to that island like somebody dressed me in an iron suit and placed a giant magnet in Cape Tryon…A few hours later I was already sitting on a plane.

XXXVI. CAPE TRYON

I WAS LOOKING AT THE WAVES ROARING SOME ONE HUNDRED AND SIXTY feet below me. The strong wind tousled my hair and I felt some sort of happiness for the first time in a long time. The entire fame circus around me had died down, I got rid of a domineering manager – albeit just for six months – I was on vacation and on the brink of discovering something that had driven me through the entire last half of the year…I had already spent a day here, in this peaceful place. The kind manager of the house I was staying in let me know on several occasions that there were numerous scenic points around, where he could take me to for a small amount of money. And that there were a lot of tourist attractions too… But I was interested in only one…the lighthouse.

He told me there was nothing special about it. That it still operated, but had no special properties besides its neat appearance. Three steps led to the gate. Above the windows there were red jutting roofs, creating an adorable old-fashioned appearance. The roof was recently renovated too.

I walked up to it twice on my first day there. Once in the morning – right after I woke up following my arrival – and once in the evening. Now that I was staring at it on the second day, it seemed a bit different…I got closer to it.

The wind blew harder again and I instinctively protected my neck with the jacket. I walked to the lighthouse door and put my hand on the doorknob. *That's pointless*, I thought, having tried to enter twice already only to find the door locked. The lighthouse was empty and was supposed to stay empty until our meeting. And that was five days away.

And yet something was different this time. I could hear some sort of group singing, a murmur behind the door. Like a smaller group of people was trying to hit the same tone or something like that. Maybe a local choir practice…? The manager never mentioned anything like that.

I decided to try to open the door. The doorknob gave in to my hand unnoticeably and inaudibly, much easier than one would expect from a seemingly rusted door. I quietly cracked the door open and peeked inside with the corner of my eye. The big round room, from which the staircase was leading upwards, was illuminated from the middle. A group of people was sitting around the light – whose source I couldn't determine, but was probably some sort of light bulb – singing a precisely defined tone. They were very absorbed in their doing and I was pretty sure nobody noticed me.

I started to observe the people inside the circle and I recognized most of them! They were my high school classmates: Gina was sitting next to Ravi and Ina, and there were also George, Elliot, Sienna, Jeanette, Hannah and some kid, who reminded me of Ravi's father, the principal of our school, Aaron Davies.

They were still singing, only the manner of singing had slightly changed. From a sharp sound they moved to a deeper sound, a deeper manner of performing the same tone. They gently raised their hands and the light in the middle became bigger and more oblong. The light bulb in the middle must've been a pretty expensive one considering the ability to change shape and the use of the remote control. Soon it changed into a five feet tall pillar.

As they were singing, I also started hearing very high tones, like somebody was playing a flute. I hadn't been a very attentive student in music class (I preferred practice to theory), but I did remember the day when we talked about aliquot tones. I don't know why I was so attentive that particular day. I guess I simply found it fascinating that people were capable of producing two different tones at once. And our teacher also played us a video, which kept us quiet for at least fifteen minutes. Watching videos was always much more attractive teaching method than listening to the teacher's monotonous voice that you heard every day anyway. And the documentary was really interesting.

The pipes were creating an interesting and vivacious solo and I saw two parts branching off from the pillar. The whole thing slightly reminded me of some sort of an arrow. I started looking around for the cable that was powering this thing. I also knew that it could be a wireless thing, possibly operating on sound frequencies. The things that money can buy! A light bulb for a better choir practice!

A five feet long arrow started changing into small dots, like it was made of couscous or polenta grains. The point of each part divided into five smaller parts and the top of the arrow assumed a more oval shape…Slowly a silhouette of a human figure made of small, unconnected grains started forming in the middle of the circle. I hadn't seen anything like it before.

They continued to sing and the grains started to stick together, slowly forming larger parts. Two hands formed, then a torso with a white cover over it, a neck, a face and blonde hair. The figure that softly floated in the air at first finally touched the ground and nobody was even slightly surprised by that. Quite on the contrary, they smiled! While some of them continued to sing, the lady I'd already recognized disappeared and then reappeared a few times with lightning speed: first she was at the top of the stairs; the second time she hung from the ceiling upside down, with her long skirt spread over the ceiling, like she was actually standing on the ground; the third time she appeared right behind Ina and attacked her from behind.

A fight ensued and went on with an exceptional speed: the girls demonstrated a sort of kung fu in the middle of the circle and it looked terrifying. If I was attacked with such speed and such powerful punches, I'd surely go down to the ground and wouldn't pick myself up again. When Ina's fist slightly touched the blonde's cheek, they ended the fight and respectfully bowed to each other.

Without any warning the blonde turned towards me and pierced me with her gaze. I wasn't prepared for that! I really thought that nobody could see me. The others turned their heads almost simultaneously. I closed the door and started running like the Devil himself was after me...*It's not true, it can't be true*, I fought the voices in my head. I was amazed and despaired over the fact that I had managed to create such a realistic fantasy world. *Did I hallucinate all through the high school? Was I crazy? Would I have to take the stupid medication for the rest of my life?* I admit that I used to make fun of people who had problems with depression, mental illnesses and such. I thought it was funny how they rolled their eyes and generally acted weirdly...Never, but really never would I've thought that I'd become one of them. All my thoughts focused on the absurdity of my own life.

Who do I live for, I thought. *For my mom, who is a robot anyway and won't be in the least hurt by my disappearance? For my dad and Terry, who are gone? For Rodney, who got tired of me after all the little squabbles on buses and planes? For myself, even though I was obviously much crazier than I'd thought?*

I was still running, now with even greater determination. Considering what I just saw I suspected I wouldn't be able to escape them. But I wanted to get as far away from those hallucinations as I possibly could. I heard voices behind me and I knew they were following me...

XXXVII. THE CLIFF

I RAN UNTIL I LEFT THEM BEHIND ME. It seemed so real and at the same time so...impossible. I panted up the hill astonished at my own weakness. When I got to the edge I caught sight of her again and although I don't scare easily, I shrieked loudly.

»Get lost, you freak!« My threats didn't drive her away. She stood calmly on the edge of the cliff looking straight into my eyes. When I took a step forward she moved towards me. She was less than three feet away. I started to shake again. As her arm reached towards me I quickly got around her, ran ahead and found myself on the edge of the cliff. *My hallucinations have obviously come back*, I thought. *It doesn't matter now if this world is real or not.* I wanted to leap forward.

»You don't want to do that,« she continued.

»I said get lost,« I screamed and stared at the rocks. I would surely get smashed to smithereens if I jumped. I sensed her gaze at the back of my head and turned towards her. I cried in anger and fear.

»It doesn't have to be this way...Please understand...« she slowly drew nearer. Her pale face looked even more divine and more terrifying. I knew what she was capable of. She took another step and I instinctively drew back. Suddenly I realized that I had actually stepped into an empty space.

I panicked, because I wasn't ready yet. *I don't want to leave this world,* I screamed inside, *no matter how terrifying it is...*

It was too late. The blackness started to engulf me and I felt the pressure in my stomach – the kind one experiences on a roller coaster. Except that this time it wasn't a game...it was real.

I felt the falling more and more intensely and it seemed like it lasted forever. Memories started flashing through my mind of all the unimportant details that happened in my short life…The earliest memories of my childhood…How Terry and me played and did everything together. My dad taking me to a game and buying me ice cream for the first time. Elementary school, where I was pulling a sour face most of the time because I felt completely lonely. It simply wasn't fun without Terry. High school, where I felt better, because I had left Quebec that reminded me of my childhood behind me…High school seemed like a flash of a second…The fame that wasn't at all what I thought it would be…My dad. Regardless of the fact that this was just a projection in my head, I still felt pain in my heart…Now I was about to discover whether afterlife existed. Or maybe I'd wake up all sweaty in a New York hotel bed and realize that everything had just been a dream…

I got my courage back and opened my eyes. Too late. A huge rock that was part of the beach was hurling towards me. It was obvious that I missed the water. In the last moment I regretted not leaping further – maybe I'd reach the water and survive. I heard my own vertebrae crack as I hit the rock. Then the silence engulfed me.

Part two

Keisha

»WITH ALL DUE RESPECT, I'M NOT DOING THIS!« I said. I knew that what she wanted me to do was actually similar to becoming a kamikaze. »It wasn't a request,« she said with conviction. »You are a part of a larger plan.«

»But that's madness!« I insisted and tried to understand how my going out to a mad army of people could be a part of a bigger plan.

»You are thinking too much,« she smiled, »or rather you think too much like *him*,« she said emphatically. Did she really always had to remind me of my failures? Trample all over my ego? Her statement hurt me more than anything she had ever said before. Even if it seemed much more innocent than the others. It was *true*. And painful. I thought I had already got over him.

»But you haven't,« she said having read my thoughts again. »You are still a part of that negative magnetic field and it's time you cleaned it. It is time for you the cleanse the world.«

It seemed pointless asking why my death should cleanse the world.

She laughed broadly. But I didn't think it was funny. »Maybe one day you will see the plan like I see it and you will find it amusing how much resistance we can put up against this brilliant and infallible plan of the universe.«

She looked at me again and all of a sudden I felt weaker. I felt cold all over my body and I hadn't felt that for 120 years. Was that possible? Was the universe taking my powers away? In my despair I begged her with my eyes to stop what she was doing.

»The choice is really *yours*,« she replied. »You can either revolt against the plan of the universe and change sides or you can surrender and trust the light which will always lead you to higher levels…«

I had no choice. To become a vulnerable human being again seemed so… unacceptable. How could I have strayed so much from my path? I closed my eyes, took a deep breath and asked all forces to help me.

»OK,« I said pacified although I knew I was going to my death, »I will do what you ask.«

When I opened my eyes again my leader had already disappeared. Only the wind, which was pleasantly caressing my eternal body again, proved that I had spoken to Timeless.

I. FACING THE TRUTH

S INCE I WAS BORN INTO A WEALTHY FAMILY I NEVER KNEW ANY SHORTAGE.
At least not in the material sense. Nevertheless, in some way I did
feel different from the others who liked playing cricket, drinking tea and
throwing Sunday parties. On sunny days I was completely satisfied with
a nice walk by the sea.

In the year our island was named Prince Edward Island I fell in love
for the first time. It was during the time I started noticing that my body
started responding differently to the young gentlemen than before. I
became fragile and euphoric when my loved one approached me and I
wasn't used to that. But somehow I felt that he liked me too.

It happened soon that he met with my father and asked him for permission. Although I wasn't quite sure what the outcome of that meeting was – I
wasn't supposed to know about it – I could feel that from then on my father
started acting differently towards me. My mother also suddenly became
busier. And finally the time came when the young man started courting me.

Even though he was young, Philip, Duke of York, had inherited a
lot of wealth by the time he was twenty-three. A lot of girls – and their
parents – had hoped probably because of that that he would choose them.
It was different when he chose me. I *really* liked him. It wasn't important
to me how much he was worth; you can't measure love with money.

Oftentimes there would be a beautiful message wrapped in silk waiting for me at home. On numerous occasions he would send his friends to
serenade under my window at the back of our little mansion. Each night
there was something inexplicable in the air; I prayed each night before I

went to bed that we would be united in front of God as soon as possible. He finally granted my wish and set the date.

My father called me to himself and told me what I already knew: I was to become Philip's wife in a month's time. I was overwhelmed with happiness, my entire body radiated with excitement, and preparations for the wedding began soon.

A couple of weeks later we had our engagement party. All the members of the nobility on the island and beyond came to congratulate us. That was the first time that such a party seemed perfectly reasonable to me. Usually I found the rest of them to be monotonous and boring. This one, though, was…something special to me. When I stood by his side, seeing him in his shiny regalia, while the sound of violins was coming from the next room and we were greeting friends and relatives together…That's when I realized how stupid I had been by not accepting my beautiful life as my own. These timeless parties, these beautiful smiles, these wonderful dresses…

And then a strange thing happened. Our young servant girl, who shouldn't have even been there, joined our guests' queue. Even though I treated her with respect, I nevertheless – for the sake of our good relationship, her honor and her position – wanted to warn her to leave before my mother of father saw her. I directed my gaze at her and waited for her to look at me. Amazingly she kept looking at the floor and waiting patiently for her turn. So I decided to tell her what I thought about this when she offered her hand. I sincerely hoped that nobody would notice her until then.

I proudly glanced at my husband-to-be, whose complexion changed slightly. He seemed worried and had turned completely pale.

»Is everything in order, Philip dear?« I asked – I was already allowed to call him by his first name.

»Of course my darling Keisha,« he answered kindly and smiled to prove that. Since I was madly in love with him that smile calmed me down and I thought that the blame for his paleness might be attributed to the salmon we had for lunch that day. I too felt slightly sick afterwards.

It was the servant girl's turn to congratulate Philip. Luckily, he used the opportunity and pulled her out of the queue. After that I only heard his words:

»What for God's sake are you doing here!?«

And her stifled sobbing. He needn't have been that aggressive. I'd have handled her much more gallantly and with more respect. He escorted her out and it took him several minutes to come back. He took up his post again.

»You didn't have to act so roughly, you know,« I berated slightly him even though we were still smilingly greeting the guests. He leaned his face towards mine, so I'd know he was talking just to me:

»But a servant girl in the queue, that is unacceptable, you should know that!«

»Maybe she just wanted to wish us luck,« I was almost defending her.

»As you wish, dear,« he smiled routinely and kissed the hand of the next duchess.

The evening soon turned into the night. I had a feeling that I hadn't danced enough when the butler already announced the end of the party. In the meantime we – or should I say my Philip – announced that the party was held in honor of our future marriage. I had a feeling that the older guests were happy for us, while some younger ladies...I knew that they liked Philip too and that they found the situation difficult.

The time for the wedding arrived soon. I was happier than ever before. It seemed like my life was turning into a perfectly composed jigsaw puzzle that was unknown to me before. I thought I was being a fool for ever doubting the happy love, when it had always been within the reach of the hand. I had never asked myself whether Philip had chosen me because of my wealthy family, my not so bad looks or love. Since I was in love with him, I believed love was his reason too. And since I was basking in his attention – or the attention of his choir or his string quartet – under my window almost every night, I believed that he felt the same way.

On the happy day, which was to mean the uniting of two important ducal families to some and the happiest day of my life to me, I was getting ready in my room. Six chambermaids were taking care of my appearance. When I looked in the mirror, I didn't see just a blonde girl in a white dress...I saw pure love. The girl, who simply glowed under the blonde curls and in the white dress, her beauty accentuated by a glow that only a bride in love could possess. I truly liked what I saw. I could feel that my future husband and I belonged together.

Some fifteen minutes before the start of the ceremony my mother came to check whether everything was going according to the plan. She hugged me and I thought she shed a tear. Like that was some sort of a motherly duty: when a turning point in her daughter's life came, the crying was almost obligatory.

Then she sent my chambermaids away and left the room herself with the words: »Let's leave the bride alone for a moment so she can prepare for the ceremony!«

And she was right, I needed that moment! It was hard to be surrounded by all those people. Social etiquette didn't allow me to dance in the middle of the room, or to scream my lungs out of happiness or simply to wait calmly and relaxed in a position that was comfortable to me. I was relieved when they left the room.

Finally I managed to relax and I looked around the room. The red curtains covering the walls were rimmed with golden pattern, thus creating festive impression. They reminded me of the brocade in the dance hall where festivities were to be held. I closed my eyes and took my long skirt by the hem...In my mind I imagined the sound of violins and my husband...The large dance hall, shining brightly, welcoming the newlyweds...Him taking my hand, leading me to the dance floor for a dance of two lovers...Happy to the end of our days...

I was spinning in the rhythm of a quartet and suddenly got really frightened when I felt a real touch of hand on my palm. Somebody obviously saw me dancing. I opened my eyes and saw my private tutor, professor Harriet. We'd been close since I was little. During my teenage years we bonded even more and she became a real friend. She taught me foreign languages, as well as the mysteries of astrology. I had a feeling that nobody understood me as well as she did. She always radiated some sort of wisdom…Except this time. This time she held me by the wrist as hard as she could and radiated one single thing: fear. Her slightly gray curls were dangling from under her brown hat and I could see that she obviously didn't have time to clean herself up before appearing in front of the bride. I was about to ask her why she came in such an unusual manner, when she pushed me towards the back door of the room.

»Quickly, duchess, there's no time for explanations!«

She dragged me to the door and immediately closed it behind us. She told me to be quiet no matter what and slightly opened the door again. A couple of soldiers slowly entered the room through the front door, holding crossbows in their hands. A dark curtain was covering the mirror I was looking at myself in just a few minutes ago. After all, that was the changing area and the mirror needed to be covered, so the looks of the wrong people wouldn't get caught in it. They pointed their crossbows in that direction. They weren't looking for me, were they!?

When the weapons were fired we heard the glass breaking, which meant that arrows hit the mirror. I wanted to scream in terror, but Harriet put her hand over my mouth just in time, making sure I was quiet. She quickly dragged me down the stairs. We reached the back exit where a carriage was waiting for us.

»To the forest!« shouted out Harriet.

When we left the town behind us and I managed to catch my breath at least for a moment, I gave her a bewildered questioning look.

»I'm very sorry that you have to find this out in such a cruel way…« she started. »I want to tell you so many things…Unfortunately we only have a few minutes for me to tell you what I recently came to know. The Duke of York regretfully…doesn't love you.«

The words came out of her mouth with great difficulty – especially because she knew that my feelings for him were quite the opposite.

»The other day, at your engagement party, I wanted to take a breath of fresh air and I went outside to the tree-lined lane. I stopped by the hedgerow and listened to the crickets. Two figures started approaching me rapidly and I instinctively decided to hide. After all, it doesn't befit a middle-aged lady to be caught in the bushes like that.

I realized that it was Philip with some other lady. They stopped awfully close to me when they…kissed.«

Tears started filling my eyes. She knew that even little details of that nature could hurt me very much and decided to shorten the description of the devastating scene as much as possible, although judging by her awkward tone of voice I suspected that it must've been rather passionate.

»They talked about their eternal love and also about the lady being pregnant. Then he called her by her name and I knew immediately it was our young kitchen maid…«

That's why he was so pale that time. The spring of tears in my eyes intensified and turned into a stream of tears flowing down my cheeks.

»He told her that he had an argument with his father about her and that his father told him he could marry a girl of lower class only if his current bride miraculously disappeared. And so…Philip hired a couple of soldiers stupid and greedy enough to accept the task…« She started to sob, but soon tried to regain her composure, »They're probably looking for you. Surely by now everybody is looking for you.«

I was shocked. *Where can I flee on the island? The fleet is closely guarded.*

»Where should I go?« I asked her confused. If I hadn't seen her tears and felt her unconditional motherly love, I probably wouldn't believe her. The story was too horrible and unjust. It was also true that I saw the proof with my own eyes. The world that not long ago seemed like a perfect jigsaw puzzle crumbled into a million little pieces in an instant. »I'll have to be brief here too,« she quickly continued because we were nearing the forest.

»I know it'll sound odd, but you'll have to trust me. This morning I had an unbelievably vivid dream. I was talking to an incredibly wise woman exactly in the middle of the forest, and she was explaining the mysteries of life to me. Her name was Timeless. She told me that my protégé will soon need her help. When that happened my protégé should turn to her. She'll know the way. As a proof she gave me an ivy twig, which I still held in my hand when I woke up.«

I should believe her because of that? On the base of an ivy twig?

»Don't be afraid, I'll accompany you,« she continued. We reached the forest and the carriage stopped. Harriet wrapped me in a dark green cloak and drew its hood over my head.

»Try to remain hidden,« she said.

She paid the driver, who gave the impression that he didn't know who he had just driven. She asked him to wait for her, promising to be back shortly. We hurried off into the forest and after a few minutes we arrived at the clearing with a large tree in its center. Under the tree a woman with shoulder-length brown hair sat quietly. Her simple robe softly fluttered in the breeze; she was barefoot, sitting with her legs crossed, like the Turks did. Her peaceful face of indeterminate age was adorned with red lips, a slightly more tanned complexion than I was used to seeing in our parts, nicely shaped eyebrows and symmetrical features.

Harriet nodded at me and hugged me.

»From here on you're on your own,« she said. »I really love you, my child; I hope that we'll meet again.«

»So do I...« I said deeply moved. At the same time I was still shocked because the day unraveled so unexpectedly. I should've been Duchess of York by now and not a girl thrown at the mercy of some unknown woman in the middle of forest.

»Everything will be all right,« said Harriet and patted me on the cheek.

»Thank you for everything,« I managed to utter before her shadowy cloak vanished in the misty forest.

II. UNUSUAL COMFORT

I HELPLESSLY FOLLOWED HER DISAPPEARING FIGURE WITH MY EYES and again became painfully aware of my hopeless situation. What had I done to deserve exile, not even being able to say goodbye to my parents? Why did my…I mean, Duke Philip betray me so shamelessly? What was love anyway? In my desperation I reached out my arms towards my only true protector and once more writhed in pain that engulfed my entire body.

The leaves behind me rustled slightly and I turned around. The woman that I saw sitting down thirty feet away just moments ago was standing behind me.

»You've scared me,« I jerked. She gave a comforting smile and put her hand on my shoulder.

»I apologize for that. Would you come into the shade with me? We'll talk easier there.«

I wasn't exactly sure what she meant by that since the forest was covered in fog. But in a few seconds the sky cleared up and the sunshine lit up the clearing that started glowing in bright colors.

»With pleasure,« I managed to utter in surprise. We sat down under a tree. She in her own way and I in the way that befitted a young duchess. With my legs sidewise and my back always straight. I haven't sat in any other position since I was twelve. It simply wasn't right. And I got used to it.

»Well, you can relax now,« she said clearly. »You don't have to pretend to be somebody else in front of me.«

»Excuse me?« I was surprised. We hadn't even started the conversation properly and she already started insulting me. I didn't realize that was just the first of her outrageous statements.

»What I want to say is, you don't have to live your life always following the same patterns. Life is vibrant and colorful – like this clearing. No animal here wonders how it appears to the others. It just lives. It just is.«

The word 'living' reminded me of the castle Philip and I were supposed to move into after the wedding. I shriveled into a lump of misery and started crying hot tears of sorrow and resentment.

»I already prefer this posture,« my new acquaintance smiled. »But not your way of thinking. You are responsible for everything that's happened to you. You alone.«

Nobody had ever said such a preposterous thing to me.

»Have I hired and invited two murderers in my own room? Have I asked that…vulgar servant girl to seduce my fiancé? Have I betrayed myself?«

»The answer to all your questions is: YES.« I had the feeling that she found our little dialogue quite entertaining. Even though she somehow seemed completely at peace.

»Ha!« was all I could say to such nonsense.

»You can ha-ha all you want, it's still true.« She turned her head aside and smiled.

»How much do you really know about Duke Philip? How much do you really know about yourself? How much do you really know about life?«

How much did I really know about Philip? About myself? About life? I really didn't think that was important.

»The events in your life match the answers to those questions. Until now you've been nothing more than a well-brought-up little girl that wasn't meant to know any bigger emotions than naivety. Now you have the opportunity to learn what the game of life is actually about.«

Since I didn't think it was reasonable to continue arguing with her, I remained silent while tears were rolling down my cheeks. She became silent too. So I kept crying for about an hour, until I got tired. She was sitting still the entire time, closing her eyes from time to time.

When I couldn't cry or talk anymore, I lied down in the grass. My last memory of that day is Timeless taking my hand. I heard her sigh:

»We have a lot of work to do...« and then my head started spinning and I immediately fell asleep.

III. THE CAVERN

I WAS VERY COLD WHEN I WOKE UP. Even though I was wrapped in a blanket I was shivering all over my body; that probably woke me up. I could hear the wind howling outside and when I carefully looked around the place it became more than clear to me that I wasn't on the island anymore.

I decided to be perfectly honest with the woman that brought me here: no more polite remarks. She wasn't even trying to be courteous to me – why should I be different? Besides, she brought me to a place that couldn't possibly be better than Prince Edward Island; at least there I wouldn't be freezing from cold. I was wondering where to find the woman in white when I heard a few stones crackle near me. I realized that this place wasn't just cold and wild – it was some sort of a mountain cavern.

»So, you are awake,« she said calmly and placed a bowl of rice in front of me, »you must be hungry too.«

And how true that was! Without waiting for any further invitation I immediately grabbed the bowl and started eating. She also gave me some sort of narrow sticks, but I pushed them aside and tried to eat as quickly as possible.

»Well, all right. Since it's your first day I'll let it pass,« she was lenient.

»Where are we?« I asked as I slowly collected the last grains of rice. »And why is it so cold?«

»Hmm, that question requires not quite a logical explanation. Can we leave that for later? As I already said, we have a lot of work to do. It'll be easier for me if you're interested in the subject. After all, I've been waiting for you a really long time.«

Not one sentence in that answer made any sense to me. So, all of that – me almost dying, what happened yesterday, the betrayal – was agreed upon in advance?

»Yes and no,« she said slowly.

»Did I say anything out loud?« I asked. It seemed impossible that somebody would be answering my thoughts.

»Let me explain. Fate…is like your personal lesson plan. You did go to school, didn't you?«

»Of course.« And to the most elite one – with my personal tutor.

»Well, it's possible to foresee some things in advance. Unless a person is strong enough to decide differently. Until now you didn't have a choice. If you want I can show you the way out of this labyrinth. I think it's high time for that. That's why I said we had a lot of work to do. You have to stop playing a victim. What happened to you is just a test.«

I wrapped myself in the blanket even tighter. The woman in front of me seemed cruel and it was more than obvious on whose side she was. But since I knew that I was completely dependent on her in this godforsaken place, I just smiled at her and kept my thoughts to myself.

»It'll be hard to continue like this,« she said and then walked to the snow-covered entrance to the cavern.

»I'll come back when you're ready,« she concluded and then bravely stepped into the deep snow.

That's fine with me, I thought. *If you want to trudge in this snow, be my guest.*

Out of pure curiosity how far she'd get, I got to my feet and looked outside after her. Several footprints were obviously deeply imprinted in the snow at the cavern's entrance; further out the footprints were getting shallower until they eventually disappeared. Was that possible? Has the wind really swept all traces of her that quickly? Did she start running right after she said goodbye? Has she disappeared into thin air?

After my investigation of her footprints yielded no results I retreated from the cold back into the cavern. I was satisfied with my loneliness. Now I could think about everything that had happened in peace and simply be alone! Without needless companions.

That day I had all the time in the world to thoroughly relive the injustice that had been done to me. I mourned my lost life, my destroyed marriage – before it even began, the family I could've had and the peaceful life in the castle. Handsome duke Philip disgusted me more than I could ever imagine; the way he treated me filled me with bitter resentment. I'd gladly have cursed his future bastard children and his false life, had had I enough of his malice in me!

I looked around myself again and felt every fiber of my lonely body. I decided I'd never ever fall in love again. *And I'm not going to get a chance for that here*, I thought with a bitter smile. In the middle of the cavern I looked like a beggar in my own eyes and when I became aware of my miserable state again I screamed even more loudly. Nobody could hear me in that storm anyway.

And so it was until the evening. I became hungry again. And awfully thirsty after the river of tears I cried. I looked towards the cavern's entrance, hoping that my new guardian would come back after all. I started to call her. I remembered her name even though I uttered it with difficulty. It seemed so…unnatural. *Timeless.*

I went to the entrance and tried to call her more loudly. There was no answer. Just mountains staring back at me, returning my own dull echo. When I realized that I was getting colder and colder, and that I could die of cold here, I went back in the cavern and sobbed in vain. I lied down in the corner that seemed the warmest, and feeling utterly exhausted, closed my puffy eyes. It was growing dark outside. The wind was howling around the cavern's entrance. My last thought, before I managed to fall asleep, was dedicated to a new bowl of rice and a large stream of water…

IV. THE LAST BATTLE

I̲t was still night when I woke up. I had had a nightmare and when I opened my eyes the wind that penetrated the cavern was howling around me. It was pitch black. Suddenly I heard some sort of animal moaning outside and I wondered if I wasn't in the way of some animal in this cavern. I became frightened and at the same time I remembered again that I didn't even know where I was.

I could hardly wait until the morning. I was hungry like never before. And thirsty at the same time. My lips were stuck together and it felt like I didn't have them and couldn't use them anymore. I could hardly move my tongue around both sides of my mouth to produce at least a little bit of saliva…without success.

When I was just about to burst into tears again from my distress, I stopped, realizing that I wouldn't be helping myself by shedding the last drops of fluid from my body…So I tried to calm down. At the same time I ruminated about the last words my cruel hostess uttered before she left: »I'll come back when you're ready.«

What was that supposed to mean? Wasn't I ready yet?

Since I didn't have the strength to sit or stand up anymore, I lay down for the better part of the day. In the evening I suddenly realized that the snow that was surrounding me, was actually water in another form! I rushed outside wondering why I hadn't remembered that sooner! I scooped it up and started eating it. The snow had never tasted better before! After dining on snow for about an hour I wrapped my numb hands in the blanket again. I couldn't feel them anymore, but I did feel better because I got at least a bit of water, even though it was frozen…I got a fresh impetus and tried calling Timeless into the empty snowbound landscape…Nothing.

As I prepared to go to sleep – in my corner – I started noticing that my body was getting weaker and weaker. After eating all that snow I also started noticing my throat that was hurting more and more. I squeezed into the corner and hoped that the pain would be gone by the time I woke up.

The next day it was even worse. It became very clear to me in the morning that the pain from the previous day hadn't just stayed with me, but had intensified. My throat was extremely painful and I treated it with the only thing that I had at hand – the snow.

Soon I was unable to talk or stand up. I was shaking with fever, lying in the corner, waiting to die. I could feel how very different my soul was from my body. How I was slowly losing the ability to move my arms, my legs, my head…My throat hurt so much that I was surprised at the fact that I was still alive. Smarting pain started to spread to the other parts of my body and they started to feel more and more numb. I could hardly feel my arms, legs, ears, nose, face…

I'm not sure how I managed to last out through the night and to the third day. I could think only about how I wanted this to be over as soon as possible. I knew I was going to die. My guardian has obviously deserted me, but I didn't resent her anymore. I was contemplating reconciliation with the world.

Why am I leaving this planet? Who am I? Who are the people I have lived with? What is the meaning of everything that's happened? Can I forgive them? What is forgiveness anyway?

I thought about how there was quite a lot of us and that the world possibly didn't revolve just around me. God was probably having a lot of fun watching my little story and seeing me banging my head against the wall because of the things that happened to me. Or seeing me cry because of other people. I realized that I was like a little ant on an anthill. Sometimes it gets upset, sometimes it falls in love, then it thinks the entire anthill has conspired against it...But it's still just a little ant!

I instinctively smiled at the thought of a little ant getting upset with its whistling little voice in the middle of an anthill. My facial muscles hurt when I did that, reminding me that they were close to freezing up entirely. My throat also burned and brought me back into reality.

When I meet death here in a few minutes, I won't be ready, I thought. Back home anybody battling their last battle on their deathbed got a visit from the priest who performed the last rites. *How should I get ready?*

I remembered that our priest used to talk a lot about forgiveness, praying for our loved ones and approaching great beyond...

Maybe I could perform some sort of ritual myself, I thought. *Just like that. In my head.*

I didn't have enough strength for anything else anyway.

First, I started praying in my mind. As much as I knew how. Then I thought of everybody that had been close to me in my life...my mother, my father...Harriet. Poor soul. She thought she could save me, not knowing that she was sending me to my death...

In the end I thought of Philip. And Adele. I had a hard time recalling her name, because it seemed much more appropriate if I just called her dirty, adulterous...

No, Keisha, I thought. *You're dying now, you don't have any more time for ugly thoughts...You have to forgive now...*

I thought how Adele was probably just...in love. Like I used to be. Which probably wasn't unusual, taking into account that Philip was a really handsome man. And he...was obviously just trapped. That's right, yes. Trapped between what he was told to do and what he wanted to do. How would I act if I were in his place? If I fell in love with someone of lower class? No, never, I'd never act like he did...

Calm down, Keisha, you're dying now, I reminded myself.

Let me die if that's my fate, I thought. *But I don't intend to leave this world angry and disappointed! I'll leave with my head held high! All right, I forgive you! I FORGIVE ALL OF YOU!*

»I For ... give...all!« I whispered to confirm my statement. I always wanted to know what my last words would be before I left this world. The ones I chose seemed quite appropriate. I smiled, satisfied with my choice and realized that I was really ready.

Goodbye, world; thank you for everything I have been allowed to experience here.

»I'm glad that you're better,« I heard suddenly.

I opened my eyes. In the dim haze that was clearing rather slowly in front of me I caught sight of Timeless. I didn't know exactly what she meant by saying that I was better, when I was on the brink of death.

»You're finally ready. Come on, we've got work to do,« she said quickly.

I thought she was kidding. I wanted to tell her that my throat hurt and that I was dying of fever. To prove that, I slowly coughed. The pain had disappeared completely. I moved my legs, to check if they were still nearly frozen. To my amazement I could feel them much better! I moved my head that suddenly felt well and clear. Nor a trace of fever. I actually felt better that ever before!

Timeless offered me a bowl of rice and a cup of tea.

»Even though you're not exactly famished, you'll surely enjoy this.«

That was also true. Even though I hadn't eaten in three days, I was as hungry as I used to be at home before the afternoon tea. Not more. I even decided to try eating using the sticks she offered. It was pretty difficult at first, but I soon got a hang of it. The dinner was delicious even though it looked rather frugal. It had a sort of...inner taste, like I was actually eating risotto instead of plain rice. The tea was also slightly sweetened and very tasty. Feeling refreshed I felt I too could leave the cavern and wade through the snow. Especially if I continued to feel this great.

Timeless looked at me from time to time and smiled. When I finished eating she quickly said:

»You are solely responsible for what has happened to you. You needed that experience so you could feel the delight of forgiveness. The emotions you felt before that are like poison. You've experienced that on your own skin – as a disease. I think the time has come for you to stop looking into the past. You've got a very bright future ahead of you.«

Her words completely calmed me down. I was…drained. The pressure in my chest and all the burdens that weighed on me before were gone; I truly wished all the best to everybody I knew. And I couldn't wait to start living again myself.

»That's better,« she said. She stood up and offered me her hand. »Come on, so I can answer your first question!«

»You mean, *where are we?*«

»Exactly!«

V. THE HIMALAYAS

WHEN WE STEPPED OUT OF THE CAVERN I FELT THE WIND ON MY SKIN. I was surprised by the fact that I wasn't cold anymore. Even my feet, which followed Timeless into the snow, felt warm and safe in light wedding shoes, like I was wearing the best-padded winter boots.

»Timeless…how come I'm…«

»Not cold?« she finished my question. By now I was used to her finishing my sentences. If I had been in her shoes, I'd have probably guessed myself what a young clueless girl, who had just arrived, wanted to ask me.

»That's my little trick, which you'll come to understand later. All I can say is that without it it'd be difficult to survive here.«

That was very much true. In addition to the wind that was howling across the icy slopes I could also see steam coming from my mouth every time I exhaled. It was incredibly cold. I imagined that only the end of the world could be this cold.

»We're at the other end of the world in comparison to where you were before,« she answered my question. »Have you ever heard of the Himalayas?«

»Is that a mountain range?«

»Yes, the highest mountain range in the world.«

»How did…we…« I wanted to continue: »…get here so quickly«, but she interrupted me once again.

»We'll get to that when the time is right.«

We walked in silence for a while.

We were walking across a mountain pass between two mountains.

The snow reached up to my knees and it grew deeper with each step. My white dress blended with the snow-white landscape and if I was to trip and roll down the slope I surely wouldn't have been found. We reached a vertical rock wall that was entirely impossible to climb.

»It's time for high-mountain exploits again,« she joked. She seized the rope hanging from the rock wall and asked me to close my eyes.

»For your own safety,« she explained.

I closed my eyes and felt being lifted up. The rope must've been connected to some sort of a pulley system or something. After a few minutes a warmer wind started to blow. Since my eyes were still closed that feeling surprised me even more. Soon we stopped and I could feel solid ground under my feet again. I opened my eyes and widened them even more in surprise.

A wide landscape opened up in front of me, full of greenery and much warmer than the one preceding it. I looked back and discovered that the snow-covered mountains were far behind us; we had also left the mountain pass behind us.

In front of me on the right was a small cabin made exclusively from materials that could be found in nature: the walls were made of logs, the roof of leaves, the door was made of boards from local wood.

»Welcome home,« she said with conviction.

I looked at the cabin in front of me. In my previous life – if I could call it that – such dwelling would've seemed entirely unbecoming a lady of my stature. But now it grew to my heart immediately. I was surprised by my new and refreshed outlook on the world. Suddenly it seemed that I felt really wealthy for the first time in my life. The birds' singing around me only accentuated the all-encompassing splendor I was witnessing. The plants around me flourished in the sun and I was truly happy. Like I'd been waiting exactly for this my whole life.

»I'll let you settle in,« she said peacefully. I agreed.

»Take care of yourself, go for a walk and become acquainted with your new surroundings. I'll come back tomorrow.«

I was glad that she told me when she'd be back. I had the feeling that we started out right this time. I didn't think she was cruel anymore. I actually felt gratitude towards her.

When I entered my new home I discovered that it had everything I needed: a room for washing up; a room full of food; a room for sleeping and a room that was entirely empty – it was decorated only with a simple carpet with a golden pot in the middle. Since I didn't know what it was for, I decided to ask Timeless about it the next day.

The rest of the day went by very quickly. After a walk I got ready for bed. I felt completely refreshed. Before I went to bed I listened one more time to the birds' singing which started to mix with the chirping of crickets in the grass…There was absolutely no sign of the beasts that encircled the cavern…Just peace and fragrances of spring. Immersed in the newfound gratitude I closed my eyes. The scents of greenery and flowers and animal sounds gently lulled me into sleep…

VI. THE VISIT

THE NEXT PERIOD OF MY LIFE WENT BY IN A FLASH OF A SECOND. Soon I discovered that life on this side of the planet went on entirely differently than I was used to. The people were good-natured and friendly, although there weren't many of them living there. Soon I completely forgot who I was before. It simply didn't matter anymore. And I discovered what Timeless meant when she said that we had a lot of work to do. Soon she began to teach me.

The basic language of communication here was a smile. But at the same time one was completely helpless in the huge jungle if one didn't master at least one martial art. Timeless was teaching me two of them, which I later learned were called kung fu and jujitsu. I also learned that the inhabitants of this place had one more common characteristic: some sort of all-encompassing peace. When I looked in the eyes of anybody that lived here, I saw only a sea of confidence in life. There was no struggle to dominate or fake behavior. Everyone radiated exactly what they were. Without exceptions.

»Wouldn't it be wonderful if the inhabitants of the entire planet could live this way?« I asked my teacher on an occasion.

»They will,« she smiled. »And you'll be the cause of it. That's why I'm teaching you.«

I wasn't quite clear on what she meant by this causality.

»It doesn't matter whether you understand or not. You'll see.«

That was the most Timeless would ever tell me about the purpose of my existence on this planet.

But she did teach me so many other things! In addition to altering my body so I didn't feel cold or gotten sick anymore – she'd always remind me of some sort of awakening and preparedness. She kept watching over me the entire time and never allowed for any digressions from the truth.

My training was hard, but at the same time I couldn't imagine my life without it. I didn't know how many years had passed since I came here. I completely lost the sense of time. One day she called me to herself and told me:

»An important moment has come. I think that you need to visit somebody. Come sit next to me and take my hand.«

I sat on the carpet next to her. We sat in perfect peace – I discovered a long time ago that the carpet was intended for the relaxation of one's mind – and I took her hand. When she gave me a signal to close my eyes, I closed them. I felt very relaxed and soon I saw a flash of white light behind my eyelids. The flash was growing stronger and stronger and it suddenly expanded to me too. Soon I was engulfed by the light and I wasn't able to feel my body anymore. Just so I wouldn't get scared Timeless reminded me again: »Relax and surrender. You're safe.«

I sensed the floor under my feet. We were standing. We were standing in the room whose walls were covered in red brocade with golden trimmings and there was a large bed in its center. There was nobody in the room except an old woman lying covered with sheets. I sensed that she was very ill, because a heavy, gurgling sound was coming from her lungs. We stepped closer to the bed. The woman opened her eyes. Two eyes peeped from behind the gray hair, still full of sweetness and kindness, even though they were surrounded by a web of deep little wrinkles...

»Harriet!« I cried out. The memory of days long gone awoke in me.

»Keisha!« smiled the old woman weakly. »How nice to see you again! Look at you. You haven't...« Her eyes were now wide open, »you haven't changed at all!«

»She was in safe hands, as I promised,« said Timeless.

»That's true. Much safer than here,« said Harriet. She looked again at Timeless. »Does she know…?«

»Do I know – what?« I asked.

»It's war, dear child. Maybe it wouldn't be a bad thing if you left as soon as possible. I'll leave – as you can see – another way…« she coughed. I winced.

»No, Harriet, you won't, it's not necessary…« I looked at Timeless. She could perform a similar trick as she did on me several years ago and save her! »Help her, please.«

»There's no need, my child,« said Harriet. »Sometimes it's destined to be this way. I'm glad you're in good hands…« she looked at me once more. For a moment I thought that she saw something behind me that I couldn't see. I turned around, but there was nothing there. The squeeze of her hand weakened a bit. A smile rested on her face.

»Some people are destined to cross over differently than you,« Timeless reminded me. »Don't worry, she's all right.«

For a brief moment I felt a strong pain. I remembered that the woman lying in front of me really meant a lot to me. Timeless put her hands on my shoulders and told me to close my eyes. As I did that I suddenly saw Harriet in front of me. She was calm and truly happy.

»It's really nice here,« she was pleased. »It's nothing like death. Thank you for visiting me, my dear Keisha.«

»They're waiting for you,« said Timeless.

»Oh yes, just like we talked about,« Harriet smiled lightly.

Timeless placed a hand on her and Harriet vanished in the light.

»Since she's done a lot of good in her life, I enabled her to experience a special and very safe crossing onto a higher level of existence on Earth. Not everybody is that lucky.«

I wanted to ask her something else but there was no time.

»Come, quickly!« I heard her say as she pulled me by my shoulder towards the red curtain on the side. The door opened and a couple of older gentlemen entered the room. Hidden behind the curtain we waited for something to happen. They bent over the bed while two candlesticks illuminated their gray heads.

»She's gone,« said the first one, who I assumed was the doctor. He closed Harriet's eyelids with his right hand and covered her up. »I'll call the priest even though it's too late. My sincere condolences, Duke of York.«

»That's all right,« quickly answered the second old man. I couldn't believe my eyes. Was it true, was this really him…?

»I'll go and tell lady Adele,« said the doctor, »we have to prepare everything necessary for the funeral.«

»It had to happen now of all times,« said Philip reluctantly and they left the room.

»I think you've seen enough,« said Timeless. »Close your eyes and relax.«

This time I did it harder than before. I couldn't stop wondering what year it was and how long I had been away.

»Fifty-six years and now relax because you're disturbing the flow of energy!« She said quickly. She took me by my shoulders and told me once again to close my eyes. This time it went by faster. We were at my home again within a second. When I became conscious again I was very surprised at everything that I've witnessed. I had a thousand questions.

How did we travel? How did everything happen? How was it possible that I was obviously over sixty, yet I hadn't changed? What happened to Harriet? What happened with Philip?

»So many questions!« my companion raised her voice.

»You'll receive the answers soon. Before that I'd like to introduce someone. Come on.«

She set off towards the forest and I followed her with interest.

VII. THE FRIENDSHIP

WE SOON ARRIVED TO A BRIGHT CLEARING. We sat down in the middle of it and waited. On the northern edge, the leaves started rustling and a couple of figures approached us through the thicket. There were two older gentlemen, looking quite happy in red monastic robes, even though one of them had a large skin-colored tumor on the back of his neck. They sat down next to us and we formed a small circle.

»You've really decided, haven't you?« said my guardian instead of a greeting.

»It's not just our decision, the Rulers also agree,« smiled the one with the tumor.

»This way there'll be many more possibilities for development,« continued the other one.

»Namaste, young woman, my name is Seraf,« said the first one and slightly bowed in front of me, pressing his palms in front of his chest.

»And I am Lahiri,« continued the other one. They appeared to be very coordinated, like they were twins or something.

»You could say that,« said Timeless and turned towards me.

»These gentlemen are the masters of the next discipline you're going to be learning if you want to understand some day what happened an hour ago. This discipline is called yoga. They are my friends of many years'. They came to say goodbye, because they're going to leave their material bodies.«

My eyes got wide again. *Not again*, I thought, because I already witnessed such a departure that day and I really didn't know anymore what to think about it.

»It's all right, young woman,« said Lahiri, »We'll see each other again. We're actually staying here, on Earth. We'll travel to Europe and America.«

Travel? Is that what it's called now? I was confused.

»We'll take our teachings to where it's most needed. You see, there's a war raging all over the world. Wouldn't it be nice if mankind could open its eyes and recant this madness…?«

That was true, even though I knew very little about what was actually going on.

»It's better that you don't know,« concluded Seraf.

»We wanted to ask you a favor,« continued Lahiri. »It's very important that you remember us. You'll stay here and we'll meet again in a few years. Then we'll work together a lot.«

»S-sure,« I managed to utter, even though I didn't know what they were talking about.

Timeless stood up and I followed her lead. Seraf and Lahiri did the same. »Excellent,« said Seraf in good mood, »I'm looking forward to our cooperation, dear friend!«

We said goodbye and went home. On the way I kept looking inquisitively at my companion who still didn't answer my questions.

»Well, all right!« she said when she saw that I wasn't and couldn't be at ease.

»Today we experienced teleportation. It's an old movement technique given only to the most developed souls. The Earth's magnetic filed is too strong for everybody to practice it. It's been given to those who truly work in the planet's best interest; not just in words, but also in actions. Someday you too will know how to do that.«

I was speechless.

»Duke Philip grew old because he lived like he was *taught* was right.

He submitted to human beliefs and wants. He lived without the awareness of what life really is. That's why the majority of people on this planet are born and simply wait to die, in a way.«

Since I was still silent, she continued.

»And you're a part of a bigger plan. Working together with the gentlemen you've met and some other friends, you'll create something great. That's all I can tell you.«

And so we walked in silence. She didn't speak to me anymore that day.

VIII. A SHORT CENTURY OF MEMORIES

I N THE NEXT PERIOD OF MY LIFE I TRULY STARTED TO APPRECIATE and respect the secrets I learned from my teacher. Soon I discovered that we had lived through two world wars in the safe shelter of the woods. It was never quite clear to me why people even decided to wage wars. Just before we entered the twenty-first century, Timeless called me to herself again. I've been long since used to communicating with her through thoughts and I had also undergone teleportation initiation.

»I too am about to ascend to a higher level,« she announced. »I've got a choice: I can leave this planet and join the Rulers, or I can stay and help clean this planet. Since I can see that you're strong enough to take over that task, I have to say goodbye here.«

»No…I'm not, don't go away!« I managed to babble, completely con-fused. Every time I thought that some things were clear to me, the universe turned them upside down again, like it was doing it purely for my benefit.

»Don't worry, I'll visit you if necessary,« she reassured me. I hugged her and felt great gratitude because she had taught me so many things. At the same time I felt tears running down my cheeks. I hadn't cried in ages, but this time I had a very good reason.

We hugged for a while, resting in each other's arms. But she soon said:

»I haven't got much time left. Listen carefully to my instructions. You have to find the following people…«

She listed three important names and added that those were the souls of the Rulers, living in the bodies of teenagers currently residing in America.

»The first two have already been informed that you're coming. The third one is the key to your mission. Well, you'll see it for yourself. Do you remember Seraf and Lahiri?«

»The monks?«

»That's right, but they don't resemble their previous form even remotely now. When you look for them, look with your heart.«

I carefully listened to her instructions, trying to remember them.

»I love you.« That was the first time that Timeless rendered such words, even though I had known that for the longest time.

»I love you too,« I realized when I fell into her arms again. Then I started to feel the fabric of my teacher's clothes beginning to wrinkle between my fingers; at the same time I experienced prickling behind my eyelids, caused by the light engulfing her body. Soon only her cloak remained in my arms.

I slowly got up and headed home. I knew that the task I was given was almost beyond my abilities. I needed to get ready. Thoroughly ready.

IX. NEW YORK

WHEN, BEFORE THE TELEPORTATION INITIATION CEREMONY, THE
Rulers were choosing a special dress for me that I would be wearing during each process of such method of travel, they chose a dress of white color, which was some sort of reflection of my consciousness. How I saw myself subconsciously. On the one hand, it seemed reasonable: I did think of myself as some sort of »eternal bride«. At the same time the dress was timeless, in a way. I could wear it in any time period and I'd still blend into my surroundings.

My first task was to follow the photograph that was given to me by Timeless. It was a photograph of a really beautiful and bright house. The lower part was paneled in wood, while the upstairs windows were made of smaller triangular parts, composing interesting geometrically accurate shapes. The doors matched the windows and looked contemporary. The driveway was made of stone, while the staircase seemed very familiar, almost archaic. Some were of the opinion that such a staircase couldn't appertain to such a contemporary building. But to me the staircase seemed well known.

After looking at the photograph for a few minutes, I closed my eyes. Soon I was there. I stepped onto the middle of the driveway and compared the building with the photograph I held in my hand one more time. I was in the right place. I was surprised at the sounds that were surrounding me; the world had really changed in all those years! Above me, far away in the sky, an airplane was flying and although my teacher had informed me about them years ago, its presence slightly confused me anyway. Like watching a metal bird in the sky. The road, that wasn't far away from the house, was full of noisy machines that Timeless called cars. I knew all that, I had seen all that through projections in my consciousness, when I was learning about the modern world. But still...to experience all that with my own senses was quite a challenge for me.

I walked up to the door and found the doorbell. The door opened and a brown-haired man of fair complexion and roughly thirty years of age stood in front of me.

»Mister...Davies?« I asked. Those were my first words in this unknown place.

»Keisha, right?« he smiled and revealed slightly askew, but still very symmetrical teeth.

»Come on in, we've been expecting you.«

He opened the door and I saw two figures standing behind him. A young man, whose appearance was very familiar – everybody I came to know during the last century was Indian like him – and a young woman with bobbed brown hair. They appeared to be one in some way...Both beings looked very familiar, like I've already seen them...As they came closer I finally recognized them!

»Seraf...Lahiri!«

»Ravi and Ina, actually,« the young man playfully corrected me.

After the introductions and hugging we all stepped into the round living room, where Mr. Davies – he told me to simply call him Aaron – served tea. Ravi and Ina described to me the plans for our near future. Most of that Timeless had already explained to me. I also remembered her words: »People will live in peace. And you'll be the catalyst of that. That's why I'm teaching you.«

I still wasn't sure what she had meant by that. But I did possess a thousand years' worth of knowledge that Ravi and Ina urgently needed to refresh. They wanted to prepare as many people as possible for the upcoming new era. They warned me that the transition into the new era would be similar to a war. And that as many people as possible needed to be taught how to act when that happened.

»That's why martial arts, relaxation techniques and peace need to be a part of every individual's consciousness,« explained Ravi. »So we could be prepared for the transition between two eras. We'll need to train as many people at once as possible.«

I was prepared to collaborate. I've been learning for that, after all. With Ravi and Ina we selected training locations and divided our tasks. After the meeting finished I slowly got ready to go home.

»Keisha, wait,« said Ina. »Did Timeless tell you about…Jesse?« she was uncertain.

»Yes. I've already connected with him once, through dreams. As she ordered.«

»He's in danger,« she explained. Thanks to the image in Ina's mind I could see what she meant by that. He took some sort of pill that could be dangerous for him, because his body wasn't used to such substances.

»Please, dissuade him from that. We need him.«

I smiled. He didn't even properly start with his mission and he was already in trouble. Just like Timeless had predicted. »All right. I will.«

When I left, I thought of the place I saw in Ina's mind: a large room with a lot of people. A lot of unusual lights and loud music. I sincerely hoped that I'd be able to quickly adapt to such surroundings. I closed my eyes and the light engulfed me…

X. THE DISCOTHEQUE

THE LIGHT WAS CHANGING MORE AND MORE INTO A RAINBOW-COLORED haze until it morphed into a very loud sound. I felt the aggression of loud rhythms and at the same time sensed that the entire room was saturated with euphoria.

I remembered that Timeless warned me most about that feeling: »Euphoria is in essence a strong disbelief that you can make it. You don't expect your success, that's why you become excessively 'happy', and then you surrender to your ego. What follows is depression from which some people can't find the way out.«

I decided to get the boy out of this dark and loud room as soon as possible. I noticed him jumping in the middle of the surface they called the dance floor. I remembered what dancing looked like once and smiled bitterly. Who'd have thought that the style would change so much in a single century. I decided to try to blend in the crowd, and at the same time to attract and direct him towards me with my thoughts.

He finally noticed me. I could see that the drugs he took had already considerably worn him out. I wondered what it would be like if such substances were available on our dances a hundred years ago and smiled again. When the boy came close enough I headed towards the exit.

It wouldn't be good if the guards of this building noticed me, I thought and concentrated solely on Jesse. Timeless also taught me, among other things, how to reveal myself only to those I really wanted to see me. And this time that was just him.

He really followed me. I could sense that he liked me, even though I couldn't say that the feeling was mutual. The boy really had a very low soul vibration and he was in danger, just like Ina said. I could feel his powerful ego that craved fame, but I didn't know how to open his eyes.

He took his jacket by the exit and tried to stop me: »Wait!«

I went far enough so the guards at the entrance couldn't bother us. I had a hard time maintaining my own peaceful state in this dark place that was buzzing with low frequencies. Timeless warned me that it was going to be hard, but I didn't know that it would be *that* hard.

I decided to leave as soon as possible. Making him leave that dangerous place was big enough of an accomplishment. From here on he'd have to manage by himself. I could feel that the big guard wasn't going to let him back in for sure. I was relieved.

»Who are you?« he asked as he came puffing towards me. I saw him. I *really* saw him. Even though he was a slave to his own ego, in this weakness I could sense a great strength, which the young man wouldn't or couldn't admit to himself. Now I knew what Timeless meant when she said that he was the crucial piece of the puzzle. But at the same time I knew that another century could very well pass before Jesse was able to admit to himself who he really was.

He was standing in front of me so helpless and covered in sweat that I didn't know what to say to him. I could feel all his misery, disappointment and disbelief in success. His goals were completely baseless and his life revolved around his own ego. I could feel how his low frequencies were trying to get a hold of me and I decided to leave really quickly. But before that I really wanted to warn him about what he needed to recognize. Like how magnificent he could be, if only he was willing to open his eyes! I looked at him and put all the energy I still had left in my words:

»It's important who *you* are, Jesse,« I said with emphasis. Then I couldn't fight all the negative energy that surrounded me anymore. I thought of home and the light engulfed me. In an instant I was bathing in the light of the sun in front of my house. At my place, on the other side of the planet, under the Himalayas, it was still daytime. I looked around and there were no more dark sidewalks, asphalt streets, loud rhythms or big black guards. I sighed with relief.

I hope you're satisfied with me, Timeless, I thought. I took my time and prepared for the evening relaxation.

XI. TELEPORTATION

I MATERIALIZED AGAIN IN THE MIDDLE OF THE ROUND LIVING ROOM. This time it was easier than the day before, because I knew where I was going. The surroundings were more familiar. They were waiting for me in the circle, as we had agreed. When I completely connected with their vibration, I slightly descended and felt the ground under me. I sat in the middle of the circle. Then we spent some time in silence. To be able to emphasize my words even more, I decided to speak instead of communicating telepathically.

»Several levels of knowledge exist,« I began.

»The knowledge of health is the first one. Then comes the knowledge of money. When you transcend that, the knowledge of energy and the knowledge of eternal youth follow. And only then comes the knowledge of special abilities such as teleportation and flying. Not just in the sense of the soul, but also the body.«

»If I understand correctly,« said Aaron, »this is intended more for the young people…?«

I smiled, because I could see his concern as well as great desire to participate in this project.

»Actually – yes. But who *is* young? Who is *eternally* young? And why?«

There was silence in the room. Even their thoughts quieted down. I remembered that this gift was practically given to me as a present. And I had to remember why.

»Timeless taught me that eternal youth was an award for an individual's morals. It's not even remotely something that can be attained by surgical procedures and knives. The Rulers decide about such things.«

»The Rulers…?« It seemed that Aaron was the least prepared for the lesson.

»The Rulers are beings that lead the flow of life energy on this planet. At the same time they take care that there's always more light than darkness and help us when we decide to fight the lower frequencies. Their substance is crystal-white and some of them are even incarnated on this planet and look like humans.« I pointed at Ravi and Ina and continued:

»But since the human body has its limitations, they have to learn these truths like everybody else. Like I did.«

»Well, all right. I understand,« said Aaron. His thoughts quieted down too. *So I just need the right morals*, I could hear the conclusion of his recognition.

»Yes, *just* the right morals. For some that's as easy as pie, but for the others such challenge can last for centuries…« I smiled.

Ina and Ravi had learned some years ago what the test looked like; a test that was so hard that you could die under its weight if you were not ready to fight your sadness, ego and mourning. Aaron also went through all that, only his path was longer. All three were awarded higher morals level. But they had to learn how to use it.

»I'm not going to talk much more. We'll start with the practice.«

That seemed most appropriate. I sat in the middle of the circle again and called Ina to me. I asked Ravi and Aaron to just watch me. I imagined three of the Rulers being present at my teleportation ritual. They were with me in an instant, in the middle of the room, sitting within the circle just like me. Their help was urgently needed before a person could acquire the body with such abilities.

I asked her to extend her right arm. Two of the Rulers took a hold of her – each on his side – while the third one directed a beam of energy at her. Ina slowly relaxed. Her extended right arm started to glow in the white light, and then she slowly gave in to the vibrations she was receiving from the beings standing next to her. Soon we couldn't see her

fingers or her palm anymore, because they disintegrated into small white particles. These particles floated near her forearm as if waiting for further instructions. The third Ruler soon redirected the white particles to where they were before and the shape of the hand reappeared. All three of them slowly backed away. When the procedure was finished, I thanked them. They said goodbye and simply disappeared.

The room vibrated in silence once again. I was glad that the first lesson proved to be so successful. Those present were filled with peace and nobody seemed overtly surprised. Except maybe Aaron. After the final relaxation he came up to me once more.

»I've been wondering how I could earn higher morals, I mean, for... eternal youth?«

I knew that he was struggling with this issue. It sounded fairly simple; but turning such a thing into reality...that was another story entirely.

»You need superhuman willpower. A fierce determination, every second. You have to ask yourself every second: am I happy, am I peaceful, am I behaving in accordance with the rules?«

»The rules?«

»The Rulers too have their own rules which they must consider before allowing you on a higher level. The universe is scanning our souls – every moment of our existence on Earth. And when the Rulers receive the assurance that a particular soul is cleansed enough, they award it with the transition to a higher frequency. One of such transitions is the acquirement of the body that is eternally young and resistant against every type of weapon on Earth: knives, swords, pistols, even the atomic bomb.«

He was amazed and impressed. I could feel that had he not experienced so many changes in his life, he wouldn't have been able to believe the infallible theory I just presented to him.

»It's all right,« I concluded. »You keep practicing as we agreed and you'll understand soon.«

»Thank you, Keisha,« he thanked me and then said goodbye. They sat down in a circle again and I went home. I enjoyed such lessons much more that confrontations with Jesse. But I knew that I wouldn't be able to avoid that either...

XII. REPRIMANDED

AFTER A FEW MONTHS OF KEEPING COMPANY WITH INA, RAVI AND Aaron, I was meditating at home. I felt so happy, because our plan was coming along nicely. Ina had already received her teleportation initiation, and Ravi was about to receive his in a few days. Aaron had taken his training absolutely seriously. As he got out of bed each morning he started controlling each thought that went through his mind.

Am I living by the rules? Am I reacting to the truth? Every time I connected to the vibration of his thoughts, I'd listen to these questions in his mind and I almost began to have fun. It was only a matter of time before his patience would bear fruit.

Moreover, after only a few months the Rulers already started working on his body: each day there were fewer little wrinkles around his eyes and his cheeks started to regain their firmness. Even the area above his eyelids had been lifting little by little each day, although maybe just for a tenth of a millimeter. His forehead completely straightened out. It seemed to me that he didn't even notice all these changes – he was too busy for that. Next to relaxation, regular yoga and martial arts practice and watching his thoughts every second of every day, he didn't find the time to look in the mirror and discover that he already looked like a twenty-year-old. And the best part was: he didn't find the opportunity to fall under the spell of rapturous complacency.

During my own relaxation I sensed certain familiar thought vibrations that I hadn't sensed in quite some time…

Do you think avoiding your responsibilities is a smart decision? I heard a clear voice in my mind. I recognized it immediately.

Hello, Timeless. I wanted to play dumb as if I didn't know what she meant by that, when she already answered me.

You've got a single protégé and you're ignoring him. He's in danger again. He's been submitted to a powerful euphoria of a large number of people and you're reveling in a small training success. Why do you think I gave you this task?

Her voice was strict and relentless.

Because I have to finish it, I know.

...And not so he could be constantly submitted to negative energy, taking substances that harm him! She concluded.

Not again! I moaned.

Maybe you can change something, protect him. From now on watch him every day.

I realized that I'd been really trying to avoid this task as long as I could. But, like I already knew, the universe knew no exceptions. The Rulers were scanning my soul like anybody else's. And if I wanted to hide something, it stood out all the more.

You'll thank me someday, she concluded her speech. *Go now, it's urgent.*

In addition to the clear instruction of what to do, I also received the image of the place I was supposed to go to. It was a dark place, full of people again, with nicely arranged tables on one side, with microphones and bottles of water on them.

The band members were sitting at the table, with Jesse and their producer and manager in the middle. Once again I felt the strong pressure of low vibrations, like it was some sort of interrogation.

They call it a press conference, Timeless interrupted me. *Reporters ask famous people about their work and life, so they can write about it. Then a much bigger crowd of people reads this information, admires them and mostly creates a euphoric magnetic field. A few can see through this vibration. That's*

why you need to go there. Clean the space, divert Jesse. Save him. He's a very...
I know, important part of our chain, I repeated rebelliously. Timeless sighed almost disappointedly.

Some day you'll understand. Hurry now!

I saw the light and was already standing in a darkened room. I was glad that nobody noticed my arrival. I was standing in the back row and all the attention was directed at those sitting at the table.

I'd better start, I decided. I closed my eyes and started working...

XIII. CLEANSING

I CLOSED MY EYES AND STARTED SENDING OUT LIGHT. First to all that were sitting at the table and then I spread it over the entire place. It'd be a big help if this interrogation ended as soon as possible. I could feel that I didn't have much time left. I wanted to interrupt the conference so I could save what could still be saved.

I remembered the instructions Timeless had given me. *Divert Jesse.* I decided to focus on him. I wanted him to see me, but at the same time I didn't need the attention from the other people. So I concentrated just on him.

I noticed that people around me started raising their hands and I didn't want to stand out. I raised my hand too. It was obviously part of their ritual during interrogation. Jesse's frequency changed and I could feel euphoria.

He pointed towards me: »The lady in the back, in a white dress,« and the wave of negative energy started to spread again. »Well, don't be afraid,« he added. Since I wanted this process to end as soon as possible, I looked at the floor, while Jesse looked at his producer who was asking him something.

As he looked away I used the opportunity to hide again from everybody. *What did I do wrong?* I was asking myself. I did everything as I was supposed to. *Why did he drop to such a low frequency?* I wanted to protect myself, so I could correct the mistake that was made. I materialized in another corner of the room and watched the people behind the table. I decided to check the thought frequencies of everybody sitting at the table, so I could discover the mistake…It all took just a few seconds.

Tim: *Finally, it's over. I'm all sore from this sitting. I hope it'll be different on the tour.*

Jessica: *Rodney is rather withdrawn today. I hope nothing's wrong. He's acting arrogantly again...How do I talk to him in all this hustle and bustle? He likes that dark-haired reporter, I know it. That's why he pushed forward so hard to answer her, even though that's Jesse's job...*

Sam.I.Am.: *Damn it, the boy's started hallucinating! I can't wait to get my hands on Ian and ask him what kind of medication he's been giving him! Incompetents, every last one of them! Do I really have to do everything myself?! Of course, I'll smile for your stupid cameras, but nobody will get away from me on the bus! Damn! And I believed in this band so much! Maybe it can still be fixed, we just need to get on the damn bus.*

Rodney: *I can't wait to leave. Jesse's really changed lately. I hope everything is still all right. Why is Jessica staring at me like a stuck pig? I hope I didn't do something wrong again. Ah, this is how it is when you take your girlfriend on tour with you. Your every step is monitored...But it'd be boring without her, he, he.*

Jesse: *Maybe I could even invite her to dinner. Ha, everybody's looking back now. Let them see the possible future Mrs. Roy...Where did she go? Damn it, she was back there a second ago! Where the hell is she? She even raised her hand!!! I saw her with my own eyes! What's wrong with me? Am I crazy!?*

I could feel euphoria mixing with fear and I didn't know where to place these vibrations. I decided to withdraw for a moment. I managed to interrupt the interrogation, because I heard the producer start saying goodbye. I went home to figure out what had just happened.

Soon I was taking a walk in the woods behind my house. I oftentimes found answers there. I went through everything that'd happened once more in my mind. Suddenly I heard leaves rustling behind me. It had already happened once that I was surprised by a mountain lion that way. Thanks to the ancient teachings about calm and concentrated movement in martial arts I managed to skillfully avoid the animal. The teleportation was helpful as well. I turned around prepared to fight. Once again

Timeless stood in front of me.

»I'm quite often here today,« she smiled. »The Rulers obviously think that you're in need of more detailed explanations.«

»They couldn't hurt,« I admitted.

»To tell you the truth, it's about a very simple thing. It's about an emotion that you've experienced yourself, although a century ago. Now, that you've progressed through so many levels, you feel it as a strong negative energy. The truth is simple, really.«

I raised an eyebrow.

»The boy is in love with you, Keisha,« she smiled.

»That can't be true!« I contradicted. »He's supposed to be my student, my protégé. And besides, I'm a hundred years older than him!«

»Well, you don't look like it,« she teased me and it seemed that she was having fun with all this. Like the universe had prepared a role just for me in this dramatic soap opera.

»How…how do I make him see through this emotion?« It was hard enough without it.

»Any which way you can,« said my mentor, »just remember that tests we're presented with never surpass our ability to solve them.«

I thought about how blind I was when I fell in love with Philip all those years ago. Infatuation and love are indeed completely different emotions. One is a perfect illusion and the other pure truth. Darkness and light. Yin and Yang.

»I think you've heard enough for now. From here you can carry on by yourself.«

She hugged me again. »I believe in you,« she said with a smile. »Just stick to your instructions and you'll always get the right directions…« She disappeared as quickly as she appeared.

I kept standing in the middle of the forest and decided once again not to give in that easily. I sat down and spent quite a few hours stocking on sunlight. When I felt strong enough, I decided to go back. At least now I knew what to expect.

XIV. THE PROTECTION THAT FAILED

I MONITORED JESSE EVERY DAY, JUST LIKE TIMELESS HAD INSTRUCTED ME.
I didn't reveal my presence to anybody, of course. Inside the crowded bus
I did my best to cleanse the low vibrations that were constantly attacking
the bus. I also felt the vibrations of people reading tabloids throughout
America and sending their energy to the bus that was transporting the
rock stars. It was really hard work. I may have felt their fame more than
they did it themselves.

Even though I knew that I wasn't allowed to influence the people in
their immediate vicinity, I did try to direct the course of events that would
at least mitigate certain situations. Sometimes I even supported events
that seemed negative at first sight. I was glad when Sam.I.Am ordered
Jesse to take another sedative, because I could see the sequence of events
that were about to follow: less pills, Jesse would have more freedom and
that would enable him to develop more. Nevertheless, I was trying each
day to balance the energy within the band as best as I could, which was
very hard to do.

I too was very grateful when the tour finally ended. My efforts were
obviously awarded and I intended to contact Jesse again quite soon. Then
I was surprised by the new attack of low frequencies: the euphoria of some
sort of music awards and the illness that – instead of Jesse who had been

constantly under my protection – struck his father!

This is never going to end, is it? I thought helplessly.

Since I couldn't be in two places at the same time during the ceremony – I was protecting Jesse, while in the meantime his father left his body – I failed again. In the end Jesse too fell into the frequency of mourning and anger.

After a few months of trying I decided once again to withdraw. I had to find out what I had been doing wrongly. At home I was met by Timeless again.

»Tell me, what have I done wrong? Where was it that I failed to consider the laws?« I quickly asked. I was really interested what her answer would be.

»The higher we go, the more demands we have to take into consideration. Your mistake was that you've been trying *too hard*.«

I should have known that already, at least such was the tone of her voice that accompanied her instructions. But I was firmly convinced that I had been trying as best as I could.

»That's right,« she continued decisively. »You didn't *know* that you'd make it; you *tried* to the best of your abilities. Well, nobody's interested in your best abilities. You should know that by now.«

I became silent. My thoughts quieted down too. I was really looking for a way out.

»What should I do?« I asked seriously. I was really interested in her answer.

»Go back and fight! Don't just surmise that you'll make it; *know* that you'll make it!«

I imprinted her instructions in my consciousness and was grateful that she was helping me so much.

»It wasn't meant to be like that, you know,« she reprimanded me again. »My frequent visits prove that you don't have the desire to solve the test. I'm leaving now. If I have to come back again, that'll mean a fall of your frequency. You don't want that, do you?«

»Of course not,« I said quietly. I was almost sorry that I disappointed Timeless like that.

I sincerely decided to win this fight. No more trying. I widely opened my eyes and prepared for a fight with a bright outcome.

XV. DECISION AND PREPARATIONS

I DECIDED TO FIGHT FOR JESSE'S SOUL UNTIL I SUCCEED. I realized that the world of the famous was full of low frequencies, therefore I admitted to myself that I needed help.

Our little group that consisted of Ina, Ravi and Aaron, was making an excellent progress in training, therefore we decided to invite a few of their friends to join us. Ina mentioned a few of her and Ravi's former classmates that they had kept in contact with and that could be of great help to us. So their friends Gina, George, Elliot, Sienna, Jeanette, Lance and Hannah started practicing with us.

I was thrilled watching such a broad spectrum of different powers developing with delight under the supervision of their owners. I saw Elliot's incredible speed that would always come in handy. I was completely taken over by Gina's keenness to fight for light. Sienna was able to recognize the low vibrations even before they'd attack us. Jeanette could find answers where I couldn't even see them with lightning speed. Her ability to project herself into the consciousness of others and to find the simplest solutions surprised me again and again. George was the first one to undergo, in addition to the teleportation, the flying initiation ceremony. And Hannah was helping us with her clairvoyance. She was able to predict the events that were meant to happen very accurately; our task was simply to decide whether to let them happen or change them.

While I was preparing my army, Jesse went on another tour. This time I only asked the Rulers to retire his band from the public eye for a while. That way I was able to prepare much better for the events that were about to unfold, while at the same time my protégé was much less exposed to the low vibrations. I was very grateful for the universe's help: the band actually almost slipped into oblivion. And so another three months passed by, during which time we managed to prepare the last details for *the most important link of the chain*, as Timeless called him. The big task, that was to be entrusted to him, remained unknown to me. My part was only to – prepare him. And I took my role absolutely seriously.

When our preparations of several months were completed, I looked at my new friends and assistants: we were truly ready. Even the last member of our secret army passed the teleportation initiation. Aaron. After months of training he was completely changed. And not just because his body was completely rejuvenated and he looked like a seventeen-year-old. He had also transformed his way of thinking and developed the reaction speed; he *lived* high morals every second. In any case, he felt the whole time that he didn't have the time to be too proud of his appearance or his work. Here too he managed to outsmart his own ego. He was truly one of us now. It was quite possible that I was more proud of him than he was of himself.

We decided to invite Jesse and Rodney to the high school reunion. We thought that sort of a meeting would appear much more casual than inviting them to a meditation or relaxation session, where Jesse could misunderstand something and his timid consciousness could get frightened again.

Ina designed neat invitations and made sure that they got into Rodney's hands. He then handed Jesse's invitation over to its addressee. All we could do now was wait.

I was very pleased when I connected with his consciousness and saw his decision to attend the reunion. I could feel that the absence of the low frequencies of euphoria and fame did him a lot of good and that he might be almost ready to meet me. I was actually looking forward to the evening when we would meet. Ina and I decided that I should show up later, when the others already had the opportunity to see whether Jesse was ready or not. I was supposed to materialize in the ladies' room and return to the restaurant with Ina. If the boy were calm then Ina would introduce me as her friend. And if he were attacked by euphoria, I would withdraw until the negative vibration abated. I really wanted to direct him so he would find out for himself what he needed to do and how. I also wanted us to finally start with the training. There had been enough of waiting.

Now I also knew what my mentor felt when she told me the first day we met: »I've been waiting for you a really long time. We have a lot of work to do.« That was exactly how I felt the entire day as I was preparing for the »high school reunion«. I knew that I had done everything right this time. And now I could only wait for the appropriate moment...

XVI. HIGHLY ANTICIPATED
»HIGH SCHOOL REUNION«

I LET INA AND RAVI CHOOSE THE APPROPRIATE LOCATION. After all, they knew best where such an event could be held. They booked the entire restaurant called Rigoletto's Pizza and waited. They also took care of the music and were soon joined by the others: Gina, Hannah, George, Elliot, Sienna and Jeanette.

We didn't have to wait long for Jesse to arrive. His vibration was much cleaner and he was in a good mood. I was maintaining the telepathic connection with everybody in the room the entire time.

Jesse walked up to the door and entered. They immediately started scanning his vibration.

Sienna: *Nothing suspicious so far. He's in a good mood.*

Jeanette: *Although it seems like he's expecting something. Maybe he knows subconsciously...?*

Sienna: *That doesn't matter now. What's important is that he's relatively clean. I'm not detecting any low frequencies.*

George: *Ina, will you let Keisha know?*

Ina: *Right away. I'll just shake his hand so it doesn't look impolite. Keisha will be glad; I think he's ready.*

Ina quickly stood up and offered her hand to Jesse: »Hi, Jesse. Please forgive me, but I really need to go to the ladies' room.« *I hope I didn't leave to soon. I really can't wait for Keisha to get here.*

Ravi: *It's all right. I'll distract him.*

»Hi, Ravi,« continued Jesse.

Ravi looked at him and smiled relaxed. We were still mentally connected. »Hey, musician – I'm glad you could come.«

They somehow managed to engage in a relaxed conversation like a couple of former classmates who hadn't seen each other for quite some time. In the meantime I prepared and materialized in the ladies' room.

Even though I could already sense through their thoughts that the general response of my army was positive, I wanted one last confirmation from Ina.

»Everything is really all right, even the room is quite cleansed. Sienna is taking care of that. We'll make it.«

Nevertheless, I had a hunch that we hadn't considered Jesse's instability.

»If that happens, you know what we need to do,« I told her once more. »We'll find the solution eventually.«

We looked at each other.

»Are you ready?« she asked.

»As ready as I'll ever be,« I concluded and took a deep breath.

We left the ladies' room. We walked across the dining room and I took a quick look at my protégé. He noticed me.

Sienna: *Keisha, we have a problem. I can feel low vibrations again. His heart is pounding heavily.*

Jeanette: *Cleanse the room and I'll go and see what's weighing on him...*

Jeanette entered Jesse's consciousness. Since her intention was pure help, his frame of mind immediately opened up to her. All in all, it didn't last more than two seconds...I could see images and movies that Jeanette was browsing through and I became sorry that I didn't explain his frame of mind in more detail to the others...

H ER DIVINE BODY, AS SHE GREETS ME IN THE CAVERN…HER BRIGHT and smiling face, as she notices me on the other end of the dance floor…Her presence at the press conference, which brings meaning back into the completely meaningless world…And now she's there, ten steps away. And she really exists! Really! I love her, I can't live without her! I'll touch her, if it's the last thing I touch in my life! I'll address her and I don't care what it takes! I have to catch up with her, I have to!

Jeanette stopped browsing, as she comprehended the sequence of events in a moment. I looked at her.

Please forgive me for not mentioning this to you earlier. It didn't seem…decent.

This is not about what's decent, she answered, *we would've been much better prepared, had we known that he's that much in love. That's all.*

I know, I apologized again.

We have to abort this task, thought Sienna, *unfortunately we weren't prepared for this.*

All right, I'll be back in half an hour, I thought.

Ina and I walked to the door.

»I'll see you,« I told her. She too had been connected to our thought flow the entire time anyway. »I'm sorry,« I concluded.

She slightly shook her head. »Well, all right. See you.«

I walked through the door and focused hard. I had to make myself invisible. I stepped aside just enough to give space to Jesse, who came rushing through the door even though Ina tried to hold him back at least a little.

»What's your hurry?« I heard Ina's voice as the restaurant door opened again.

He came rushing through the door like the wind. His mind was racing in crazy-fast vibrations. I had to divert him from reentering the room where the others were; I was responsible for the way he behaved. And I also didn't take care of the safety as well as I should have. If I had been smart I'd have told my assistants everything. But some sort of old-fashioned sense of discretion awoke inside of me and Jesse's condition and thinking simply didn't seem…honorable.

I focused on his body. What I did next I also learned from Timeless. Since people often can't see past our bodies, we think that our body is everything we have. Consequently, we are easily influenced by the people with the power of greater awareness.

Timeless often compared such state of control with a mouse that can't see further from what's on the ground. Where *it* is. The hawk that is flying above the mouse has a much better view of where the mouse is and where it's going. If the hawk wanted, it could catch the mouse or direct the mouse anywhere it wanted, and the mouse still wouldn't know why and where it's going.

I used that technique on Jesse. I focused on his body. Regardless of how much he wanted to go back from where he came from, I'd allow his legs to move only when he was walking away from it. When he wanted to come closer to the restaurant, he couldn't move anywhere.

He was very persistent. His crazy desire was mixing with euphoria; he wanted to return to the restaurant and start asking his classmates about me: who I was, what I was doing, where I lived…I really didn't need that right now. Finally, after half an hour of trying he lost all hope and went away.

See you, Jesse, I thought and returned to the restaurant. A group of people was waiting on me there, waiting for an explanation.

XVII. PLAN B

»I'D LIKE TO APOLOGIZE ONE MORE TIME FOR THAT,« I SAID AGAIN. »It's your project after all,« said Ina. »Actually we could have guessed ourselves…«

They laughed but at the same time I could feel some sort of resistance. I felt pretty uncomfortable being associated with such…a person of low morality. I remembered Timeless' advice…*You'd experienced that emotion yourself, even though it was a century ago.* I had to face the fact that I had been at the same frequency of thought, as he was now. And I had to try to understand him if I wanted to conquer him.

After several hours of consultation, we decided to invite him for an hour of practise and explain the whole thing to him. We decided it was a whole lot better if he learnt the truth and saw it with his own eyes. It would be easier for him to get over the euphoria of being in love if he realized who I was even if he was frightened. We had to choose a good spot where the demonstration of our abilities could take place since we didn't want to attract attention. It had to be a place that was remote enough to keep our privacy in case the boy started screaming or doing something silly.

I don't know why the place where I grew up came to mind. Harriet and I enjoyed visiting that place and she would tell me stories of mermaids and sailors…

»How about…Prince Edward Island…?« I asked.

»What about it?« said George.

»Well, I know places where we definitely wouldn't be disturbed. I grew up there.« I showed them a part of my memories through the projections in my mind. They closed their eyes and suddenly their faces softened. They looked like they were watching a movie made based on a novel by Jane Austen or Charlotte Bronte.

»How beautiful,« Jeanette sighed. »All those parties, dresses, long walks…and carriages. Now I can better understand why you thought that some things were undignified…You come from a different century.«

»Actually, a different millennium now,« I smiled. It'd gone by so fast.

»I'm all for it,« said Ina with conviction when she saw the lighthouse. »I'm sure nobody will bother us here. I can invite Jesse myself.«

I thought that was a good idea. I looked around the room.

»What do the rest of you think?«

»We all agree,« said Aaron who was observing the whole scene from the background but was as thrilled as the rest of them.

»So, Cape Tryon it is,« I concluded. We agreed on the practice time, the date of the meeting and divided the tasks. This time we were ready for anything.

XVIII. CAPE TRYON

PREPARATIONS BEING WELL ALONG THE WAY, I WANTED TO BE EVEN more prepared than the rest. I would meditate for days at a time. I asked the Rulers for help, I asked for more power and ability. As if I felt I would be faced with a test I had never passed before. And that was beyond my capabilities. I felt something bigger than myself approaching and I felt insecure even though our plan had been carefully thought out and double-checked.

The only person who really understood how I felt was Hannah. When I was meditating on the cliff by the lighthouse, she sat next to me.

»You can feel it, can't you?« she said.

»What?« I tried to make the conversation less serious and simple. I didn't want to talk about it.

»I can see it too, you know. You are forgetting I'm clairvoyant,« she went on. »But I can understand you don't want to talk about it.«

»Hannah, I don't know what to do,« I said earnestly. I felt that what was about to happen was too huge and important for somebody to understand how I felt being faced with it. And it was getting closer even faster than we had planned.

»I do understand you,« she recapped, »I just don't know how to help you. It will take a giant leap in your abilities...«

»I know. You can help me by sending a lot of light into this event. At least you know lies in wait for us.« This was true too. I didn't want to bother anyone else with this...

»OK,« she said. »I'll help you. If nothing else, in this way.« She went away and I was left alone on the cliff.

Keisha, please come here, there's been a change of plans, I could hear Ina's voice in my head. *Jesse is already here.*

He surprised me. Because I had been preparing so fervently for the events that were about to follow I failed to connect to the frequency of his thoughts often enough to find out he was already on his way over. I went into the lighthouse immediately. The others had already waited for me there.

There are more possibilities, I thought. *We can reveal who we are sooner than planned or we can wait.*

We heard knocking on the door and Jeanette looked at me. *Don't worry, this time the door is locked.*

We heard some voices.

»There is nothing to see here, sir. But if you want, there are many interesting tourist spots nearby where I can take you. For very little money...«

»Well, I'm actually interested just in this lighthouse,« we could hear Jesse's answer.

»Well, if you change your mind, just let me know,« the older voice said.

We heard them moving away and we instinctively let out a sigh of relief. We decided to speed up the process. If Jesse was so interested, why shouldn't we be?

»Tomorrow,« I said. »And we will try to be as informative as possible.«

We decided to demonstrate the process of teleportation as slowly and graphically as possible. We would use voice movement as help – to make the process feasible in slow motion. I had taught them a couple of techniques how to create special waves of two voices by singing in a single voice, which would make the procedure precise and explicit. Jeanette sensed that Jesse decided to come again tomorrow.

»OK. We'll be ready tomorrow,« I concluded.

XIX. A LESSON

I MEDITATED EVEN MORE THE NEXT DAY. I stayed at home and for the last time I asked the Rulers to help me. Soon I got that interesting feeling that I wasn't alone. I opened my eyes and I saw a completely white being standing in front of me. It was glowing in a way I had never seen before. It was clear to me that I hadn't seen it before, it also wasn't present in any of my initiations. At the same time, I could feel its fondness of this planet.

»Hello, Keisha,« he greeted me.

I felt honored but I didn't know why. This being was emitting a higher frequency than the rest of the Rulers. As if he were their leader, president, god or something. His presence lighted up the atmosphere wherever he looked. I didn't know how to answer.

»The answer is simple. You asked for special help and I came.«

»Who are you?« I asked bravely.

»This is not so important. What is important is that I can do something you will need in the next couple of hours. And there are not many who can teach you this skill.«

»I see.« I felt very small and unimportant. The being in front of me could feel that and opened his heart even more.

»Don't admire me because this could block the flow of our learning. If this helps you, I can tell you that I used to be a part of this planet and this magnetic field, too. This was a long time ago. I *know* exactly what you are going through. And what you will be going through when you have to face death. Through somebody else's eyes. I went through that myself.« I had a million questions.

»You really only need to believe. When you feel like running away because you are so scared, you just need to surrender. You must get rid of every shred of doubt, or you could end up trying in vain for centuries and never succeed. Do you understand?«

I nodded.

»It really helps if you somehow connect with the person you want to heal. You could place your hands on the person of just look at them. You need to sink into their consciousness just like you need to dive under water when you are trying to rescue a drowning person. When they are bidding farewell to life, you need to enter their mind with your own strong will. You need to give them a gift of realizing that it is possible to be reborn instead of dying. This part of transformation is very important. Rebirth.«

I could barely follow.

»When you are doing this it will be easier then trying to *grasp* it,« he smiled. »Pretty soon all the people on this planet will be able to do this – if they choose to open their hearts. I'm looking forward to this time. Finally they will *really* understand.«

»When I've convinced them they can be reborn, what then?«

»Then just believe they will follow you. Follow your faith. Anything is possible,« he said with conviction, »and when there is no doubt left, what people describe as miracles, starts to happen. We could call it common sense: what we believe, happens,« he said smiling.

»There are no miracles,« he explained. »There is only truth. When we describe something as a miracle, it means we didn't believe it was possible. You have already outgrown that, Keisha. Don't perform miracles. Perform the *Truth*.«

I felt relieved. He managed to explain the secret that had puzzled me for such a long time.

»Thank you,« I said comforted.

»Glad to be of assistance in any way,« he said smiling. »The transition into a higher level is just a state not worth admiring. It is worth living.« He got up and I followed him.

»I'm leaving because you no longer need me.«

He looked at me with a pleasant glow in his eyes. He joined his hands together in front of him and said »Namaste«. He disappeared as fast as he arrived.

XX. THE INTRODUCTION AND JESSE'S TRANSITION

WHEN I FELT THE APPOINTED TIME APPROACHING, I AGAIN CONNECTED with my »army« who were totally ready now to face Jesse. When they began to feel his presence they stared singing.

I slowly got ready for the slowest teleportation procedure to date. Even when Timeless was teaching me, it didn't go that slowly. Some things in life are just simpler if you do them quickly. But this time we wanted to be as demonstrative as possible. Ina and I also agreed to do a martial arts demonstration so that Jesse would know exactly what kind of practice he would have to undergo.

While I was imagining the place to materialize, I knew that I shouldn't place my body in the right place just yet. I stopped in the middle of the circle, in the air. I did my best to remain concentrated to be able to stay in the state of light as long as possible. The high and low tone vibrations helped me a great deal.

Gradually I allowed my material body to start appearing. From the silence of the thoughts I had grown used to, I could feel a thickening of my physical body until I could feel my entire body. I slowly descended to the ground feeling grateful that we had succeeded. I materialized in different parts of the room a couple of times and then Ina and I started to perform the martial arts demonstration. It was easy and playful. While we were fighting we remained connected in thoughts. It felt like fighting myself, just for practice. We decided that she would defeat me. Afterwards we bowed to each other, as the rules demand.

Finally I looked at him. The decisive moment that nobody but him could influence lasted for a second. He opened his mouth and we saw that he didn't expect we knew he was watching us. He closed the door quickly and started running. This was the reaction we had expected.

I decided to follow him. I materialized on the cliff. How many times had I seen that event in my head! And I knew what followed. I hoped against hope that he would somehow change his mind. But sadly by that time he was overflowing with terror and suicidal thoughts. I tried to chase away the low frequencies that had started to attack him. The others helped me from a distance. Despite our efforts, Jesse chose fear again and again. This definitely is one of the downsides of free will.

When he noticed me on the edge of the cliff, he shouted in agony.

»Get lost, you freak!«

I knew his words were just the consequence of the delusions he had created for himself. I kept looking at him calmly and tried to connect with him. The transition gate remained closed. I got closer to him. To chase his fears away I extended my arm towards him. But this time my gesture had the opposite effect. Instead of grabbing on to my hand and chasing the fears away, he started shivering even more. He dashed to the edge of the cliff.

Obviously the hallucinations have returned, he thought. *Now it doesn't matter if this world is real or not.*

I could feel his despair and sense of helplessness. Although I could sympathize, I knew I had to do what was in my power to prevent him from doing that. The darkness surrounding him made his life seem more gloomy and hopeless than anything else in the world. When I got even closer to that frequency I could feel all the misery of his world but at the same time I knew that everything he felt was an illusion.

»You don't want to do that,« I said slowly.

»I said get lost,« he threatened me again. Although I knew that the decision what to do was solely his, I tried to summon the help of all the forces to relax. I felt that he held in his hands the most precious crystal chalice that had been entrusted into my care, and he had the power to smash it into smithereens...I slowly tried to get closer to him.

»It doesn't have to be this way...Please understand...« I managed to say when he moved backwards again and unintentionally stepped into nothing.

I had wished too hard he wouldn't do that. *And what we are thinking about, this is what we attract*, Timeless would say.

I materialized at the bottom of the cliff, next to a rock. I saw his body falling towards the sand and I knew where he would land.

I closed my eyes and connected with him. This time the flow of thought was much clearer. Jesse was bidding a farewell to the world. I could still hear the voice of the being that had been teaching me that day in my head, *if you want to save a drowning person you need to dive under water...*I dove into his consciousness.

I CAN FEEL THE FALLING MORE AND MORE INTENSIVELY AND IT SEEMS to take ages. I see pictures...First memories from childhood...Terry and I play and do everything together. Father, who takes me to the game, and buys me my first ice cream. Elementary school where I have a long face most of the time because I feel utterly alone. Without Terry there just isn't any fun. High school where I am feeling better having left Quebec which reminds me of childhood...High school seems to pass by in a split second...Fame which by far wasn't what I had expected...Father. Despite the fact that he is just a projection in my head, I feel a stinging pain in my heart...I'm about to find out if life after death actually exists. Or maybe I'll simply wake up in a New York hotel, all sweaty, and find out it had all just been a dream...

I open my eyes. Rock. If I had jumped farther, I might have reached the water...I can hear the breaking of my own vertebrae as I hit the stone. A moment of pain. Silence.

I felt totally at home in that silence. My hands rested on his body. I completely connected with him. I started to imagine the light. I knew I was able to do it. I *became* Jesse.

M Y NAME IS JESSE ROY AND I'M SUMMONING ALL THE FORCES OF THE UNIVERSE. I summon the light. My soul is pure and my body is totally healthy. Health is the truth. My cells follow that truth.

We were surrounded by the light and we were both calling it: me consciously and he on an unconscious level. I *knew* he would follow me. His cells started to move away from that light and they followed the flow of our united thoughts. The muscles returned to their places, broken ligaments between the vertebrae became whole again. His bones became firm again and his skin was renewed. Calmly I made my next demand.

Rebirth. I know it is possible. My body is reborn.

His body surrendered to the frequency of the light. Suddenly I could see his flawless healthy body lying in front of me. I returned to my state of awareness but Jesse was still asleep.

Hannah, who had been helping me together with the others from a distance, sensed my wish to carry him to a cleaner place.

Thank you for your help, I thought.

Anytime, they answered.

I'll see you again when he is ready, I concluded and then took Jesse in my arms. I imagined the cavern where Timeless had brought me the first time. A place for initiation. After the physical rebirth he had just experienced, I knew that was the place where he would be totally safe. We were there in an instant.

He lay on the ground. Just in case, I took a blanket and covered him. I sat next to him and waited for him to wake up. I went into myself and decided to reveal my presence only when he was ready for that. Gratefully I listened to his heartbeat and gave thanks for the mysterious visitor I'd had that morning...

Jesse stirred gently. I felt he was waking up and that he was completely healthy. I eagerly awaited his first reactions in his new body.

XXI. THE MEETING

JESSE STRETCHED HIS ARMS AND OPENED HIS EYES. When he realized he was lying on the ground, he quickly lifted his torso to find out where he was. I was sitting next to him but I didn't reveal my presence to him. I wanted him to get used to the environment first.

He got up and looked around the room. I felt he was assessing it. I remembered how I was feeling when I was first here. It seemed so long ago. And still…Was Timeless at my side at that time too? Was she there the whole three days? I'd never asked her that.

Jesse lifted his shirt to check if his body was OK. It's no wonder that he wanted to know since his clothes were still soaked with blood. Pulling his shirt down he went to the exit.

»Where the hell am I?« he said silently to himself. *I don't remember planning skiing or mountaineering*, he thought. I decided he'd had enough time to get used to the new environment. Since I wanted to save him from guessing and since we were in a hurry to make up for the lost time, I got up. I focused on him again and prepared to be seen by him. I felt relieved that his mind hadn't woken up to that extent that he would remember his entire life. I would have to help him with that. And hope again he doesn't become too euphoric.

I took a step in his direction to make him hear me. He turned around. He just looked at me for a while. I smiled.

»It's great to finally see you, Jesse,« I said. He was still trying to place me.

»Who are you?« he asked me after a couple of seconds. I was getting closer to him.

»That's not important now. What is important is that you have finally arrived…«

»Where to?«

»I think it'll be best if you sit down,« I said to him. I didn't know how to explain it to him. I decided to tell him the truth.

We sat in silence opposite each other for a while.

»I want to show you something. You are a part of a bigger plan…But you have to promise me to stay calm no matter what happens. Promise?« I asked tentatively.

»OK. I promise,« he said determinedly.

»First try to relax as much as you can.«

He straightened his spine and relaxed his shoulders. I led him into a relaxed state calmly asking him to relax each part of his body. He followed my instructions. Soon he was ready. I decided that the easiest way to tell him what had happened was transferring data thought my consciousness.

I thought of the events of the previous months and surrounded them with light. My body started to vibrate in the frequency I normally use for teleportation. But that was not the purpose this time. I raised my left hand to the level of his face and pointed my index finger. I gently touched him in the middle of his forehead and light atoms entered his consciousness like electric current.

FAME. Discotheque. Gigs. Tour. Sam.I.Am. The band. Am I OK or am I sick? Do I need treatment? Why? She. Apparition. Her eyes are ocean-deep. Press conference. *So she is a journalist. Let them see her, maybe she is future Mrs. Jesse Roy…*Shrink. Medications. So many people!

Look down, Jesse, everything will be fine…Rise and fall. Grammy. Father! Could I have prevented his death had I arrived on time? The law suit. Sam.I.Am sends us on tour again. *If I want artificial-tasting pastry, I will buy it from a machine…*Memory card…Is it possible to take it out? Holidays. Reunion invitation…So she is real! I must touch her, I must speak to her! Cape Tryon. Fear. *Who is she really?* I'm falling but I don't want to leave the world just yet. I can hear my own vertebrae cracking… Then…Light. I can hear my own voice speaking as if it had a will of its own and I agree with everything it says. *Rebirth. This is possible. Anything is possible. My body has been reborn.* I merge with light again…

We worked through the data and I saw everything was coming back to him. We sat for a while and then we opened our eyes. He looked at me completely calm. The flow stopped again. I was happy that he was able to take the information he was given so well. Finally we could start with training.

I was just about to tell him we were going to head towards the jungle when something completely unexpected happened. He extended his right hand and drew me closer to him. Then he put his lips on mine.

After the initial shock, I drew back and pushed him away from me. I felt very disappointed with my failure.

I headed towards the exit. I didn't have a choice.

»Wait! I'm sorry!« he shouted.

»It's not about that. But I can see that you have totally misunderstood me.«

»What was I to think about you? I've been trying to find out who you are for the last six months. I don't know if I'm sick or I'm losing it! I've been stuffing myself with stupid drugs because of you. I demand an explanation what is going on!«

Me too, I thought feeling powerless.

»You are not ready yet, that's all,« I concluded. I felt that no explanation would do the trick. I remembered Timeless and myself in this same cavern. I hadn't understood her either then. I didn't want to understand her. I clung on to my ego up to the time my body was ready to die. Was this how it was going to be now too? Is it really necessary that we reach the threshold of death, the brink of despair to allow ourselves to recognize something that is more than obvious?

»I'll come when you are ready,« I said finally. I thought of my cabin and I was immediately there.

XXII. DOMESTICATION

I SAT IN FRONT OF MY HOUSE MEDITATING FOR A WHILE. I really wanted to understand how to proceed. An important link in the chain was so close and at the same time so far away…Instead of developing his powers and potential he chose to succumb to low vibrations and focus his attention on me…

In a way, I could understand him. If somebody had ordered me a hundred years ago to learn something from Philip, without feelings of love and rapture, I would have thought it cruel too…But at the same time I didn't want to encourage his feelings for me. If he really loved me and if the frequency of his thoughts and body was the same as mine, we maybe could work together as one. But this…meant my chances of fulfilling what Timeless had instructed me to do were diminishing from moment to moment.

I decided not to let him die in the cavern. Every morning and evening I brought him a bowl of rice and some tea. I didn't let myself be seen, of course. I monitored his way of thinking. At first he was pretty angry that I had left him so fast. But gradually he came to accept it. He made for himself a cozy dwelling in the cavern he inhabited. The fact that he was regularly being supplied with food gave him hope that I would come back soon.

Sometimes I would sit in the cavern and send him light. But I never let my presence be known to him. Up until day 7. It was then that I noticed that the frequency of the cavern suddenly shifted gently. As if somebody else had entered the place. The vibration seemed very familiar…

»Hello, Jesse,« said a shadow dressed in a cloak. She took off the hood and the wind that blew in the cavern, gently ruffled her brown hair. Jesse, who was lying down and napping, woke up immediately. Finally he had company.

»Hello,« he said with a husky voice. »Have you been bringing me rice and tea?« he asked meekly.

»No, that was Keisha,« smiled the girl.

»Keisha?«

»Blonde girl you had a…«, she looked in my direction, »a misunderstanding with.«

I had no clue what she was doing in this cavern, but I felt defeat and a slight drop in the frequency of my body…

Oh, that's her name, he thought. I felt defeated again at his amorous thoughts of me.

»I guess I don't have to introduce myself,« he said smiling. »And you are…?«

»I'm Keisha's teacher, her mother almost. My name is Timeless,« she said calmly. Although her introduction was very cordial, I couldn't help but notice certain strictness in her voice which pointed to the fact that I had failed to do something. Something that looked so simple but was at the same time almost impossible!

»Do you know why you are here?« she asked him. Her question was straightforward and honest. There is only one way to answer such a question – the truth.

»Funny you should ask me that,« he answered. »I think I do. A part of me knows, at least. But the more I think about it the less I know. And in the end I'm clueless again…Keisha…« this was the first time that he actually said my name, »…told me I was a part of a bigger plan.

»I'll show you something now that will be our little secret,« Timeless said smiling. She looked towards me, smiled and looked the boy in the eyes again. »Relax and wait…«

Jesse closed his eyes. Timeless was soon surrounded by a beam of light and I knew she was preparing for data transfer. No matter how much

I wanted to see what she was about to show him, her power managed to cut off the frequency of my thoughts completely. I felt powerless and fragile…I was amazed that the frequency of my body had fallen so much… What had I done wrong?

Timeless touched Jesse's forehead and transferred a large wave of energy into his body. Since I had carried out a similar procedure with him a couple of days ago to make him remember his past, he was already used to the flow of energy. His body didn't convulse like when touching electricity and it was much easier for him to let go. When they finished they sat in silence for a couple of minutes.

They opened their eyes and Jesse was smiling. He looked like he had just learnt the secret of all existence on Earth, the meaning of life. I didn't know why Timeless had decided to share that secret with *him* and not with me. Was it possible that I was less ready than he was…?

»Gorgeous,« he answered calmly. »Now I do understand.«

»But this is our little secret, OK…?« she gave him a conspiratorial smile.

»And Keisha…knows that?« he asked her. I felt totally excluded.

»Why don't you ask her yourself?« She looked towards me and said condescendingly, »Keisha, that's enough of hide and seek now.«

She took away my power to remain invisible. Jesse noticed my outline immediately but, surprisingly, he stayed calm. I accepted the fall of my vibration. Obviously there was no other way. But I was hoping that the lesson the universe was trying to teach me would end soon.

»No, I don't know,« I answered. »I will find out when I am ready.« I wanted to sound as responsible as I possibly could. But I didn't think it was fair that Jesse knew.

Jesse looked at Timeless on more time. »Thank you very much. Now I really understand.«

»I know,« she said and smiled. »I knew you would understand.«

»Can we start with training now? If you still think I can do it, of course,« I asked.

»Of course I do,« said Timeless smiling. My defeat felt all the more bitter because she succeeded to bring Jesse out of the low frequency state in a matter of seconds. And I hadn't been able to do it in six months' time.

»Jesse, are you ready?« she asked him again.

»Sure,« he answered calmly. I felt he wasn't in love at all anymore. But he was absolutely eager to learn and couldn't wait for us to get started. Because I was so curious what Timeless had shown him, my frequency dropped further. Timeless noticed that.

»Keisha…why don't we take a short walk? We need to prepare everything before we take Jesse into his new home…«

»No problem, I'll wait,« said Jesse calmly. I still couldn't believe the transformation I had just witnessed.

Timeless headed towards the exit and I felt she wanted me to follow her.

XXIII. PAYMENT

WE WALKED ALONG THE PATH BEHIND MY HOUSE LEADING TO the forest.

»Why?« That was all I managed to say. I was totally disarmed.

»Things are never as they seem,« she said and smiled. »When we think we are at the top we are already falling. You've lost your modesty, Keisha. That's why your vibration plummeted. You thought you were better than Jesse. More developed. More important. That's why I've been sent to you again. To remind you.«

»But I thought…«

»I know how you felt. We all have had to fight our narcissism sometime. You thought you owned the powers you had had all those years. You thought you were better than others. And this is a big offence in the eyes of the Rulers.«

I started to think. I didn't feel my own narcissism. But I knew I had more knowledge than Jesse. Was that wrong?

Timeless smiled again. »The two of you are so alike!«

Her statement confused me again. It was true that my vibration had really plummeted. I hadn't felt such feelings for years. How was I to get rid of them?

»Firstly, you need to admit certain things to yourself. Total honesty.«

»OK,« I was completely convinced that had to stop. »Can you give me an example?«

She giggled again as if she were asking me things a child would know.

»Your narcissism.«

I tried to dissect my consciousness one more time. In the end I had to admit to myself I had been looking down on Jesse. I would never have thought that he would learn about important plans of the universe before me. Was this a sign of my narcissism? Was he really cleaner than me in that respect?

»Yes,« she answered succinctly. »As we speak, he is cleaner and braver than you.«

These words hurt me a lot. It was me who had saved him from the depths of misery. I remembered him all sweaty in front of the discotheque and I felt better again. I helped him then.

»And who was it that sent you there? The next level you need to reach is humility.«

Is he better then me in that, too?

»Yes. He has really been looking forward to this practise ever since he was born. He didn't know what was missing from his life. First he thought it was fame. Then it was you but today he has learned what led him here. He would give anything for that. His life, money, love, health…anything. Because he knows how priceless this gift is. I can't say the same for you anymore. You've started to take all the abilities you have acquired so far for granted…«

When I realized she was right I let out a silent cry. If that was true, was there anything I could still teach him?

»And thirdly,« she said strictly, »self-pity! Of course you can teach him, that's why we are actually here! That's why I taught you! When you become aware of your flaws, there is no time and place for self-pity and guilt! You just didn't know how to protect yourself from lower vibrations, you couldn't protect yourself from narcissism. The time has come to make the decision: everything will be different from now on.«

I sobered up. »OK. I didn't know. I wasn't able to do it. It will be different now.«

»That's better.«

»When do I start?« I asked. It was the first time after a while that I saw in her eyes that she was satisfied.

»If you want, you can start immediately. Do you see the cabin at the foot of the hill?« she asked me when we came back to my house. A house similar to mine was located on the opposite side of the hill. The walking distance between them was about 5 minutes.

»That one is for Jesse?«

»Yes,« she said.

»I'm sure your training will go smoothly from now on.« I sensed relief in her voice. »I will leave you to it. If you need me, just give me a call.«

I didn't want to do that. She had already done too much work instead of me.

»Thank you for everything, Timeless,« I said gratefully. That day I learnt things about myself I didn't want to know. Although it hurt at first, the experience had a cleansing effect. You can never, never be safe from feeling superior.

Timeless gave me a knowing smile and then disappeared into sunlight.

XXIV. LESSONS

I IMMEDIATELY WENT BACK TO THE CAVERN. Jesse was sitting in a lotus position, his spine was straight but he was still wearing his blooded pair of jeans and T-shirt.

»It's time to start with the practice,« I said conciliatorily. »And to find some decent clothes for you.«

He agreed and we headed towards the jungle. I chose exactly the same path where Timeless had led me years ago. At the crossing I asked him to close his eyes. I didn't want to brag with flying. The time will come for that.

I led him to his cabin and invited him to make himself comfortable. I gave him a tour of the cabin and provided some clean clothes. He thanked me and I told him I would be back the next day.

As I was leaving I could feel some sort of relief. On the one hand, I was grateful for everything that had happened that day: Timeless' visit, the fact that I had come to realize some things about myself, the fact that Jesse was ready, really ready to start learning. I could not have wished for better gifts. I turned back to the cabin gratefully and saw that he had already gone inside. I realized again that his euphoria had left him completely and I felt silently victorious although I couldn't take the credit for it.

Soon we started with our first lessons. Jesse frequently smiled when I would explain something to him and mumbled something to the effect of, »Oh, this is what Ravi meant!« I tried to remain grounded and calm all the time. I really wanted to rediscover my humility and modesty. I was too attached to my life to throw it all away because of some moments of narcissism. I tried to silently remind myself about that.

Jesse was a really fast learner. He loved martial arts; he surprised me by knowing the basics. He told me he had already taken some lessons mainly due to his fear of being attacked in the street again. When he explained what had happened, I found his story quite amusing.

»It wasn't at the time, though«, he replied laughing.

Soon we started training martial arts blindfolded. He had to listen, feel and learn to see in a different way. He had to sense every blade of grass. He had to learn to surrender to his abilities. And he wasn't afraid anymore.

I taught him to trust by having him follow my voice. Many times he only just avoided a tree trunk or a precipice under the path. I knew he would succeed. But if his legs should have accidentally chosen a wrong way, I would have saved him. Soon he was able to not only walk but run following my voice. And soon he didn't even need my voice anymore. He totally surrendered to his powers and his connection with the universe – he called it *universal GPS*. After only a year of practice he was ready for his initiation into teleportation.

When the Rulers gathered at the initiation ceremony, the one who had taught me healing was present, too. This time he led the ceremony. Jesse joyfully surrendered to their procedure of changing and transforming the body. He received a great-looking outfit consisting of dark denim trousers and a white shirt and jacket for the teleportation process. When they finished, I felt I had accomplished a larger part of the task that I had been given.

Jesse gratefully shook my hand and I saw that he had changed a great deal in the previous year. The bags under his eyes, results of tiredness and worry, had completely disappeared. His skin, which he had been wearing out with constant partying and euphoria, acquired a youthful look. His soul was reborn into a completely fresh and new frequency. He realized who he really was. I got the feeling that he didn't need me anymore.

»Thank you for everything you have taught me...« he said to me.

»It was a pleasure,« I answered. »I think our training is slowly coming to an end...«

»Well...yes and no,« he winked meaningfully.

»What are you saying?«

I wanted to connect mentally with him but this time the line went dead.

»I want to tell you this in person,« he smiled.

OK. By now we had become almost equals and there were even moments when I began to feel weaker...

»What Timeless told me a year ago...« he started, »was truly wonderful.«

»Yes...?« I asked.

»Keisha...« he started slowly, »I really love you and I want to work with you.«

I could see the film from a year ago in my head and I instinctively moved backwards.

»Don't worry, I'm not going to kiss you,« he said smiling. »But you should know it is our destiny to be together. It is our destiny to work together and perform together. *That's why* Timeless taught you!«

I moved back again. I didn't know what to say to him. Everything Jesse had had to go through – all the euphoria, danger that he faced, all the negative vibrations of fame and money-hungry people – *that's* why I was here? *That* was my mission?

I had to leave. I left my protégé without saying a single word. I had to speak to Timeless whom I hadn't seen for a year. I materialized in the cold Himalayan cavern where she had helped Jesse. I called her in my mind...When she appeared at the back of the cavern, I took a deep breath to stand up to her, maybe for the first time in my life.

XXV. A DECISION

»WITH ALL DUE RESPECT, I'M NOT DOING THIS!« I said. I knew that what she wanted me to do was actually similar to becoming a kamikaze. »It wasn't a request,« she said with conviction. »You are a part of a larger plan.«

»But that's madness!« I insisted and tried to understand how my going out to a mad army of people could be a part of a bigger plan.

»You are thinking too much,« she smiled, »or rather you think too much like *him*,« she said emphatically. Did she really always have to remind me of my failures? Trample all over my ego? Her statement hurt me more than anything she had ever said before. Even if it seemed much more innocent than the others. It was *true*. And painful. I thought I had already got over him.

»But you haven't,« she said having read my thoughts again. »You are still a part of that…negative magnetic field and it's time you cleaned it. It is time for you the cleanse the world.«

It seemed pointless asking why my death should cleanse the world.

She laughed broadly. But I didn't think it was funny. »Maybe one day you will see the plan like I see it and you will find it amusing how much resistance we can put up against this brilliant and infallible plan of the universe.«

She looked at me again and all of a sudden I felt weaker. I felt cold all over my body and I hadn't felt that for 120 years. Was that possible? Was the universe taking my powers away? In my despair I begged her with my eyes to stop what she was doing.

»The choice is really *yours*,« she replied. »You can either revolt against the plan of the universe and change sides or you can surrender and trust the light which will always lead you to higher levels…«

I had no choice. To become a vulnerable human being again seemed so…unacceptable. How could I have strayed so much from my path? I closed my eyes, took a deep breath and asked all forces to help me.

»OK,« I said pacified although I knew I was going to my death, »I will do what you ask.«

When I opened my eyes again my leader had already disappeared. Only the wind, which was pleasantly caressing my body again, proved that I had spoken to Timeless.

XXVI. THE ROBOT

I SAT IN FRONT OF MY CABIN. I had left my things, which were not so many, inside. If I come back, I will be able to find my peace here. Anytime. Jesse did the same. I locked the front door and prepared for my trip. He came to me and offered me his hand to help me get up.

»Ready?«

»Los Angeles?« I asked conciliatory.

»Yes.«

We closed our eyes. Jesse established a mental connection and I saw a cute house in a row of great-looking houses. There were flowers on the flowerbeds and some nicely pruned trees. The façade was white with light blue decoration around windows and doors.

We surrendered to the light and we were there in an instant. Jesse walked to the front door and knocked. The nice lady, who opened the door, had a different soul vibration than people in India. I felt some sort of confinement and I couldn't explain it at the time.

»Hello,« he said.

»Oh, Jesse, hello. We haven't seen you in a while!« exclaimed the woman.

»Actually, I wonder if you have any idea where Jessica is. Or Rodney.«

»Well, I only know where Jessica is. They haven't been together for quite some time now.«

How is this possible? thought Jesse. *They used to do everything together!*

»Jessica is staying with a girlfriend.«

She gave us the address and I could still feel that she was happy but somehow reserved at the same time. Jesse recognized the frequency of her soul immediately. We said goodbye to Jessica's mother and when we were far enough from the house he started speaking.

»This soul is trapped in the frequency of machines,« he started to explain. »I felt this with my mother and now I can feel it even stronger…You know there is this thing people have implanted in their central nervous system. In their heads. In order to live simpler and happy lives without having to make an effort. It is called a memory card.«

I couldn't believe that was even possible.

»I was surprised at first, too,« he went on. »But thanks to our practiceI am now able to sense this even stronger and clearer. I suppose it must have become even more popular since I've been gone.«

We reached the address the lady had given us. It wasn't far from the house where we had been. We rang the bell. Jessica opened the door.

Jesse looked at her and shuddered. The girl, who wasn't much different from other girls in America, smiled broadly.

»Jesse, finally we have found you! How are you doing?« She was very pleasant but I could feel the same sense of confinement I had felt in our previous visit.

She too? How on earth is this possible? thought Jesse and I could feel his frequency drop with sadness.

We mustn't let these emotions overflow us, we should try to find a solution instead, I advised him.

You are right, he admitted.

»I'm fine, thanks. I was wondering…I had been traveling and was gone for a while. And now I would like to assemble the band again.« He tried not to feel the emotions that welled up inside of him when he was in contact with the people who were led with the help of a memory card. He tried to put as much power and compassion in his words as it was possible.

»That won't be so easy,« she answered smiling. »Rodney and I broke up a while ago.«

»I heard,« he looked at her again. »Do you still want to be in the band?«

She leaned against the front door and said, »I don't know, really. That fame thing wasn't for me anyway. That's for boys. For you and Rodney. Oh, and who is this?« she noticed me.

»I'm Keisha, nice to meet you,« I introduced myself and extended my hand.

»Your girlfriend?« she asked as if that was self-explanatory.

»Not really,« said Jesse reticently and looked at me. »Right?«

I decided to change the subject. »That's not so important. And where is Rodney?«

»Where he was when you two started,« replied Jessica. »Why do you think I dumped him, the slob? He wasted all the money and now he is where he started. And I don't feel like supporting him in that«, she concluded quickly. »If you go looking for him, look for him there. And good luck!« she said as we moved away. We had seen enough. She even waved at us.

We felt the weight of the vibrations that Jessica was subject to. Confinement. I felt I could have guided her thoughts had I chosen to do so. I would just have had to harmonize with the frequency of her card.

»I felt the same thing, you know?« Jesse said completely amazed. »I could have hacked into the frequency of her memory card and think, 'scratch your left ear' and she would have done it! But I wasn't brave enough to actually go through with it.«

»This is called high morals. You can't take advantage of the people who are caught in the frequency of machines. That simply isn't allowed.«

»I know.« I just wanted to say that such a card could turn out to be a much bigger burden than you could imagine…«

»Let's hope that at least Rodney still uses his head.«

»According to Jessica, he probably does,« he smiled.

Soon we arrived to Jesse's ex place. Even from very far away, we could hear loud music coming from the basement…

XXVII. JUNKIE

JESSE PUSHED THE DOOR MAKING IT FALL OFF THE HINGES AND HIT the floor noisily. What we saw in front of us was a dark room that hadn't been aired for a very long time. We sensed heavy substances of low frequencies which mixed with a smell that I could not breathe for a long time, much less live in. In the center of the room, there was a young guy who had black hair arranged in a ponytail. He was leaning over a coffee table and holding a small white tube in his hands. On the table, I noticed some kind of white powder organized in two orderly lines.

He closed one of his nostrils and using the tube sniffed one white line and then repeated the procedure through the other nostril. I could feel a strong wave of low vibrations. Since Jesse and me arrived too late to stop him we tried to at least do something.

»Rodney, what are you doing?«

»Oh, Jesse, you of all people!« said Rodney. »I was just about to fly,« he said and sniggered. He took a little bag from his pocket. »Do you want to come?«

»No, thank you. I'd rather wait here for you to come back,« he replied.

I turned down the music and sat next to him.

I could try to neutralize the effect of those substances, I thought.

How? he asked me while we were sitting next to Rodney who had already surrendered his body to the expected feelings.

It's only about vibration, I explained. I thought of the time I had rescued Jesse's body that had smashed against the rock.

We must go after him and then fill his soul with light. He will think it is the effect of the drug he took. Then he will follow us and return.

He agreed. We relaxed. We descended after Rodney who was sinking into the darkness. When we reached his soul we embraced him and started to create light. Soon the effect was so strong that all three of us were bathed in light. The shadow moved away and there was silence all around us. Our bodies floated in a creamy mixture of energy and it was wonderful. We thought of the place where we were and filled it with light, too. We returned Rodney into his body and we reattached too. We sat relaxed in Rodney's sofa for some time after the procedure was successfully carried out. The silence was broken by Rodney's shouting.

»Bad gear!« Rodney said dissatisfied and threw the bag on the floor. »Damn it.«

He was really in a bad mood but at least he was sober. Jesse couldn't help himself and he hugged him. He was tremendously pleased to discover that his friend had kept his own mind and the ability to make his own decisions, which people with a memory card had lost.

»Rodney, how did this happen?« said Jesse when he let go of him.

»What do you mean?« asked Rodney who was still not showing any happiness that Jesse had finally turned up.

»You, Jessica…all this.«

Rodney pushed Jesse away and started explaining.

»The whole thing is quite simple, really. After six months we met with Sam.I.Am, as we had agreed. All of us except you, the *big star*.« I could feel strong resentment. »We tried to revive what was left of the band but, without you, that wasn't possible, of course. Sam.I.Am tried to find a new frontman in a desperate attempt to keep the band alive. Impossible, if you ask me. Who can be the singer in the Jesse Roy band if not Jesse Roy? As if Brian Adams suddenly became the frontman in Bon Jovi. That simply doesn't work. Nobody could sing like you. After two months, Sam.I.Am disbanded us. We were all pretty depressed, you know. You didn't bother to tell Sam.I.Am and obviously *we* didn't deserve to know where you were either!«

»Rodney…« Jesse tried to put his hand on Rodney's shoulder.

»Get off!« shouted Rodney. I read the mixture of pictures surrounding his consciousness. All the misery of his existence was revealed now; the dreams Rodney had shared with Jesse, were shattered. And the girl he really loved had left him.

»You don't need me, you have clearly showed that to me!« he continued sadly. »You don't care about what we have created, you only care about your-self and your interests!« He looked in my direction. »And you have found yourself a girl…« he said with a fake-friendly voice. »At least now I know why you've been so busy the last six months! I hope she is worth it,« he added.

Jesse's vibration dropped slightly as he fought human emotions.

You don't need that anymore, I tried to calm him down. *This is not him, it's resentment speaking from him. Let's try to defeat it with love…You know the truth.*

You are right again, he thought.

»Rodney,« he said affectionately, while I was sitting on the sofa and sending them love, »You are right, I should have let you know where I was. I know I can never make up for that – there is nothing I can say. Anyway, I ask you to forgive me.«

Rodney was silent and stared at the floor.

»I don't expect you to believe me. But please just listen to me. When I was traveling around the world, I came across a certain practice course in the Himalayas…I know it sounds crazy. It sounds like science fiction. But it's true. And the year went by so fast. I couldn't make contact with Sam.I.Am. And I couldn't tell anybody else. It was all too…unbeliev-able. I'd never thought that kind of environment could feel so familiar to me…I'm even thinking of moving there. When you visit me there sometime, you will understand.«

Rodney lifted his eyes and looked sharply at Jesse.

»You could have told me,« he insisted.

»I'm telling you now,« replied Jesse, »and you are the first to know all this. We came here because we want to bring the band together again.

257

Without Sam.I.Am. Only us. Maybe it was meant for the band to fall apart under his leadership. In this way, we can build our own band, just like we want it!« his answer was so inspiring that it was really hard for Rodney to stay cold.

»What do you say, my friend?« asked Jesse. »Are you with me?«

Rodney's lips curled up a bit and he couldn't hide a smile coming. Jesse asked again.

»Are you in?« and put his arm around his shoulders.

»You aren't going to disappear again?« Rodney asked somehow childishly.

»No way!«

»Really?«

»Really. There is only one tinny little condition,« said Jesse firmly after seeing how much Rodney wanted to be in the band.

»And that is…?«

»You will have to give up those powders. And you will attend practice with Ravi.«

»You mean our high school mate…?« Rodney asked doubtingly.

»Exactly. You will see what I've been doing the last year…«

XXVIII. PRINCE

T HERE IS ANOTHER PERSON WE MUST VISIT, THOUGHT JESSE AFTER WE said goodbye to Rodney.

We found a secret place where nobody could see us and we held hands. Jesse telepathically sent me a picture of a beautiful mansion house surrounded by a big garden. Although the building was old, its inhabitants were dressed in modern clothes. So it wasn't a picture from the past, it was the present. This mansion actually existed somewhere.

Even in this time there are princes and princesses, thought Jesse. *It is just that their function is a bit different from what it used to be. You will see what I mean. Just follow my pictures.*

I surrendered to Jesse's vision. After a short flicker of light we found ourselves on the edge of a garden. In reality it was even bigger than in the picture.

Finally you will fit somewhere wearing that dress, Jesse teased me and I knew he was right.

We headed for the front door where we saw two guards. Although they were standing totally still they pointed their spears in our direction when we wanted to go past them and enter through the front door.

»I'm very sorry but is there any way you could let us through?« Jesse started politely, »we are here to see prince Tim.«

The guards didn't even look at us.

»I think it is necessary that you call in advance,« I offered feeling much more familiar with the situation that he did.

»How am I to do that?« he asked me pointing at the guards. They don't even want to look at me.«

»Do you happen to have Tim's phone number?« I asked wanting to help.

»Actually I do.« Jesse had left his cell phone on Prince Edward Island but in fact he knew the band members' numbers by heart.

We headed to the restaurant called King's Court that was just across the street. Jesse asked if we could use the phone and they were happy to oblige.

»Your highness,« he said joking, »how are you, dude?«

I could hear laughter coming from the phone. Tim seemed to be in a good mood although he had to follow royal rules of conduct. Obviously he wasn't alone.

»I'm great, thank you very much,« I could hear him answer.

»Can we meet in about half an hour?«

»What...? Are you here?« I heard a surprised voice from the other side.

»Yes, I'm here with a friend. I'm trying to bring the band together again and we've come to ask you to join us. This time it will be just us. Without Sam.I.Am. What do you say?«

»I can't discuss this right now,« he said officially; but I could still feel he was happy about meeting an old friend again. »Shall we meet in King's Court? In half an hour.«

»Deal.« Jesse hung up the phone. »Now we just have to wait.«

We sat down at one of the tables. A waiter appeared immediately. We looked at each because we didn't have any money. We hadn't used it at all in the past year and this time Jesse reacted faster than me.

»Two glasses of water, please,« he said. And when the waiter left he added, »I'd better look for my credit card...« Knowing that he was becoming a part of this civilization again he smiled feeling relaxed.

How different my perception of the world is now than it used to be, he thought. He was so relaxed and at peace that I also sank into his vibration of peace. I really enjoyed myself in his company. It was different than anything else I had ever experienced in my life. This merging simply made me feel good...

»So we are making progress,« he said smiling. He surprised me and made a mental connection again. And of course he managed to hear my last thoughts too.

»Well, I'm not suffering in your company or anything. Is there something wrong with that?« I asked. He held my hand and I felt peace descend on me. I felt I couldn't resist him much longer. I didn't want to resist him anymore. But I did want to find something out.

»Jesse?«

»Yes?«

»What did Timeless show you?«

He smiled again. I must have looked quite helpless.

»Definitely not helpless,« he disagreed. »More…really curious.«

»Please…I'd really like to know.«

He looked around the room which was packed. »Now?«

»We won't be doing anything illegal. And ordinary people don't even notice these things. It will look like we are just focusing on each other.«

His eyes were glowing. »OK.«

I closed my eyes and drew my face closer to his. He leant his forehead against mine and prepared for data transfer.

XXIX. A MEETING

IN THE WHITE LIGHT SURROUNDING ME I SLOWLY BEGAN TO RECOGNIZE sounds. Many people screaming Jesse's name…I could hear music being played, but I still couldn't see anything. The picture remained blurred no matter how hard I tried to bring it into focus.

I can't see, Jesse, I thought. *Think harder…*

You're no ready yet, Keisha, I could hear a familiar voice that didn't belong to Jesse. *When you are ready, you will find out.*

I suppose Timeless was omnipresent. Even in King's Court.

And besides, you have company…

»Jesse, is that really you?« we could hear a familiar voice from behind my back. Jesse opened his eyes in surprise and I could feel that the sudden disturbance bothered him. But he hugged his friend happily anyway.

»Tim, this is my girlfrie…friend Keisha,« he quickly corrected himself.

We almost said too much, didn't we? I said joking in my mind while shaking Tim's hand.

Yes. I'm sorry, he said seriously.

Maybe…I don't really mind, I thought.

Still. I want to introduce you properly, he answered. We sat down and the waiter brought us two glasses of water.

»Well, you can take that away,« said Tim good-spirited, »three glasses of champagne, please. We are celebrating today. This is on me.«

The waiter bowed respectfully. Of course everybody knew prince Tim.

»Thank you very much,« I said.

»Don't mention it,« he said waving his hand. »Tell me how you are? Where have you been all this time, mate? What are you planning to do?« I could feel that Tim considered Jesse his true friend even though they hadn't seen each other for a year.

»First, thanks for not giving me a hard time,« began Jesse. »And thanks for seeing us so fast. Before I answer your questions, please tell me what happened after I left and how did you manage to keep a straight head?«

I knew exactly what he meant. Jessica and Rodney had both lost the battle with the low frequencies of fear and resentment.

»The thing is pretty simple,« said Tim. »Why should I blame you? I had also tried to run away from Sam.I.Am a couple of times but I just didn't know how. To tell you the truth, a weight was lifted off my chest while you were gone. I said to myself if I played again, it would be because I wanted to and not because somebody wanted to make money off me. And this was exactly what happened.«

»And what happened to the others? » Jesse asked curiously.

»Well, the others didn't take it so well,« started Tim. »When I told Jessica and Rodney what I thought about the whole thing, they were furious with me. Actually, we desperately tried to find a new singer for quite some time. Our search was futile, of course. How could we have found a new Jesse Roy? Even if we had changed the band's name, things would never have been the same again…So one day Sam.I.Am had to admit the battle had been lost. We broke up. Jessica and Rodney were still pretty mad with me. And things between them were not too rosy either; at least that was my feeling at the time. I haven't heard from them since. I'm so glad you are all right. I had been pretty worried about you for quite some time since you seemed to have vanished into thin air. But I have always had a good feeling. Deep down I knew you were all right. And I am so glad to see I was right.«

»How about your…status, your royal highness?«

»You've noticed, haven't you?« Tim said joking. »After all that all I wanted was some peace. I couldn't stay in the music industry where everyone fought everyone for success. This type of fame is not for me. I started going to Sam.I.Am's studio less and less frequently. And finally I stopped going altogether. He didn't care much about me either. I came back home where I was greeted with open arms. My mum was happy to see me succeed as a musician. She even said to me that she would support all my efforts in connection with music, which I considered to be a miracle. Of course I also reclaimed my old status. Now I'm officially a prince.«

I felt somehow honored. In my times it was considered a privilege to associate with a prince. Jesse sensed my thought and I could see a smile creeping up on him.

»If I told you I was trying to bring the band back together...would you want to join us?«

Tim's answer was clear, calm and definite. »Sure. Definitely.«

»Excellent. So there are just a couple of things that need to be sorted out – Jessica and new lyrics. Let's talk in a week or so,« concluded Jesse.

»What about Jessica? What do you mean?« Tim asked curiously. I could see what Jesse was about to do through the projections in his mind and I wasn't sure it was wise to share his idea with the others.

»Well, nothing really,« he concluded shortly. »They had an argument and I think we should try to make her change her mind.«

Good explanation, I thought having seen what he really wanted to do. It looked pretty dangerous. But Tim was pacified.

»I knew they would fight. They were at the end of their tether at that time. Good luck to you,« he said to us.

»And – I can hardly wait for our first jam session. I will grab the sticks today! It will be great joy and honor for me to play with you again, Jesse Roy. And I guess also with you, Keisha?«

For the first time I felt like a part of a band and the feeling was pretty unusual. I nodded.

»I look forward to that!« he said and kissed my hand like a true gentleman.

So times haven't changed that much, thought Jesse playfully.

I guess not, I smiled.

When we said goodbye in front of the restaurant, he reminded us again to call him.

»This time I'll be angry if you don't inform me about how to proceed. I don't have your phone number, you know!«

Right, thought Jesse, *there is still that to sort out.*

Welcome back to the civilization, I thought. *I never needed that…*

After we had said our goodbyes we decided to arrange everything connected with his return. Personal documents, credit cards and everything else we needed for Jesse to become a member of society again. To do this, we had to go to Quebec.

*I would also like to try something there…*thought Jesse. Again I had a feeling he was about to do something dangerous.

XXX. THE INTRODUCTION

WE MATERIALIZED IN FRONT OF A BRICK-COLORED HOUSE WITH A blue garage door. The front door faced the sea.

This is my home, thought Jesse. *This is where I spent my youth.*

It's nice, I thought.

»Keisha, I'd like to ask you something,« he said. »I'd like to ask you for help.«

»OK. Anything.«

»I really want to save Jessica. And before that, I want to save my mom. Can you help me with that, please?«

I connected with the pictures flooding his mind another time. »It won't be easy…but I'm with you.«

We knocked on the door. A friendly-looking woman answered the door and I immediately knew this was his mom. I felt a strong sense of confinement.

»Jesse, my baby,« she said kindly. »I knew you would be OK. The media really hype everything, like you had told me before.«

Jesse held me by the hand and introduced me.

»Mom, this is my friend Keisha.«

»Oh, nice to meet you. Jesse has never brought a girlfrie…friend home,« his mom was trying to be nice not knowing what this introduction meant. Actually, it wasn't cleat to me either and probably not even to Jesse.

He entered the house and I followed.

»Mom, I'd really like to talk to you,« he started bravely. »Where did you have your memory card implanted?«

Jesse's mom was a bit surprised but she answered quite calmly, »Well, I had it done here, at our hospital. But they have subsidiaries in all hospitals around the world. It's pretty sophisticated, you know.«

»I'd like to try something. Do you remember when you dialed my phone number using your card?«

»Of course I remember. But the reception would have been much better had you had a memory card, you know.«

Jesse inhaled deeply. I sensed he wanted to try something big.

»I know, mom. Thank you very much,« he replied. »Can you do it again? Can you try again?«

»Sure.« She closed her eyes and with her right hand she touched her temples. She was obviously trying to get a connection because the frequency of her ethereal body changed a little. It became even more visible as it pulsated in the frequency of machines. Like a giant cell phone. Looking at her I got an even stronger feeling of confinement.

It was simple for Jesse to harmonize with this frequency and subdue it. His mom suddenly opened her eyes and said:

»I don't want the card anymore. Can you remove it, please?«

I looked at him in surprise. He did it quicker than I thought.

Careful, he thought. *She still doesn't have control over her body. I'm operating her now. We should go to the hospital immediately.*

Now?

Immediately!

We ran to the front door and his mom followed us as if she were hypnotized.

XXXI. THE HOSPITAL

WHEN WE ARRIVED JESSE HEADED TO THE RECEPTION.
»Please, help my mom,« he said concerned. »I think her memory card has broken down!«

The clerk said kindly, »I doubt that's possible.« Both Jesse and I could immediately feel the artificial vibration of the receptionist. It must have been pretty common in the hospital.

»Look at her,« said Jesse and pointed at his mom.

»I want you to remove my card. I don't feel so good!« she said again.

»I can see now you are right. An emergency procedure will have to be carried out!« said the receptionist. She immediately called a doctor, »Emergency B316! I repeat, emergency B316!«

Hospital staff hurried towards us, and Mrs. Roy was put on a gurney. She was wheeled into an operating room.

We've done all we could, he thought relieved. *Now they will have to fix what they had done. And maybe the rules will become stricter for the others.*

I had a bad feeling but I didn't know why.

Don't worry, everything will be OK, he thought again. *We can save Jessica the same way.*

OK, I answered.

After surprisingly short time – it couldn't have been more than 15 minutes – Jesse's mom came out of the operating room.

»Well, I'm all set!« she said with a smile.

Both of us heightened out senses and we realized she was still under the influence of the magnetic memory card.

»But how…?« Jesse wondered.

The doctor approached us.

»Hello. Young Mr. Roy, I presume?«

»Yes,« replied Jesse disappointedly.

»You mom's card had lost its magnetic charge. It had to be replaced. Don't be afraid, it's a totally routine and painless procedure.«

»It really is. Thank you, doctor. I feel great,« Jesse's mom said emphatically.

Oh, no, he thought bitterly.

I thought it wouldn't go so simply, I joined in.

What now?

»Let's go home,« said Jesse seemingly calm. »I'd like to ask you just one more thing,« he said to the doctor.

The man, one of the rare ones who didn't have the robot vibration, turned around. »Yes?«

»What about…have you ever had a case when you had to remove the memory card completely? I mean, should it lose magnetism again…«

»No need to worry. This will not happen.«

»But…have you ever removed a card?« Jesse repeated his question emphatically. The doctor looked at him carefully.

»If we were to do that, there would be a high risk of injury. We inform everyone about that before they sign the contract. Emptiness appears that is difficult for the body to accept. As if somebody cut out one of the vital organs for managing the nervous system like hypothalamus or even part of the brain. The removal of the card is almost impossible and therefore undoable. But even if it were possible, it would cost you a fortune.«

»How much?« Jesse said prepared to bargain.

»About $50 million,« the doctor said coolly.

»OK then,« said Jesse resigned.

I thought of something else.

»Excuse me, doctor. I have another question,« I started. I remembered the big lump Lahiri or Ravi had 50 years ago on his neck before he decided

to leave his body.

»My uncle has a big lump on his neck and many experts claim it's a tumor. What about this kind of surgery? Is it expensive...?«

»Not at all, young lady,« answered the doctor kindly. »Such procedures are routine. The patient just needs a valid medical insurance.«

»Great. Thanks a lot.«

Please come with me. I thought of something, I gestured to Jesse.

»You're welcome,« said the doctor and headed towards his office.

»Let's go, mom,« called Jesse. His mom almost danced towards us.

»What kind of card did they give you this time?« he said almost gently.

»Even better,« she said playfully. »Now I'm really feeling great, I didn't before.«

She'll say exactly that when the card is no longer inside her, he thought.

You're right but we will have to join our forces and knowledge to succeed, I answered. Soon we arrived back home. Jesse and I headed towards his room. We asked to spend the night. Jesse's mom was thrilled, of course. She was thrilled about almost anything. In the evening we sat on the bed and I showed Jesse my plan that could succeed...

XXXII. TUMOR

*I*F WE JOIN POWERS WE CAN DEMAGNETIZE THE CARD, I THOUGHT. Just in case we communicated by using telepathy. We didn't want to risk his mother hearing us.

And once it is demagnetized, we just take it out, right?

I'm not sure it will be that simple, I replied. *I don't have any experience with memory cards or any implants. I've only healed natural injuries. If you make a cut into human body and implant a foreign object, it is much harder to undo the damage. It would be much easier and less dangerous if the person who implanted it took it out as well. Because the vibrations are similar...* I tried to explain.

Do you think my mom could die because of two vibrations that are too different?

I'm afraid I do, I thought. *If our healing frequencies of light met the low frequency of steal...well, I'm not sure what could happen. Natural tissues usually respond well to such healing but with artificial ones it is usually quite the opposite.*

Let's give it a try, thought Jesse. *There is almost nothing...to lose anyway.*

We waited for silence to cover the house. We heard Jesse's mom turn off the TV and go into the bedroom. In an hour or so we followed her.

We sat on the edge of her bed and started relaxing. The room filled with light immediately. We joined the powers of our thoughts and focused on the circuitry of the card. It became demagnetized immediately like it did earlier that day. But it was a bit different this time. The frequency of the card fell so dramatically that Mrs. Roy lost consciousness. We were too strong. And the card burned out somehow. And because it didn't fuel the body it was attached to anymore, it lost its functionality. The body was still showing vital signs – breathing, heartbeat…but that was all.

We felt how the tissue surrounding the circuitry of the card started to treat it as a foreign body. The cells around the card started splitting to protect the body. A lump started to appear surrounding the card.

»To the hospital, quickly!« I said.

»Quebec?«

»No, we must go some place else. Montreal,« I replied. We had to go far away in order not to look suspicious.

Jesse had to drive again after a very long time. Because his mom's vibration was too low, it wasn't possible for her to travel in any other way. In about half an hour we reached the hospital. In the glass surface of the Hôpital Maisonneuve-Rosemont we could see the twinkling of the stars. The vast parking lot allowed plenty of space for the family Chevrolet we used to drive there.

Jesse prepared all her documents and demagnetized her health insurance card.

»You'll see,« he said as he lifted up his mom's body and carried it hopefully into the hospital building.

XXXIII. AN OPERATION

WE REPORTED AN EMERGENCY AGAIN. Surprisingly they were less concerned this time.

»Oh, it's just a tumor,« a friendly nurse said. »Do you have her medical insurance card?«

»I'm afraid it's become demagnetized,« said Jesse.

»Let's have a look,« the nurse said and put the card into the machine. »You're right. Can you tell me same basic information, Mr ..?«

»Jesse Roy. I'm her son. Sure I can tell you her data. Her name is Justine Roy, her address is Rue de Champlain…«

When he gave her all data, the nurse asked, »And does she have a card?«

»Sorry? Oh, you mean memory card? No, she doesn't have it,« he lied quickly. »She's always been against it. When she developed this lump they tried to talk her into having one implanted. But you know how older folks are. It's hard for them to keep up with new things. My mom is definitely one of those.«

»But my records show…« the nurse went on.

»Yes, I know. It's a mistake,« Jesse corrected her. »It was just her doctor's suggestion. But she refused. She doesn't have a memory card. That's why her lump grew so much. Please remove it.«

The nurse deleted the data. »OK, then. I'll let the doctors know.«

Now all we can do is wait, thought Jesse.

I've got a bad feeling. What about the X-ray? I thought.

You're very much informed for a 19th century girl, he joked.

I must keep up to speed with many things, I replied. *And I'm known to be very good at absorbing data from the environment. This is just another thing I've had to learn if I wanted to do any good here.*

Then help me prevent them from doing the X-ray, he thought.

We sat down on one of the benches in the waiting area. We knew what we had to do. We closed our eyes and left our bodies. We left our bodies sitting in an upright position. If anybody came by, they would think that we just closed our eyes or nodded off while waiting.

We went to the operating room.

»Scalpel, please, nurse,« said the main doctor. »I still don't know how it is possible that this darn thing is growing so fast,« he mumbled to himself. »I've never seen a tumor like this.«

»What about if we are really dealing with a foreign object in the body?« asked the nurse.

»Maybe an X-ray should be done,« she suggested.

»There is no time for that. Before we can make a diagnosis, the tumor can overgrow the entire neck area! You better help me.«

Mrs. Roy was lying on her stomach and the doctors used electronic appliances to establish how deep they could cut.

»Ready?« asked the doctor. »Now we need to ask ourselves whether we believe in God or not. I advise you to be as humble as you can, no matter what you believe in. Only a higher force can help us save this lady...«

What a beautiful explanation, I thought. *Actually our methods are not that different. In both cases it's about positive messages...*

But I haven't noticed tweezers or knifes in your case... added Jesse.

I know. It's good to see they are making an effort.

Making an effort is not always enough, he reminded me. *How about we offered a helping hand?*

But...

I know we are not allowed to influence her, he thought. *But we can influence them*, he said pointing to the crowd of people around her bed.

You're right, I admitted.

We focused and started to work. I imagined a strong beam of light shining into the room. Like a thick soup, the dazzling fog spread around the room. It surrounded the bed and started feeding the doctor and his assistants.

Anything is possible, I thought. Suddenly everybody was inhaling the light and I sensed they had received my message.

The doctor managed to cut the last strings that connected the lump to the body. Then he quickly took an appliance used for enlargement. They observed the behavior of the cells on a screen beside the table. They sprinkled some fluid that looked like a disinfectant all over it. We still persisted with the flow of light.

After a few minutes the doctor announced, »I think we can relax now. The operation has succeeded.«

All those present let out sighs of relief and started clapping spontaneously. We got ready to go. And since the doctor would soon be coming to tell us that the operation had succeeded, it would have been a good idea to wait for him in our bodies.

When we focused on ourselves and not on the bright river surrounding the table, I noticed that the body on the table had become brighter than it was before. It was surrounded by a stronger vibration. One of the Rulers was standing near her and had lifted her soul above her body. The machine started emitting a well-known beeping sound announcing that Mrs. Roy had lost consciousness. We were there immediately.

»Don't worry,« the Ruler tried to calm us down. »Justine needs to go through a thorough process of cleansing, the cleansing of her body and soul. You two can help me. And you just let go,« he said to Jesse's mom.

The doctors came running and started with resuscitation.

We directed a beam of light into her body and tried to cleanse her ethereal wounds caused by the surgery. We reactivated the centers that had been responsible for supplying her body with energy. The sense of confinement that had been suffocating her before evaporated. Her nerve

cords and energy centers came back to life and assumed their roles again.

The Ruler now let Justine's soul enter the now cleansed body.

Thanks for your help, I thought.

Never be afraid to ask for help, the Ruler reminded me. *Lower frequencies rule this side of the planet and that's why the work with energy is hindered. There is no shame in asking for help.*

I know. OK. I'll keep that in mind, I replied. He was right, I was really trying to do everything by myself. I even tried to force things sometimes.

The machine was emitting a sound announcing that the patient was conscious. She opened her eyes and asked: »Is Jesse OK?«

All those present smiled and let out another deep sigh. The doctor approached visibly relieved, »The question was whether you'd be OK but I guess that's clear now. You should rest now.«

Jesse and I materialized near our bodies and reattached to them. In a sitting position we opened our eyes again and looked at each other. We were glad we had succeeded although it was harder than we had expected. I embraced him.

»That's OK, love birds,« the doctor greeted us. »The operation was successful. You can see her and talk to her in a couple of minutes. She's been asking about you.«

We smiled and got up. We headed to the operating room. When we came to the door, he looked at me.

»You go ahead. The two of you need to talk,« I said.

»No, I want you to come with me,« he begged. »If it hadn't been for you, my mom would still be a robot.«

I sighed and sensed I couldn't deny his request. »Sure. I'd be happy to.«

XXXIV. A CONVERSATION

»M OM!« said Jesse happily when seeing that not only was his mother alive but sitting up in her bed waiting for her son.

»Jesse, my baby!« said Mrs. Roy in French. This was the first time that I noticed real love in her voice. Unlimited and without boundaries.

»What happened, Jesse?« she asked him.

»I don't know if we can discuss details here, mom,« said Jesse. »What matters is that you are alive and well.«

»And you, Jesse? Are you OK? I've been so worried about you. Everyone said you were dead. And I felt…some sort of numbness that I can't explain. I was really worried and afraid. I was angry because I'd obviously done something wrong since you left without saying goodbye. I felt that this time I lost both of you, you and Eugene…And I mourned both of you. But all this was covered by a thick layer of ice. As if I was swimming in an icy lake that I could never leave. I felt totally powerless. I couldn't speak, couldn't control my body. A part of me was just watching what was going on…«

Hearing this moving story I realized how the other people, who had chosen this type of slavery, felt. And seeing how fashionable it had become, I realized how much work we had to do…

Jesse hugged her again.

»Just don't tell this to anyone, OK?« he whispered to her. »You had a memory card implanted in your brain and a lump grew around it…But this piece of information had already been deleted from the files. I told the nurse you had a tumor and that was that. Don't be afraid, but I think we have just done something illegal. We had to save you.«

Mrs. Roy connected the events together and tears came into her eyes.

»Oh, Jesse, you're my hero. You needn't have done this…« she hugged him again. She remembered the procedure and the cleansing that we had done. She looked at me. »And you…you are the daughter that I never had. Thank you very much from all my heart!« she held out her hand and I joined in the hug.

The doctor entered the room.

»Mrs. Roy needs her rest, you know,« he said relaxed. I could feel that he was still very proud that the operation had gone so well.

»OK, mom. See you tomorrow, then?« asked Jesse.

»OK. Please come and visit as soon as you can!« she said happily.

»She should be well enough to go home tomorrow if everything goes well,« the doctor said smiling. »Mrs. Roy is right. You should visit her tomorrow.«

When we said our final goodbyes she looked at us gratefully again.

»I'm really very grateful to both of you. For…« we both looked at the doctor and tried to tell her with our eyes that we were not alone anymore, »…bringing me here.«

»You should consider getting a memory card in the future, Mrs. Roy. So that you are even healthier,« encouraged her the doctor.

»Thank you,« she said with distaste, »but these novelties really aren't for me!«

XXXV. JESSICA

WHEN MRS. Roy returned home the next day she felt reborn. She kept asking Jesse how he had done it and what exactly it was that we had done. After a couple of hours, Jesse gave in and started explaining to her what I had been teaching him. His mom absorbed all information she received from her son with great interest. Soon Jesse found out it wouldn't be bad if we introduced her to Ravi and Ina.

»Aaron is also part of the group,« I agreed with him, »and he is older than your mom.«

Justine packed her bags and we went to New York. She had some money left from her husband's insurance policy and she divided it into three parts.

»I insist,« she said decidedly. »If it hadn't been for the two of you, I wouldn't be here right now, at least not in this form,« she said and smiled. »I'm sure you will need the money for your projects.«

She was right about that. We definitely needed the money. Just another proof that we were on the right track: the constant support of the universe. On all levels – also on financial.

When I connected with Ravi in my mind again and showed him what had happened, he couldn't have been happier. Rodney had joined them during this time and he had made a great progress after the first week of withdrawal crisis. He discovered a completely new and natural purpose of existence. Without the help of illegal substances.

Mrs. Roy adjusted perfectly to the new environment. Because she was the only one whose body wasn't young or rejuvenated she looked like everyone's mother at first.

»You're safe now, mom,« said Jesse. »We'll be back soon.«

When we said goodbye, we knew which parts of the puzzle were still missing – Jessica and Tim. Tim was not such a problem but we were worried about Jessica. If the procedure was really so complicated as we had experienced with Jesse's mom, we would really have to work very hard…

But at least now we know what to expect. It should be easier to prepare, he comforted me.

You're right there, I agreed with him.

And so it was. When we started working on Jessica we prepared everything in advance. We chose the hospital, we prepared her documents, we discussed all possibilities. And at the same time, we asked the Rulers for help. And we also got it.

The procedure of reclaiming Jessica was carried out after a week of serious preparation. Everything was much simpler than with Jesse's mom. There were five of us, including the Rulers and everything ran smoothly. Jesse had become an expert on speaking with receptionists at the hospital. He added a few spicy details to emphasize the drama of his story. He worked his charm on the doctor and the nurses. Jessica's file was repaired immediately as if her memory card never existed.

His ease at speaking with the nurses made me feel a bit bitter…

Jealous…? asked Jesse playfully.

No, of course not, I thought. *Although we're doing the right thing, I feel that you're lying too much. That's all.*

OK, then. I'll try to be a little less dramatic, he concluded seriously.

Jessica was saved much faster and with a lot less effort. The Rulers had done almost all the work instead of us and I felt relieved that it was still possible to save people who decided to be saved. They couldn't have known what they had been getting themselves into when they had the cards implanted.

»I'd like to apologize for my behavior,« said Jessica when we were alone. »I really want to be a part of the band again. I know you can bring us all back together. But you should know that I really, really suffered when we fell apart...« Her eyes filled up with tears as she shared how she felt. »I really like being on stage with you guys. And Rodney and I had such a good thing going...but when you disappeared, I felt something was wrong. Rodney started shutting me out and I got the feeling that he loved you more than me. I became angry and jealous. And when I told him that, he said angrily, 'You're free to go if there is something you don't like!' I was already distraught because we were not going to play together anymore and his words shook me up completely. I hated you, Jesse. I could feel that Rodney left because of you...«

She was crying hard now. I felt it would be good if she channeled her feelings into more positive thoughts. But I knew she had to say out loud why she had decided to choose captivity.

»And then mom suggested *this* solution,« and pointed with disgust to the catalogue lying on the desk. »She was happy and satisfied although her own marriage with my father hadn't been good for years. He was having an affair and we both knew it. Her behavior changed completely when she had the card implanted. She was no longer angry with my father but I was still furious. I was a handful at the time. And when Rodney and I broke up it was just too hard for me. Nobody in the whole wide world understood me, nobody was on my side. Dad didn't care and mom was living in her own perfect world. *If this is the way out of all problems, why not do it*, I thought. I went to the doctor and signed some papers I couldn't care less about. The only thought in my head was to get rid of the pain.«

Jesse and I listened to her and we couldn't believe how similar Justine's and Jessica's stories were. If they hadn't chosen to think all those negative thoughts in the first place, they could have avoided the sense of captivity altogether. As if we had to die to feel lust for life again. This fact reminded me of my own resistance so many years ago. I had to get to the brink of death to be able to forgive Philip.

»Then it all just got worse. All those feelings that I got hidden away in my heart and they were ready to go off at any moment. I was burning up inside, my heart was heavy and small. I wanted to express my feelings but I couldn't find the right words. As if somebody else was in control of my body. My lips were smiling but I didn't feel fulfillment inside of me like I used to. I did all the things other people did, I would go to the cinema, read magazines, hang out with friends. But under this veneer, I was deeply unhappy. Like never before...«

When she calmed down I could feel she wanted to ask us something. »Jesse,« she stared timidly. »Is...is Rodney going to be in the band...?«

He smiled. »Would you mind if he was?«

She looked down again. »Actually...I wouldn't.« She was being honest. I felt she really loved him despite everything they had been through.

»Does he...I mean...Do you know...Does he have a girlfriend?«

»Not to my knowledge. As far as I know, he led a pretty desperate life after the two of you broke up. He started taking drugs to find compensation for what was missing in his life. In a way he did the same as you.«

Although she was worried when she heard this news, she thought: *so he really loves me!*

She lighted up. She pressed the button by her bed and called the doctor.

»Please remember, this is a secret,« Jesse added quickly. »Nobody must find out what we had done here. Otherwise we are in trouble.«

»No worries,« she replied.

The door opened and the doctor came in. »I'd like to go home now,« Jessica said quickly. »I'm fine, you see.«

»Yes, I can see you are all better,« the doctor said amazed. »Before you leave, I must remind you that you have a chance for better health...«

»You can shove that chance somewhere,« Jessica said bravely when the nurse disconnected the machines. She took her things and said: »Let's go, guys.«

XXXVI. INSPIRATION

ON OUR WAY TO NEW YORK WE PICKED UP TIM WHO HAD FLOWN in from England. He and Jessica hugged like they hadn't seen each other for ages. In a way it was true since Jessica was virtually reborn.

In New York we joined the group Ravi and Ina were training. We couldn't believe our own eyes. Justine looked half her age.

»Good atmosphere,« she said and smiled. »And great people.«

When Tim and Jessica joined in, the group got a new impetus. Jessica fell into Rodney's arms after the initial greeting and the only thing we could hear for a while among kissing and gentle caresses was their stifled moans: »Forgive me,« »No, you forgive me«.

While Ravi and Ina were busy with preparations that were carried out according to Jesse's instructions, our task was to write lyrics and music for the new band.

Jesse knew exactly what we were up against and so his plan was very clear. It included a lot of walks and relaxations during which we were to find out what the lyrics of the songs should be. At the same time he gave me singing lessons. I had always enjoyed singing but I never thought about it as my career. Timeless taught me other things. I didn't know why she hadn't taught me to sing since she new what was waiting for me.

»Maybe it is destined that I teach you,« smiled Jesse.

I was left speechless again – he was the only one to know what our destiny was. After a couple of attempts at pop-rock singing I almost gave up. In my time we sang totally differently. Nowadays it is called opera.

And I liked it. But this that Jesse was trying to teach me, well…when he started singing, it sounded quite alright; but when I tried…Well, I didn't like it at all.

One day we were sitting on a hill facing a sun-kissed New York. We were just about to give up trying to sing because I couldn't do it. I wanted to sing in my own way.

»How about if you knew what lies in store for you? If you could *feel* what I felt?« he asked me again when I opined that singing just wasn't for me.

»I had thought of that myself,« I replied, »but you know that Timeless won't let me find out.«

»Have you actually asked her for permission?« he asked me meaningfully.

I really hadn't tried that. How simple. I felt quite embarrassed that I hadn't thought of that myself.

»When you observe other people, you often immediately see what their problem is. But with our own problems we frequently don't see a solution even if it is right in front of our noses,« he said trying to make me feel better.

I closed my eyes and thought of Timeless. I heard her laughter immediately.

First I have to compliment you, she said.

I don't need compliments because I'm not doing very well, I thought almost sadly.

I'm not talking about singing, she interrupted me. *I'm talking about freeing two people, which nobody has ever done before. There are people and organizations who know exactly how dangerous cards like Justine's and Jessica's could be. But not only that they have always been silenced so far but their attempts to have the cards removed have always ended with death. They could learn something from the two of you…*

Great. Thank you very much, I said trying to contribute to the topic

Timeless had opened. I was really happy to hear her praise but I really wanted to get to the bottom of things. Public performance, overcoming mass euphoria…and also singing. I heard Timeless' laughter again.

You are sort of like Superman who has just saved the world and now he is obsessing which sandwich to choose for his lunch.

I'm glad that you find my worries amusing, I replied. Again I summoned all my humility and prepared to ask her the question.

Timeless, could I please find out what my destiny is? Can Jesse show it to me? If I feel what he felt that time, it might become easier for me…

She continued seriously: *there is a very demanding path leading to that answer and it will take a lot of effort. You will have to remove many obstacles and overcome your own weaknesses first. Only then can you witness what I had shown to Jesse. He also wishes to pass this wave of energy on to you. But a very complicated procedure will have to be carried out to do that. When you are ready, you will feel it!*

Again I was surrounded with silence that followed her voice. Timeless disappeared again and left me alone in my uncertainty.

Jesse opened his eyes and smiled.

»Did you manage to find anything out?« I asked him. I felt like a student after a particularly difficult math class asking a fellow-student if he was able to understand anything.

»Yes and no,« he replied mysteriously. »Timeless is right. When you're ready you will know.«

He got up. »I can feel you could do with some time on your own,« he said and left.

I was left alone on the hill watching the city. In comparison to what I had experienced, it seemed so big and so small all at the same time…I felt that I was always at the beginning of my journey no matter how hard I wanted to learn and how deeply I was looking for the truth about life.

When the sun came out from behind the clouds and shone on my face I got an idea to write a song.

»Jesse?« I said looking around. I wanted to share my inspiration with him. But he wasn't there anymore. Obviously he sensed I needed to be by myself. But he left a piece or paper and a pencil right next to me.

He knew. I took them and started writing…

HAPPY

I wanna see the truth that is flying above my head,
I wanna know who sings to me that future that is lying ahead is
always bright,
I wanna be the strongest in your fight of light,
I wanna be one with you.

(Chorus) I wanna be happy, happy, happy – ever after,
happy, happy, happy with you, only you,
happy, happy, happy, every second!
Let me fly there to you, up here with you.

I wanna know, why all the world is hiding in my soul,
I wanna be the one who will always bring your love to all,
I wanna dance with you and always fly right next to you,
I wanna be one with you.

XXXVII. ORGANISATION

THE FOLLOWING MONTH WAS MARKED BY PREPARATIONS THAT JESSE was responsible for. When we were talking about the name for the new band we were unanimous again.

»Jesse Roy,« said Rodney. »We are already known under this name and our frontman is still the same. The name is obviously not protected by copyright since it's your own!«

Rodney was right and everyone supported him. Only Jesse just shrugged modestly and said: »Well, if everyone thinks so...who am I to disagree? But from now on everyone will answer interview questions!« he added strictly.

I remembered the gloomy room at the press conference and a shudder went down my spine.

Jesse noticed my thoughts and came up to me.

»No need to worry. This time it will be different. It will be totally different.«

I was comforted. It was nice to watch the other so-called invisible members of the band. Justine and Aaron became our organizers. When they prepared a web page for the band and published the first news about our concerts, the number of hits started growing by the day. I thought of Timeless and the Rulers.

This must be your doing, I was sure.

We worked on our music very hard and here Justine's money came in very handy. We rehearsed in the peace and quiet provided by Davies' apartment. And when we needed recordings we hired a studio and made recordings as quickly as possible. Jesse kept saying that this time around things were much simpler than they were under Sam.I.Am's guidance. All sense of importance, ego and showing off…all this was gone.

»But al least you learnt a lot,« I offered.

»Sure we did,« he agreed. »And to show our respect, I suggest we invite him to our first concert. What do you say?«

Everybody agreed. They were really quite fond of him. And they were really grateful for everything he had taught them. Maybe this time they would be able to establish a friendlier relationship…

As far as videos were concerned, it was also pretty straightforward. Hannah discovered a couple of programs that allowed us to create and edit our own videos. We didn't really need anyone – videos were mostly shot in nature. They contained quite a lot of special effects. The only difference was that we didn't need blue screens, jumpsuits and dots on our faces. We were doing everything by ourselves anyway – flying, teleportation and disintegration. Luckily this was the age that took such effects for granted.

»We could include this also in our live performances. People would think it was special effects, anyway,« suggested Tim.

We all agreed.

We developed our songs quickly too. Jesse and I made the drafts, as we had agreed. We talked a lot about what the band should stand for and how to formulate the messages we wanted to send to young people.

»Have you ever listened to a love song and sung it in your mind to somebody else than one would expect?« Jesse asked me one day.

»What do you mean by that?«

»Well, for example, if you sang it to yourself. Or to universe, energy, god whatever you may call it. Wouldn't it be great if we were all able to grasp songs like that? In this way you could get a whole spectrum of emotions from a single song.«

I agreed and so we tried to develop that idea.

We even titled one of our songs Diversity aiming at different possible ways of understanding that song…The others also liked our new concept of the band.

XXXVIII. THE COMPANY AND FINAL PREPARATIONS

IT WAS INTERESTING THAT JESSE DECIDED TO ESTABLISH HIS OWN company because we needed a recording company for our first single. »Like I promised my father many years ago,« he said with nostalgia in his voice. And again we were glad to have his money for establishing the company.

*Like I promised, Papa: office supplies, computer, and other costs...hope you're proud of me. Even if pride is not a very useful emotion...*thought Jesse while his first office was being decorated.

Why don't you contact him? I thought, when I felt the frequency of his thoughts.

You're right! I never thought of that, he said smiling.

Sometimes somebody else can see the things that are...

...right in front of your face, I know. Thanks, Keisha. I'll ask the Rulers. I'd really like to know how he is.

And so our preparation ran smoothly and it seemed that the universe supported every step that we made. But I still wasn't sure what I would have to face on the stage. Whenever I would think of Jesse's live performances I would remember a strong wave of euphoria descending over the band. They were absolutely ecstatic after every concert but the next day they were dying of depression. Despite my protection. I really wondered how it would be now...

Our CDs hit the stores and sales increased by the day. We got more and more orders from more and more music stores and finally our sales surpassed that of the previous band.

The interest in the band rose dramatically but I could feel an interesting shift in the vibration of energies – not even one single tabloid contacted us. We were mostly approached for interviews by serious music magazines or TV programs which had managed to retain credibility throughout the years. I knew it was *their* doing. Timeless would never allow our messages to be wrongly interpreted. I was amazed at the precision of the universe. And the protection of the Rulers. We didn't need any bodyguards.

The days rushed by and the date of our first live performance was getting closer. The proceeds from the CD and other official merchandize had already covered our initial costs.

»There is no need for contracts like we used to have with our manager,« smiled Jessica. »How can we cheat each other if we can read each other's mind?« we laughed but at the same time we knew that living in such high frequency, we had to be particularly strong and, every second, conscious of our thoughts.

During the rehearsal we agreed that we didn't need any dancers on the stage. 'Special effects' would be totally sufficient. And we were planning to add some kung-fu moves…We had a great time discussing and practicing our performance.

The day of the live performance approached very quickly, too quickly for me. I spent the last day before performing on the stage meditating and relaxing. Although the Rulers had been supporting us throughout the process, I asked for their special help that day. But what I didn't know was that the universe had planned a special challenge for me…

XXXIX. THE LAST DAY BEFORE
THE LIVE PERFORMANCE

SINCE I HAD SPENT SO MUCH TIME CALLING THE RULERS, I WASN'T surprised seeing the group of visitors mid-morning. There were the Rulers who had initiated me into the procedure of teleportation, there was Timeless and also Harriet. They all sat in a circle and relaxed with me. I was extremely glad to be surrounded by so many people that I loved and I felt very cozy. Timeless was the first to speak.

»You must be asking yourself why there are so many of us.«

»Because I'd called you…« I tried reluctantly.

»We've come to bless your mission in this world. Pretty soon you will be entirely clear on what I mean. We've come to prepare you for the breaking point you are about to face. And at the same time we thought it would be smart to change your teleportation outfit a little. You know, make it a bit more up-to-date, fashionable…«

She gestured to me to get up. The Rulers surrounded me and led me through the procedure of initiation into teleportation one more time. My skirt was shortened a bit and I wore almost invisible tights that ended in the middle of my calves. They were made of yellow lace and they superbly complemented the yellow material surrounding the tight fashionable upper part of my dress. Timeless added a pair of glittery flats and some accessories in my hair which looked like little flowers. When they finished I looked at myself in the mirror on the wall.

»Wow, I didn't know something like that was possible. Thank you, » I said. I looked like I had just escaped from a prestigious up-scale catwalk.

»Anything is possible,« Timeless replied. »You might as well have learned that already in all this time I have been teaching you,« she chided me.

»I know. Thanks.«

Then Harried walked up to me. »I'm so proud of you, my dear girl. I'm so happy I was allowed to protect you all those years ago. Look at you now!« she said and we hugged.

»Thank you for everything, Harriet.« I said to her. »I love you.«

»I love you too,« she whispered. »You should know that nothing bad is going to happen. Your future is totally bright. Remember that.«

»OK. I'll do that.«

We sat in silence for a while. Then they gradually began to disappear. In a couple of minutes all that was left of them was light that mixed with the freshness of the air in my room. When I looked at my watch I saw I was already late for the rehearsal.

I decided to show my fashionable outfit to everyone. I could have worn something different but I wasn't able to disintegrate other clothing so that it could be teleported together with the body. The outfit Timeless had chose for me made that possible. When I entered the room where Rodney had already prepared everything for rehearsal, everyone's jaws dropped with surprise. Including Jesse's. And I was pretty amused. I had never been greeted like that before.

»Keisha, you look…wow,« Jessica was able to utter. »I want something like that, too.«

»Amazing, really…« said Tim from behind the drums.

»But my Jessica is still prettier,« said Rodney and hugged his girlfriend. Only Jesse was left speechless.

»So, guys, are we rehearsing or not?« he said quickly.

We rehearsed with pleasure and enjoyment. We could feel that tomorrow's performance was going to be something special. Justine reported that all the tickets had been sold out. Roadies had already finished with preparations. This time it was different from when the band had to travel together with them. They traveled long hours back then, there were many disagreements, sleepless nights…And now we would be able to stay home right up to the start of the concert. And then we would teleport to the stage.

After the rehearsal we took some time for ourselves. We went our separate ways to prepare for the next day. Some of us went for a walk while the others stayed in the room. Jesse left the room immediately after the rehearsal. I left him alone. He seemed deep in his thoughts.

After an hour or so I saw him sitting on the floor of the balcony. And there was somebody sitting opposite him that I didn't recognize. Behind them there was a beautiful view of a New York sunset. When I got closer, I heard a couple of words they said to each other.

»I know what you meant, son. I forgive you for everything. Please forgive me for not knowing how to be a better father.«

»You did a great job, Papa,« said Jesse, »but as far as being uncertain goes, you just didn't have the knowledge, that's all.«

Not wanting to eavesdrop, I coughed discreetly. They noticed me and invited me to join them.

»Hello, young lady. You must be Keisha. I've heard so much about you,« he said to me.

»I don't know about the rest but the name is right,« I replied and shook his hand.

»Actually we were just leaving,« he added and looked at Jesse meaningfully. »But I'm *really glad* that I met you, Keisha.«

»It was a pleasure for me, too,« I replied.

We got up and they hugged. When they said goodbye, Mr. Roy turned to me and waved at me awkwardly. And soon he disappeared in the light that surrounded his body…

XL. THE EVENING OF EPIPHANY

WE KEPT STANDING ON THE BALCONY FOR A WHILE. The red setting sun caused the far-away buildings of New York to light up. Lights started coming on inside the buildings to make up for the fading light of the sun. I walked up to the glass railings that separated the balcony from the vastness of the city. Jesse followed me and held me across the shoulders from behind. Suddenly I felt totally relaxed in his company. It felt like I really *knew* him. Longer than I'd thought. Much longer.

I could feel the coziness of his presence. I felt his power that was to fulfill me for as long as I lived. What was to happen the next day wasn't so important anymore. All my thoughts merged into one wish – to turn my face towards his to study it again.

Then turn if you dare, he thought.

I turned and I was greeted by his smiling face.

»Jesse…« I started timidly. I knew I had behaved egocentrically and with superiority even when he didn't deserve that. I knew I would probably have to ask him for what I wanted. But the words rolled off my tongue much more smoothly than I'd thought.

»Could you please kiss me…?«

»I thought you would never ask,« he said relieved.

He drew my face, which was totally relaxed, closer to his. The electrified atmosphere of the late summer evening seemed to have come to a complete standstill. A split second before his lips touched mine, he connected with my thoughts…and I could hear his gentle voice.

My love, now I offer you the clairvoyance of our future, resounded in my head as I felt the gentle press of his lips against mine. We merged into a flow of thoughts. We were caught up in a whirlwind which took us to a bright place where we pulsated only as frequencies, as souls. I saw him saying goodbye to me obviously planning to make some sort of transition…

»L ET ME GO DOWN ALREADY,« I SAY. »I've had it with looking at people follow their own deception. I can't wait to join them and tell them what they are doing wrong!«

»Try to curb your egocentricity,« you say to me. »It may not be as simple as it looks…«

I look at the Rulers and say: »That's alright. Just let me go down, OK? And at the same time I feel the need to turn to the soul that had been accompanying me and helping me with similar actions for millennia. »I'll see you in 120 years, my dear,« I say playfully.

»In my dimension this is just a split second, you know that…« you reply.

»I know. But still.«

I hug you one last time and we whirl in our common and so familiar dance vibration. »I can hardly wait to see you again,« I say before my vibration starts to drop and adjust to the small body within my mom's womb…

We were still meditating in the kiss when suddenly I hit present time again. I removed my lips from his and the flow of light was interrupted. I inhaled deeply.

»Are you OK?« he asked me gently.

»Yes…« I said trying to catch my breath. »Actually I'm great.«

He stepped closer to me. »Shall I go on…?«

I moved my face closer. »Yes, please,« I said passionately.

I could hear his voice again.

This is our present and future, my love…

ALTHOUGH WE HAD LOST OUR MEMORIES, WE CIRCLE AROUND EACH other and eventually we meet. I teach you great truths which both of us had known before and at the same time I can learn humility from you. Finally we get the task that had been given to us at the very beginning. To move the boundaries of the awareness of life for hundreds, thousands, millions of people…

In the light that shrinks into my body I materialize on the stage. I feel complete peace and quiet. I gently land on the floor. On my left you are already waiting for me and I join you at the microphone. Getting closer to the mike, I notice the countless number of people quietly waiting for our songs. When I get even closer, I notice the Rulers who have chosen to remain invisible. I know we are completely safe because we have an unlimited support of the universe. We couldn't possible have better body guards. I smile and give thanks for this precise plan that has been given to me. My lips shiver when I utter a single word:

»Happy.«

A wave of complete harmony goes through the mass of people. The band opens with the song that I wrote and you are standing by my side smiling and accompanying my singing on your guitar. When I sing, it is my heart that is actually singing…We are happy. We are *here.* It was destined. *This* is true love…

When I was one more time transported back to the balcony by a sea of light, I was no longer afraid. I gave in to Jesse's soft lips and ran my fingers through his golden hair…In his embrace, I felt his strength and devotion. When I finally let him breathe a little, he asked me smiling:

»And now? Do you believe that the future is bright?«

»You know I do,« I said before I became lost again in the softness of his kisses.

ACKNOWLEDGMENTS

I am grateful to my husband, agent and the most capable man I know, Jan Sebastian Srečkar. He also helped me with some great ideas, wich I used in this book.

I am also grateful to the music band Jonathan Jackson + Enation, whose music is like an angel, which has always been by my side, no matter what. I would also like to thank to Richard Lee Jackson, for having such a personal aproach to all of their fans.

I am grateful to everybody, who have led me on the path to knowledge: Polona Sepe, Slavko Mahne-Shyama, Foster Perry, Luna, Matej Škufca; Eros with his book [psi], Rhonda Byrne with her book The Secret and Vladimir Megre with his book collection Anastasia.

I thank my mom, friend, proofreader and artist Anka Kolenc. Without her wisdom, faith and unconditional support the world as I know it, wouldn't exist. My thanks go to the other members of my family: my father Zvone Kolenc, sisters Mojca Sosič and Špela Kolenc. I thank my mother-in-law Metka Zadravec, father-in-law Ivan Sečkar and friends Benko and Sara Mrđanovič, for their support and trust. My thanks also goes to the programer Edis Talundić for such a dedicated cooperation and for all the patience.

I thank everyone, who red this book and wrote their opinion about it on my web site. My special thanks goes to Maruša and Dragica Babnik.

I would like to thank the translators Mojca Lober and Alan Horvatič, who provided the English version of the book. Their translations always have a unique and special – personal touch, for what I am truly grateful.

I am also very grateful to Pia Rihtarič, the designer of the wonderful pictures and ornaments for this trilogy and Katja Pirc for graphic design.

And the most important of all, I thank the universe, wich gives us energy and inspiration every single day of our lives.

ABOUT THE AUTHOR

Janja Srečkar is a versatile artist (author, poet, director, actress, dancer, singer; a music teacher by profession) and a fan of science-fiction literature. She is especially drawn to the protagonists with special powers. She has a wide array of favorite authors and their main quality is that they strengthen the message they wish to convey with the use of love and humor. Among her favorite authors are Vladimir Megre, Eros, Charlotte Bronte, Gustav Šilih, Bogdan Novak, Richard Bach, Stephen Turoff, Paramhansa Yogananda, Shirley Maclaine, Rhonda Byrne and Stephenie Meyer. In author's own words her mission is "to mask" positive messages - that benefit our everyday life as well as our future - into packages of art (printed publications, theatrical performances, poems...) that people accept, understand and possibly even have fun with."

www.ingramcontent.com/pod-product-compliance
Lightning Source LLC
Chambersburg PA
CBHW031253170626
46807CB00001B/120